THE DEVIL'S DOCTRINE
A Hale PI Novel

Peter Fratesi

THE DEVIL'S DOCTRINE
A Hale PI Novel

A DOUBLE DRAGON PAPERBACK

ISBN 978-1-78695-480-0

Double Dragon
is an imprint of
Fiction4All

Published 2020
Fiction4All
www.fiction4all.com

CHAPTER ONE

Linda Kazinski was wrapping up her waitressing shift. The last few patrons had stumbled out into the hot, humid, New Orleans night. She loaded the final batch of beer and shot glasses into the industrial-sized washer in the kitchen and took off her apron. It reeked of beer, smoke, and the sweat of hard work. She winced as she noticed the swellings on her butt from being pinched all night by rowdy men and some women.

Buster ("Bull") Bronson, the owner and chief bartender of the Sorry Ass Café and Blues Bar, wiped down the bar for the twentieth time that night. He wasn't called "Bull" for nothing. He was a huge, bulging man—an ex-Marine sergeant who used a VA loan to finance his place. He could put the fear of God into unruly customers and wouldn't hesitate to use his trusty bat, The Persuader, always at his side. But Bull had a soft spot somewhere underneath his hard exterior. He looked at Linda sympathetically. He knew she'd had a tough go of it. Her husband had left her, and she worked hard to support her three kids, juggling another job on top of the one at the bar. She was the best damn waitress he ever had, he mused. She had a near photographic memory for customer orders and always had a kind smile or word for everyone, including the most obnoxious boozers. But the clientele at the Sorry Ass weren't exactly big tippers. On more profitable nights, he slipped a little more beer-soaked cash into her pay envelope—all under the table, of course.

He usually stood at the door, watching her make her way down the side street to Main, half a block away. It was a rough neighborhood, after all, and with these recent murders in the area, Bull kept an especially close eye on her after closing time. But tonight, he was distracted by complaints from his blues guitarist over his gig fees. The musicians were always bitching about something. But this guy was good, Bull knew. So, as Linda walked out the door, he went over to hear him out.

Linda was on edge as soon as she stepped out of the café. James Street was deeply shadowed in the faint moonlight. The sole streetlight buzzed and flickered dimly, as it had for the past two months. "One damn street light and the city can't fix it," she muttered to herself.

Her anxiety grew when she noticed Bull wasn't at his usual post in the doorway of the café. The garish red and blue blinking lights of the café faded in the murk as she walked on.

She swallowed as she looked down the narrow side street. The shops were long closed, those that could afford it shuttered with burglar bars. The doorways and alley openings were completely shadowed, and she peered apprehensively into each one as she passed. The lights of Main Street seemed awfully distant.

Thoughts of the murders, not far from there in the French Quarter, crossed her mind. Lone women had walked in dark side streets just like this. Their families would never see them alive again. She tensed as she heard a doorknob click in the dark to her left. She hurried on, checking several times for anyone following her.

About halfway down the street, she heard the roll of a tin can on the pavement somewhere near her. Her heart racing, she looked back but saw nothing in the street. She told herself she was overreacting and lit a cigarette. She was startled as the flame of her lighter illuminated a figure sitting in a doorway a few feet away, its head resting face down on its knees. The head suddenly rose. "Linda, how 'bout a quarter? I'm donatin' to the AA."

She breathed out a sigh of relief. It was only Joe, one of the alcoholic regulars on James Street. She pulled a couple of quarters from her pocket and pressed them to his hand. "That's for originality, Joe."

"It's for a good cause, ya know."

"Yeah, yeah," she said as she resumed walking. "Watch yourself, Joe," she called back. "I hear the backstreets aren't too safe these nights." Good advice for herself, too, she thought. What the hell was she doing out here alone, anyway? She should have had Bull escort her on a dark night like this.

She took several puffs on her cigarette, distracting herself with idle thoughts. Funny how nicotine seemed to lose its jolt after the first two or three drags. No matter. She was going to kick the habit anyway. Better get a move on. That pimply-faced babysitter of hers might get it in her head to charge overtime.

She was on the verge of calming down when she heard a subtle, fluttering sound behind her, steady at first, then speeding up. "Joe? Is that you? No practical jokes, now…. Come on, Joe. It's not funny anymore." She listened for a few moments, holding her breath. There was no reply.

She quickened her pace, at the same time reaching into her purse for her pepper spray canister. The fluttering sound grew louder. Her heart pounded in her ears. "Jesus," she whispered and turned abruptly to face the strange sounds. She thrust out the canister. "I don't know who the hell you are, but back off. I'm armed." She fired three squirts in the direction of the sounds, but there were no signs that the noxious streams had hit their mark.

Panicked, she started to run all out toward Main. She tripped over a raised manhole cover and fell heavily to the ground, her spray can rolling away from her. Whatever it was behind her in the dark was almost upon her.

CHAPTER TWO

It was a rainy Saturday morning on the river. Jeremy Hale relaxed in his captain's chair on the bridge of his boat docked at Bay Bayou Marina. A flotilla of drenched powerboats, small yachts, and sailing crafts bobbed forlornly at their moorings nearby.

A thick fog enshrouded the river. The passing freighters looked like hulking ghost ships pushing their way through the gloom to and from the port of New Orleans.

Jeremy had christened his boat *Mississippi Dream*. The boat symbolized his love for the river. In fact, he loved it more than most of the women who'd come into his life. He referred to the river as "she," for it was his true woman friend—certainly the one he knew best and trusted most.

But his boat was more than a symbol. Beginning as a weekend getaway, it eventually became home, his outpost on the edge of the city. His boat-home gave him refuge from the hard, tedious, and sometimes dangerous business of being a private investigator in New Orleans for the past fifteen years. It was practically an antique, built back in the 1920s. Jeremy had long ago learned to ignore the curious, amused looks from the power boaters. Only he could appreciate the history in his boat's thick hardwood timbers, lovingly coated with successive layers of bright marine paint over the years. But he was a kind of ship's surgeon as well, ever alert to the occasional spot of rot in its otherwise sturdy hull, which he would diligently dig out and patch.

The bridge featured an old wooden captain's wheel, brass compass, and silver-plated ship's chronometer. A cluster of levers jutted out, apparently haphazardly, from the control panel. Jeremy had a small cabin with a single bunk adjacent to a sitting area that doubled as a dining room. This was sparsely but tastefully furnished with pieces of antique furniture rescued from a late 1800s sailing ship, including an oak rolltop desk. A small, well-worn pool table also adorned the room. The sitting area abutted onto a tiny galley with an old gas stove.

His choice of an old boat was no accident. He had always loved things historical, sometimes feeling alienated from the high-tech world of 2017; at one time, he had even considered a career teaching high-school history. He had occasionally wondered about his attraction to the past. Perhaps, he mused, it was because the past had already happened; it was set in stone, unchanging. God knows, given what had happened with his mother and sister, he needed predictability in his life.

The river also gave him constancy. After all, the Mississippi had generally held its course to the gulf for eons. A plaque on Jeremy's cabin wall displayed his favorite aphorism: The great river will always take you to the sea.

But most importantly, the river was a place of reflection. A few times a week, Jeremy would bring the boat out for a run. He would travel upstream for hours, giving the throbbing old diesel a workout. He would then reverse course and cut the engine, allowing the boat to drift south in the current; occasionally, he'd make minor course adjustments with the ship's wheel. It was while he drifted that he would have his deepest thoughts, and at times, insights into his life. Once in a while, he'd remember Mark Twain's character Huckleberry Finn. He could not help but notice the parallels between Huck and himself. Huck, too, drifted down the Mississippi—only on a ramshackle raft—seeking freedom and discovering some deep and unexpected truths during his journey. Jeremy sometimes laughed at the comparison. Imagine thinking of himself as a modern-day Huck Finn!

But on this foggy morning, the boat would have to remain docked in the marina. Jeremy had visited Dad's Variety Store, next to the marina's repair shop and hardware, to buy Saturday's copy of the *New Orleans Sentinel*. The headline and story were disturbing: Woman Found Brutally Murdered and Raped on James Street. Thirty-three-year-old waitress and mother of three Linda Kazinski had been on her way home after closing time, Friday night, at the café where she worked for the past five years....

Jeremy's brow furrowed as he read the rest of the article. He was well aware of the half-dozen similar murders in the old districts and the three levels of police desperately looking for a sadistic sexual killer. He knew that the investigation had gone nowhere so far and that the public's fears were growing fast.

Jeremy sighed and put down his paper. In his university criminology classes, he had studied serial murderers. He knew all about their profiles and psychodynamics. But he felt he'd never understood, in any depth, their incredible inhumanity. Somehow, the theories just didn't seem to measure up to the magnitude of their crimes. At times, he wondered if there was something much more fundamental, like pure evil, at the root of it all.

Jeremy spent the rest of Saturday doing some reading. He liked some of the older detective story writers, especially Arthur Conan Doyle and Agatha Christie. He especially liked that, so far, all the criminals were caught as a result of brilliant deduction. It was a welcome relief from the real world of investigation.

Just as Poirot was about to checkmate his suspect, he heard footsteps on the wooden dock and then some whistling. It sounded like his old buddy, Tony Vasquez, coming to pay a visit.

"Ahoy, Captain! Permission to come aboard."

It was Tony taking a friendly shot across his bow. Jeremy played along. "Permission granted, matey."

The two laughed as Tony joined him in the sitting room, a six-pack of beer under his arm. Jeremy eyed the beer. "Got your boarding fees, I see."

"Here's your booty," Tony said, handing over the beer.

The two cracked open a couple. Tony spied the Agatha Christie book opened on the old desk. "I see you're spending another exciting weekend on the river," he observed. "No hot dates tonight?" He knew very well that Jeremy's dates were few and far between, and never on his boat. Jeremy's gangplank was the boundary between himself and all romantically inclined women. But Tony liked to skewer him on the matter, hoping to goad him into getting out once in a while, and if miracles existed, to date a female or two.

"Bugger," chided Jeremy.

"Well, somehow I don't think your dating prospects are too good in Bay Bayou Marina."

"Been docked all week," Jeremy complained, changing the subject. "The engine's going to rust if I don't give her a run soon."

Tony nodded. He knew Jeremy too well to miss his friend's favorite avoidance tactic whenever the topic of dating came up. The two had been close friends since they were teens and had gone to St. Vincent's High School together in New Orleans. After that, they parted ways for a while. Tony had gone on to the police academy and joined the New Orleans Police Department as a beat cop; Jeremy had won a scholarship and enrolled in Harvard University's criminology program. Tony was a family man now, with two kids and one more on the way, but he and Jeremy still managed to get together on the occasional weekend.

Tony was aware that Jeremy was only five years old when his mother left the family. Jeremy had always presented an I-don't-give-a-damn attitude about what she did, but Tony knew better. It was not that he absolved Jeremy in the matter. His mother had tried to reconnect with him when he was a teen, but Jeremy ignored her messages. Now, he was a thirty-eight-year-old man with abandonment issues he had never faced. Tony was thankful he'd never had that problem. His parents were about to celebrate their fiftieth anniversary together, along with their huge extended families.

Tony let the topic of dating pass by. He'd done his duty for the day on the matter. "Have you heard about the murder last night?"

"The waitress? Yeah. It was all over the Sentinel. Same M.O.?"

Tony sighed. "That's what Jack Claye, the lead, told me. The poor woman was brutalized: raped, strangled, and had her ovaries removed, if you can believe it. God knows in what order. There are some signs of torture, too. We're obviously dealing with a viciously sadistic SOB."

Jeremy slowly shook his head. "I heard everything but the ovaries and the torture. I gather you boys held that information back. God, when will it end?"

"When we catch the psychopath," Tony said, his jaw visibly tightening. "I'm not up on everything, but I'm plugged in to the grapevine enough to know that the investigation is going nowhere. No suspects. No decent leads. I hear there's some weird stuff at the murder scenes, too, that doesn't make sense."

Jeremy could almost feel Tony's frustration. Tony was not only his closest friend but also a comrade in arms. He had moved up to detective in the NOPD and often provided valuable police information for Jeremy's private investigations. Both Tony and the NOPD valued Jeremy's talents for solving difficult criminal cases that would otherwise languish in police files. Sometimes, Tony had permission to team up with Jeremy, but more often, budget restraints meant going the covert route and passing information on the sly. The chief knew about the practice and turned a blind eye to it. He was more interested in improving his force's arrest record and getting commendations from the mayor.

Tony had never completely understood Jeremy's claims that the river played some kind of role in his investigations. Jeremy had used a quote one day from Mark Twain's *Life on the Mississippi*, attempting to explain to Tony his relationship with the river: "The face of the water, in time, became a wonderful book … which told its mind to me without reserve, delivering its most cherished secrets as clearly as if it had uttered them with a voice. And it was not a book to be read once and cast aside, for it had a new story to tell every day."

Tony had been utterly bewildered. "Would someone please translate that?" he protested.

"Honestly, buddy," Jeremy had gently chided. "I think you slept through Literature 301 at St. Vincent's. It's a metaphor, Tony. Twain has insights while travelling the river." Tony looked even more mystified.

Tony took a more pragmatic view of his friend's investigative successes. He knew that Jeremy's deductive abilities were second to none. He also knew that Jeremy had good sources in the New Orleans underworld, a carefully groomed list of informants in the know about other shady types operating just below the police radar. Jeremy's reach extended even to several jailhouse snitches.

"How's the FBI doing on the case?" Jeremy asked.

"Well, their violent crimes unit has been analyzing the case, and there's no end to it. We have criminal profiling information from them on the murderer coming out of our ears. Don't get me wrong—a lot of it's really good stuff. Like in many serial murders, the bodies have been posed, and this has helped the FBI with their psychological analysis of the murderer. But all of this has not helped us to narrow down any suspects yet. I get the feeling that the break will come from somewhere else, and when we've got him, then we'll say, 'Oh, yeah, he fits the profile.'" Tony shrugged in exasperation.

"The pressure for an arrest must be high. Word on the streets is that people in the old districts are definitely scared, and I imagine the mayor must be getting an earful."

"Yeah. Things may get a lot worse, too. I've heard there's been an unusual number of women disappearing in bayou country. Some may turn up dead, or at least what's left of them after the alligators have their way. If it's the same M.O., then God help us all."

"I'm half glad I'm not in on it."

Tony smiled grimly. "Well, if things go downhill any more, you'll be asked to join the investigating team for sure."

Jeremy let his breath out slowly. "That should make life interesting."

"For the department, too." Tony grinned. "Just don't tell them about the river."

Jeremy laughed. "Good shot, Tony. You deserve another beer."

"I've had my limit. But I'll tell you what I deserve. Why don't you come over for supper sometime? The kids and I have some great computer games you could learn. There are better things to do weekends besides reading dusty old crime books. The modern age lies before you, buddy."

Jeremy smiled. "I'll take it under advisement, Tony."

The two turned their attention to the pool table. That usually started a friendly argument about what game to play, but tonight Tony generously settled for a contest of snooker.

CHAPTER THREE

It was the first day of the workshop in Advanced Forensic Investigation at the Colonial Building in downtown Boston. Jeremy was required to attend at least fifteen hours of professional development per year to keep his license. This was not the most important reason for registering. He wanted to stay on the cutting edge of his profession. New technology was always entering the field, and new psychological techniques of criminal profiling. A side benefit was revisiting some of the historical sites in Boston.

Jeremy felt right at home in the Constitution Room, the venue for the workshop. It was a former music hall renovated to preserve its rich history. From its vaulted ceiling hung stately, old-style crystal chandeliers, their low-energy electric lights the only concession to the modern age. The floor was a rich antique oak. A battalion of cushioned, Colonial-style chairs filled the room, awaiting most of the participants. The pastel rose walls were lined with old portraits of the original signers of the US Constitution. A copy of the venerable document enshrined in a huge, ornate frame, hung from an end wall.

The workshop had not yet begun, and people were still milling around the coffee and croissants. He recognized a few familiar faces from his Harvard days and went over to trade notes on old times and new. They certainly seemed more subdued than they had been as students—ready to take on the world then but now more likely weighed down by it.

But there was someone familiar he hadn't yet greeted, an attractive, rather sophisticated-looking woman a few rows away. But he couldn't place her. He sent a few sideways glances in her direction, wondering who she was. He even tried unsuccessfully to steal a look at her nametag during the coffee break. He knew he had seen her before—but where? He mentally reviewed his brief list of ex-girlfriends but drew a blank. She wasn't a former client either, at least that he could pinpoint.

He was in the same unfortunate dilemma during the second day of the workshop and berated himself for not having the nerve to just go over and introduce himself. He rationalized the situation. What was he supposed to do? Use the corny old line *haven't I seen you someplace before*? To his consternation, the workshop ended with this mini mystery still unsolved.

He'd soon forgotten about the incident until six months later when he opened the office door to his waiting room. There she was, fifteen hundred miles from Boston, waiting for a job interview with Hale Private Investigations. His business had been going well—so well, he knew he'd either have to start refusing new cases or hire on an investigator. He made the decision any good businessman would make and advertised.

He now knew who the familiar stranger was at the workshop. She was Monica Sauvé. She had also attended the criminology program at Harvard. He had been in his senior year when she was a junior. He couldn't miss her. She was quite attractive then, too. But he'd always considered her to be a preppy from the Bostonian upper crust. He was afraid to introduce himself then, too. So incredibly, she shows up all these years later looking for a job! Remarkable coincidence? Or could it be synchronicity? He smiled at the thought.

He had debated at length with himself over shortlisting her. She was lean on field experience, with only a couple of years as a beat cop in Boston. She spent most of her career office-bound after that as a criminal profiler. He was also concerned about the cultural divide between her hometown of Boston and New Orleans—two very different worlds.

She was the sole female candidate. He was no misogynist, he felt, but with his history with women, he seriously wondered how he would do with a female partner. However, her background as a criminal profiler could make a real contribution to his business, and she had received commendations for her twelve years of work with the Boston Police Department. They had some commonality with Harvard, as well. In the end, nostalgia and considerable curiosity about her had tipped the balance in favor of Monica. He would see what impression she would make face-to-face.

He introduced himself, finding it supremely ironic he was finally doing so under these circumstances. He invited her into his office and gestured her toward an old oak captain's chair in front of his cluttered antique desk. He took a closer look at her. She wore an unpretentious but stylish navy-blue business suit and minimal facial makeup. But that didn't detract from her looks. In his opinion, her maturation over the years had moved her from the category beautiful to stunning. She looked him directly in the eye with an air of poise and confidence. He liked that.

"So, Ms. Sauvé—"

"Call me Monica," she interjected.

"Okay, Monica. What brings you all the way from Boston to apply for a job in New Orleans?"

"It's straightforward, really," she replied. "I worked as a criminal profiler for the Boston PD, but I think my true calling is investigative work in the field. I felt I would never get a detective position in the department."

"Why was that?"

"I think that despite all the noise about equal opportunity for women in the department, there is still an old boys' mentality about women in the detective field."

"Okay. There's still the part about why New Orleans."

"I was looking for a more earthy, maybe a bit exotic place," Monica responded, "and I thought that could be afforded by New Orleans."

Jeremy smiled. "Oh, it's earthy all right. But I wouldn't use the word 'exotic' in front of the locals if I were you."

"I'll remember that.... I meant to mention, too, my family was originally from Louisiana before they moved up north to Boston—Cajun, in fact. My first name is really Moniquc, but people would just call me Monica. It stuck. So I use it."

"Okay, so you're a frustrated police profiler, looking for a field job in Cajun country, who doesn't use her real name."

She nodded, amused. “I might add that I’ve tried to keep in touch with my Cajun roots over the years. I even took French lessons privately in Boston.”

“All that’s great, Monica. I really mean that. But it looks to me like you’ve got little experience in actual investigative work.”

“True,” she said, “but I’ve got a knack for it. Some of that’s intuitive. In case discussions at the department, I would often come up with new tracks to follow or throw a different light on evidence. Even the most experienced detectives used to surreptitiously come to me when things were going cold. My motto is: follow the psychology of the crime and your gut, and you will be led to the perpetrator.”

Jeremy was struck by the cold-case reference. Much of his work was done on cases the police had filed away as unsolved. Aggrieved family or friends of victims wanted justice done and hired him to get it done. Where the police left off, he would begin. He could use a partner who could warm up cold cases, all right. Her intuitive psychological take was interesting, too. Perhaps she had her own equivalent of the whispering Mississippi. “You know,” he said, “we share an alma mater.”

She gave him a quizzical look. “You went to Harvard?”

“Yes. Criminology, too.”

“I don’t remember seeing you around,” she remarked.

“I was ahead of you, but I knew you were around.” He couldn’t help but be struck once again by her beauty. But he realized, uncomfortably, that his aesthetic appreciation of her could complicate a business relationship. If he hired her, that would have to be kept out of the mix. "Remember Professor Romney's class, Criminal Investigation 202? Anyone who could pass bumbling Bob's chaotic course must have natural investigative talent!"

She smiled, starting to feel a good connection with the man behind the desk. There was a part of her that noticed he was quite a handsome guy, rugged in his own way, yet there seemed to be a certain fragility beneath his tough exterior. She also sensed his attraction to her but somehow felt he would be business-like with her if she were hired.

Jeremy looked at her searchingly. There was another concern on his mind. Would she really have his back if it came down to a brawl with the criminal types they'd run into? He voiced the thought. "There's one thing, Monica. It's been a long while since you've been on the streets. It's a rough world out here. You or we might be assaulted by thugs twice your size. How do you think you'd handle that?"

"Well, I recently received a black belt in judo."

Jeremy gave her a skeptical look. "I know that from your resumé, but as you know, being trained and applying that training in the real world can be very different things. Has a recent situation happened where you've stood your ground physically, against the odds?"

Monica was not flustered. "I was walking alone in downtown Boston after dark six months ago when I was jumped by two men at the mouth of an alley."

"I'd say that would qualify. How did you do?"

"I managed to put both of them on their backs long enough to get out of there."

Jeremy nodded, impressed. She was getting more than a passing grade so far. He knew he'd be taking a chance on the field experience factor, but she was obviously bright and likely would be a quick learner. He also thought about the man-woman communication games and misunderstandings that could arise if he hired her and the unsettling potential for deeper feelings arising between them. He already had his fill of these in the few brief relationships he'd had with women. But he reminded himself this was not going to be that kind of relationship. The dialogue had also been going very well. He'd have to think upon it.

***

A week later, Jeremy and Tony met for lunch at a downtown café, for po'boy sandwiches and New Orleans café au lait. Jeremy couldn't wait to tell him the news.

"Remember the mysterious attractive woman at the workshop I was telling you about six months ago?"

"Yeah."

"Well, she showed up in my office for a job interview last week."

"You're kidding. What are the chances?"

"Slim at best. And I just emailed an offer to her to join the firm as my assistant."

Tony's jaw dropped perceptibly. "You? Hiring an attractive young woman? She must be attached, otherwise I'd say you've finally flipped your lid!"

"Neither. I've vowed to keep the relationship professional."

Tony laughed. "Easier said than done! She must have been a damn good candidate to bring her on."

"Yeah, she has a lot to offer. Okay, get that smile off your face. I'm speaking professionally now. I admit she's light in the investigative department, but that's manageable. I'll train her up for the state PI exam. She's got plenty of talent and studied criminology at Harvard when I was there."

"It's no wonder she seemed so familiar.... Actually, it's perfect timing that she's coming on now."

"How's that?"

Tony smiled. "I've been asked by the chief to give you a heads-up. As I expected, the murder investigation's hit rock bottom, and the dominoes have started to fall. The governor has leaned on the mayor about the case, and the mayor is pressuring the chief for an arrest. So the chief has made room for you on the team, if you want it. The pay's good, and I'll be working with you, too."

"That's great, Tony, but what about my assistant? It'd be a terrific learning experience for her to work on the case."

Tony shook his head. "Jeremy, I don't know about using someone so green in a heavyweight investigation like this."

Jeremy folded his arms across his chest. "Talking about the domino effect, you can tell the chief she comes on or I don't. Black or white."

Tony remained dubious, but he knew his friend was not going to back down. "Okay, okay. I'll see what I can do. Get her resumé to me. I'll try to sell her to the chief."

The two finished their lunch, and Jeremy ordered another coffee. He noticed that Tony was already engaged in his own post-meal ritual, happily chewing on a piece of bubble gum. Jeremy was well acquainted with Tony's long, checkered history of gum-chewing. His friend became hooked on gum after quitting smoking ten years ago. He had developed some dental issues from it, until his wife lectured him into using the sugar-free variety.

Jeremy smiled to himself. Some of the people he knew carried liquor flasks on them for the occasional discreet swig; others, now dwindling in number, had cigarette cases. He carried his stress reducer in his mind; he'd simply remember calmly drifting down the river. But Tony carried a small tin loaded with his favorite bubble gums. The habit wasn't much of a vice, Jeremy knew. However, Tony's constant chewing could be an annoyance. Jeremy thought that for his birthday he might get him a small dispenser tin with a timer to open it at respectable intervals. At the very least the gift would be worth a laugh!

However, as Jeremy walked back to his car after lunch, his mood became somber. He thought about the chief's offer and the terrible predicament the police were in. He suspected even darker times were coming to New Orleans unless these murders were solved fast. Jeremy resolved to throw himself, body and soul, into this investigation and help find the leads that had, so far, eluded three levels of police.

CHAPTER FOUR

It was their first meeting since the job interview a few weeks before. Jeremy placed a cup of freshly brewed Southern Aroma coffee on the corner of his desk for Monica, complete with an old cypress coaster. Monica had given her resignation to the Boston Police Department and now had the unenviable task of finding accommodation in New Orleans.

"How's the apartment hunting going?" Jeremy inquired.

"Nothing definite yet, but I've seen some open-concept lofts big enough to let me spread out and mess things up without cluttering up the place too much. One has a view of Bourbon Street."

"Nice. Any impressions of the city, so far?"

"It's really different. Parts of it feel almost Caribbean. It seems a more pleasure-seeking, laid-back place than I'm used to in Boston."

Jeremy nodded. "It's not called the 'Big Easy' for nothing. But you can stereotype it, too. Go down to the business section at noon hour and you'd think you're in New York."

Jeremy noted she appeared even more radiant than she had when he last met her. He flashed back to the fresh-faced beauty he was so attracted to at Harvard and felt his cheeks flush. He hoped she hadn't noticed.

"I would like to thank you, Mr. Hale, for hiring me on."

"Jeremy will do, Monica. I look around for my father when you say 'Mr. Hale.'"

"Okay, Jeremy. This is giving me a chance to fulfill a dream, and I'm grateful to you." She found herself drawn to him by more than gratitude, but she didn't have a problem with that.

"Well, you've earned it, Monica. By my estimate, you were by far the best of a whole crew of applicants I shortlisted."

"I'm honored," she said. "I hope I can live up to that."

"Don't worry. You will. We'll be spending a lot of time with on-the-job training to bring you up to specs. We start by getting you licensed as a PI apprentice in Louisiana. The next thing you'll need is a concealed gun permit, since some of the types we'll be encountering will be carrying. It's not a bad idea for general personal protection, either. We have one of the highest homicide rates in the country right here in New Orleans. Are you up on your gun training?"

"I'm rusty."

"Okay, we'll put that on our to-do list." He thought her skirt revealed a little more leg than he had seen previously, but he could be mistaken. He chastised himself for noticing. Be professional, he reminded himself. That's the key.

Monica interrupted his thoughts. "So, how long do I stay as an apprentice?"

"You have up to a year max to pass the state exam to get a full-fledged PI license. There's a forty-hour course you need to take between now and then."

"I like learning."

"Good, you'll need plenty of it to put you even near the ball park with some of the detectives we'll be dealing with." He paused and looked her directly in the eye. "This is confidential, but I just got word you'll be joining me on NOPD's investigating team for a very serious case. It also involves other levels of police."

"Is this the New Orleans serial murder case?"

"I see you've been keeping up on the news. Yes, I'm sorry to say the situation is getting desperate, and they're bringing in all the troops, including you and me. It's not the only case we'll be working on, but it will occupy a lot of time."

Jeremy smiled. "By the way, you'll have an opportunity to meet a very fine detective and my best buddy, Tony Vasquez. He's been eagerly waiting to meet you."

***

The next day on Jeremy's calendar was reserved for family matters. He prepared to pay a visit to his father, Jake, which he was in the habit of doing two Saturdays a month. Jeremy took out of his fridge several packaged meals, which were some of the "old man's" favorite foods. He knew that "old" was a misnomer for his father. At sixty-two, Jake was still in relatively good shape from his daily walks and some basketball on Wednesday nights with a group from the security guards' association. Jake's only vice was his fondness for beer, which he found in abundance at Mac's, the group's bar of choice on Magazine Street.

The elder Hale still lived in the old family home, a small bungalow in one of the rougher areas of downtown New Orleans. Jeremy tried for years to persuade him to move to safer quarters; he had even offered to buy him a new home in a gated seniors' community. His father would have none of it. He was simply too attached to his home (and its proximity to Mac's).

Jeremy sometimes thought that visiting the place was like opening up a time capsule from the 1970s. His father's easy chair faced a retro-looking standing fan, which made the hot, humid, summer days more bearable. A dated turntable sat on a stainless-steel record player stand, loaded with an interesting combination of rock and roll, jazz, and classical records.

Framed photos of Jake, Jeremy, and his sister, Kathy, mostly from the family's earlier years, lined the living room walls. Photos of Jake's estranged wife were conspicuously absent, as if she somehow had never existed. Indeed, Jeremy and his father did not talk about Mary Hale. There was an unspoken understanding between them that they never would. For over thirty years, that was fine by Jeremy. After all, there was no sense in reopening old wounds. So the two contented themselves discussing relatively safe topics like sports, politics, and Jeremy's business.

Jeremy thought such mundane conversation was ironic. His father was a self-educated man, well read in diverse subjects. The books in philosophy, science, religion, and psychology stacked on his living room shelves attested to that. Yet he had never discussed these deep subjects with his son. Jeremy vowed that, one of these days, he would ask him why.

CHAPTER FIVE

Monica and Jeremy arrived for their introductory meeting with the investigating team at police headquarters. Jeremy was collared in the conference room by Jack Claye, the team lead, before the meeting began. Monica drifted toward the coffee and French donuts, where she chanced to meet Tony for the first time.

Tony presented her with a huge smile and an equally warm handshake. "Jeremy can't stop talking about you."

"I hope it's flattering," she replied with a grin.

"Nothing but. I've heard you have some interesting ideas on investigation."

"I *am* flattered. By the way, Jeremy can't stop talking about you, either."

"I'll bet," Tony quipped.

"No, seriously. I'm really looking forward to working with you, Mr. Vasquez."

Tony beamed as he absorbed the compliment. She's every bit the charmer Jeremy said she was, Tony mused, and classy, too.

The three joined the rest of the team at 9:00 a.m. sharp. Monica took a close look around the room. There were eight other people, mostly middle-aged men in business suits. She recognized one immediately: Dr. Daryl Greenwood, an expert on serial murderers. She was familiar with his work since her university days. But two women were also present.

Jack Claye took the podium. "Okay, people. Let's get down to business. First of all, I would like to welcome three investigators to the team: our own Tony Vasquez, private investigator Jeremy Hale, whom most of you will know, and his assistant, Monica Sauvé." He then introduced the rest of the team.

Monica learned that Dr. Greenwood was a consultant for the FBI. She also learned that one of the women was a criminal profiler for the FBI; the other was a detective from state police. It seems the glass ceiling can be broken after all, she thought.

The lead cleared his throat. "Now, all of you are to be commended for your work on this very difficult case. I know you've been giving it your all, and it's paid off with some potentially important information about the killer. However, I'm sure you'll agree that we're overstretched and at this point could do with some fresh ideas. To that end, Tony, Jeremy, and Monica will operate as a subteam in coordination with the rest of the team, reporting directly to me. Their objectives are to re-examine what we have learned so far and fill in any informational holes in the investigation that they can. Any questions, so far? No? Okay, we'll proceed with the summary and updates on the case. Feel free to ask questions or offer commentary at any time. This is as much a brainstorming session as it is an update."

After the two-hour meeting, the FBI consultant came over to meet Monica and Jeremy. He was tall and well-built, very athletic for a university professor. Monica noticed he made very direct eye contact with everyone.

Monica was the first to shake his hand. "I read your dissertation on the psychology of serial murderers," she said. "It was core reading in my criminology program."

"Well, that's gratifying indeed," the professor replied. "Of course, that was my earlier work. I've since published a psychohistory book on serial murderers, if you are interested."

"It must be a fascinating read," Monica remarked.

The professor smiled, basking in her admiration of his work.

Jeremy listened politely. He, too, had read the professor's dissertation as a student but was now a seasoned PI no longer given to venerating academics in criminology.

"You two must come to see me at the university sometime, perhaps after you've read my book," the professor said. "I'm a theoretical sort. Occasionally, I need to be brought back to earth by those doing the actual field work."

After the professor had left, the three met in Tony's office for a post-mortem discussion of the case conference. "So, what are your impressions?" Tony asked the other two. "A huge pile of information to sort through, huh?"

Jeremy looked over at Monica, who took his cue. "Sometimes it's not what's said but what isn't said that's most important," she offered. "This team is clearly demoralized and mostly grasping for straws. Despite the lead's encouraging words, I can't imagine our injection into the team has helped build their confidence."

"So, what are you suggesting?" Jeremy asked.

"Well, I know I'm the junior member here, but I think we need to share a lot with the rest of the team and be supportive. I think we could start by taking an interest in their plans to put out female police decoys in the French Quarter as poison bait for the murderer. Even some of their investigations that didn't pan out—like looking into who owns and works at the local Museum of Torture and the Morbid—show that they're leaving no stones unturned. And that should be recognized, too."

"Good points," Tony commented. "They're not exactly getting kudos from the big brass these days, either."

Jeremy nodded in agreement. "It's no wonder they're demoralized. There's absolutely no commonality among the murder victims to latch on to—other than they're young women, predictable in their routines and vulnerable as they walked alone after dark. Not much to go on."

"Right," Tony said, "and add to that the usual suspects in these cases, sexually violent predators living in or near the areas of the attacks, have pretty well been ruled out."

"What bothers me most," added Jeremy, "is the murderer's preoccupation with removing the victim's ovaries and this after rape and torture. I know the FBI profiler said the murderer was likely a sexually inadequate, sadistic woman-hater. But this degree of raw hatred and the willingness to put it into action is astonishing. What do you think, Monica?"

Monica sighed. "I agree these are extreme and rare crimes. I agree, too, with Doctor Greenwood that intense hostility and anger from early abandonment or abuse by significant female figures is at the core of the murders. I wonder, also, if there's psychotic thinking behind the crimes. Perhaps young women represent some kind of delusional threat to him, and he's going to eliminate that threat at every opportunity. I've studied cases where people diagnosed as paranoid schizophrenics have turned violently on total strangers, believing they were the devil incarnate and were to be destroyed on God's orders."

"The delusion hypothesis is interesting," Jeremy said. "Another unusual thing is that the murders are not hatchet jobs. The removal of the ovaries was done with considerable surgical skill."

"But another dead end so far," Tony said. "The checks on people who fit the bill, like surgeons, veterinarians, biologists, and the like, turned up nothing. Whoever this guy is, he seems to have come by his skills in some other way."

Monica added, "It does point out, as the FBI profiler said, that the guy is likely well-educated and intelligent. Maybe he took biology and dissection in university but may not have continued into a related profession. Perhaps he even dropped out at some advanced level."

"Could be," agreed Jeremy. "This guy's hard to pin down, in general. There's a total lack of DNA material from the murderer at the crime scenes. He's either extremely lucky, or he's very careful, or both."

"I would bet on 'careful' in this case," Monica remarked. "There's increasing evidence that rape is not just a crime of opportunity or impulse. Rapists can plan their crimes and even fantasize about them in advance. Using condoms and other ways of avoiding leaving samples of themselves may be part of that planning and fantasizing."

"Well, one thing is sure," Tony commented, "neither his luck or his planning can hold up forever, and he's going to make a mistake. If he keeps up these murders, we'll get some DNA."

"It's terribly tragic," Monica said, "that there has to be more victims to get the evidence we need."

"Your point about planning likely applies to this guy, Monica," Jeremy said. "Most of the victims showed up on security cameras on the nights of the murders, but not the murderer. He must have cased the areas for surveillance. This is more evidence he's planned his attacks and again shows his intelligence."

"I think he almost screwed up in the Kazinski attack, though," Tony said. "The camera at the liquor store showed her on her back being attacked but did not get him at all. Very strange."

Jeremy was not puzzled. "Remember the audio-visual tech said that was a result of angle, dim light, and a poor-quality camera."

"But if he planned it entirely, why would he even have taken a chance of being picked up by the camera?" Tony asked.

"Maybe he somehow missed the camera," Jeremy surmised. "Let's take a look at the liquor store front at our next opportunity."

CHAPTER SIX

The trio parked on Main and walked through the crime scene on James Street. They paused in front of a liquor store, reflecting on the faded chalk marks on the pavement that marked where Linda Kazinski drew her last breath.

Jeremy located the store's external security camera. He noted it was partially hidden by a falling awning. "The murderer might have missed it," he surmised.

"Yeah," Tony agreed. "The lens is half covered—likely a factor in the murderer not showing up in the video. It's odd there was no mention of this in the investigation report." He took out his phone. "I'll put in a reminder to have the owner notified of the problem. I notice it's an old videotape camera, too. Many of the small business owners overuse their tapes, washing them out. Just in case, I'll put in a note about this, too."

As they walked on, they encountered other chalk marks in front of a pawnshop where one of Linda's heels had come off. There were more marks farther on, where a pool of pepper spray had stained the pavement. Monica paused in silence, pondering the stain. How terrifying it must have been for Linda, chased down by someone in the dark and finally savaged. Had she realized she was the latest victim of the serial killer who prowled old side streets just like this?

As the three walked on, they encountered the defective street lamp. Jeremy wondered if the situation would have unfolded as it had if the city had fixed it. He led the way into the Sorry Ass Café and Blues Bar. It was a dive—at best, a joint. A dirty, faded carpet covered the floor. There were scratched-up, wooden ranch-style tables and chairs from the seventies, their original stain finish washed out long ago by innumerable alcoholic spills. The few people around the tables looked just as worn down by life.

A big man stood eying them from behind the bar, a cigarette dangling from his lips. He wore a white t-shirt that revealed at least eighteen-inch biceps. A Marine logo was tattooed on one of them.

This must be Buster Bronson, Jeremy thought. He took a closer look at the collection of liquor bottles behind the bar. Tucked in behind some of the brand names were a few unlabeled bottles. Jeremy wondered if Buster was cutting overhead with some bootlegged liquor.

Tony took the lead. "Buster Bronson?"

Buster fixed Tony in his gaze. "Depends who's askin'."

"Tony Vasquez, New Orleans Police Department. These are private investigators Hale and Sauvé."

"Figured it was either you guys again, or the IRS."

Tony smiled. "We need to double-check on some things, Buster."

"Okay, it's slow. So I'll give you fifteen minutes. No more. I guess you guys don't drink on the job, either."

"No," Jeremy replied. He thought if he did, he'd be watching which bottle Buster lifted out of his collection.

Buster led them into a dingy little backroom with a desk loaded with yellowed tax returns. Buster wasn't kidding about the IRS. Jeremy stood as his two colleagues settled into a dilapidated cloth couch with its pawnshop tag still on it. Buster cleared away a spot on the corner of his desk to sit on.

Tony took out his notebook. "So, what happened the night of Ms. Kazinski's death, Buster?"

"Well, like I told the cops before, Linda finished her shift that night. Things were routine. The customers were rowdy, like always. She seemed all right when she left. She expected me to stand watch for her at the door until she made it to Main Street."

"Did you?"

Buster looked down. "No. I got distracted by some stuff and forgot about it." He found a half-empty bottle of rye under his papers and poured himself a drink. "I closed up and walked down James toward my car on Main. It was damn dark with the streetlight out, but I could see that Joe, the street alky, wasn't propped up at his usual spot. About a hundred feet from Main, I thought I saw a pile of trash or clothes on the pavement. But as I got close, I saw a woman spread out on the pavement. I thought at first one of our female customers had drunk too much and passed out, but her head was at a weird angle, and then I saw lots of blood. I bent down to check her pulse, but I already knew she was dead and that it was Linda. I called the cops right away." Buster poured himself another drink.

His voice lowered. "I went to her funeral a couple of days later. Her kids were there, you know…. I don't think it's right for young kids to attend funerals, do you?" His eyes teared up momentarily. Then his face hardened and the tears vanished.

"Just to double-check, Buster," Jeremy said. "You say there was no particular trouble with the customers that night?"

"None I saw, and not much gets by me."

"Okay. Was there anything different about her lately? Like her mood or any changes in her family, relationships, or finances that you know of?"

"None I knew about, and she would talk about herself a lot."

"Was there any change in her work performance lately?"

"No. She was always the best. Too good for the kind of customers we get around here."

Jeremy nodded. "Do you know of anyone who might have wanted to harm her?"

"Maybe that loser ex-husband of hers. He used to slap her around quite a bit. But he's been gone for years now. She's been turned off on men since."

"So no dates or relationships?"

Buster shook his head. "Nah, no way."

"Anything different or suspicious in the area that night or prior to it?"

"Something weird did happen with the hookers on James."

"What was that?"

"Did you see any of them when you came here? They're all gone. Not that I mind."

"So what's happened to them?" Jeremy asked.

"I think they were spooked by all the murders. I heard a couple of them say, even before Linda died, that they were scared to walk James. They felt they were being watched. I put it down to nerves about the murders. Maybe I should have kept an eye out more."

"Hindsight, Buster."

"Yeah, maybe." Buster looked down again.

"Did Linda ever mention that she felt she was being watched?" Tony asked.

"No, and I'd remember that."

"What about Joe, the alcoholic? Have you seen him since that night?"

"Joe never came back to James. I see him on Main now, near a streetlight, but I've never talked to him. I guess what went down that night scared the bejesus out of him."

"Anything else you recall about that night, Buster?" Tony queried.

Buster scowled. "I'm tryin' to forget it, if you guys let me."

This was their cue to leave Buster's company. The three left the café to look for Joe.

"What did you make of Buster?" Tony asked as they made their way back to Main Street.

"He seemed on the level," Jeremy said. "He appeared upset by the death, and I think guilty about not watching out for her that night."

"And handling the guilt by suppressing it and numbing it with alcohol," added Monica.

"What you might expect from an ex-Marine," Jeremy replied. "By what he said, there's no evidence that the murderer was known to her. From the hookers' comments, it seems that someone may have been watching the area for some time, possibly determining the routines of vulnerable potential victims. He may have then waited for the best time to murder her."

"The chase happened over quite a distance," added Monica. "He may like to frighten his victims by letting them know he's stalking them before he kills. This fits with the sadistic nature of the murders."

The trio reached Main Street and found a scruffy man fitting Joe's description dozing on a bench outside the Ace Liquor store. Joe was the epitome of the great unwashed from the down-and-out alleys and side streets of New Orleans. Tony shook him awake—at least as awake as Joe's alcohol-soaked brain could be. Joe fumbled with shaking hands in the filthy black trench coat that hung from his thin frame. He pulled out a small tin box with three quarters rattling in it.

Not too profitable for two in the afternoon, Tony thought. He placed a five-dollar bill in the tin box. "There's more of that if you answer a few questions, Joe. You are Joe Broullard, right?"

Joe nodded, his faded blue eyes hopeful but wary.

"Tony Vasquez of the New Orleans Police Department. These are private investigators Hale and Sauvé."

Joe's brow furrowed. "It's about Linda, ain't it?" He grabbed a bottle in a paper bag next to him and took a swig. "Don't recall nothin' much."

Tony held up a fresh twenty-dollar bill. "It's enough to float you for a while, Joe. It's yours if you tell me what you know."

Joe's furrow deepened as he searched for memories he'd tried hard to drown out. "Heard her scream. Can't get it outta my head…."

"Go on, Joe."

Joe's eyes widened. "Saw somethin'…. A devil in the dark. Stared right at me." The tin box rattled violently.

"Did you see his face, Joe?"

"There warnt no face."

"You mean you couldn't see it?"

Joe shrugged.

"Anything else, Joe?"

"Bull. Bull's cursin' and swearin' and the cops all over." He took another swig, and his head began to nod.

Tony put the promised bill in Joe's box and let him lapse into blessed forgetfulness.

In a few more minutes, the investigators were back in their van parked not far away. Tony put the key in the ignition and started up. "What do you make of his devil story?" he asked the others with a smile.

"Could be just a scary metaphor for the murderer," Jeremy said. "Or maybe delirium tremens talking."

"Whatever it was, he seemed genuinely frightened by what he saw in the dark," Monica added.

"It's too bad he couldn't give a description of the face."

"He said there wasn't a face," Monica responded. "The security camera at the liquor store didn't pick it up either."

"Well, we likely know what caused that glitch. So I wouldn't go running for the holy water just yet."

Tony laughed as he put the van in gear and edged it into the busy traffic.

CHAPTER SEVEN

Albert Baptiste and his adult son Willy had been out checking their bait since sunrise and were now sweating it out in the hot afternoon sun. Their small aluminum boat wove through the murky channels of bayou country south of the small town of Clairmont. It pushed its way through the occasional floating islands of waterlilies and the slimy green ferns hanging languidly in the water. Cypress trees covered with dangling webs of gray Spanish moss dotted the shoreline. Their broad, gnarled roots reached greedily down like thick, bony fingers into the spongy, moist soil.

They encountered a contrast of smells in the humid air. There were the sweet, aromatic scents of the dogwoods and honeysuckles, as well as the occasional putrid odor of still water or something rotting, perhaps in the thick undergrowth along the shore. The dark head with white stripe of a deadly cottonmouth snake glided through the water next to their boat.

To many, the bayous were indeed a creepy world to be avoided, but they were bread-and-butter to the alligator hunters. The bayous had provided abundant catches for generations of Baptistes. But the hunters were going through tough times. Demand for alligator hides wasn't what it used to be. To make matters worse, today's catch was dismal, and the two fretted about meeting their tag quotas.

Willy, in the bow of the boat, spotted two knobbly eyes poking out of the water, surreptitiously surveying them. “There’s one,” he shouted and picked up the rifle as his father cut the engine. He took a shot at the eyes, but it was high, and the bullet splashed behind its target, which soon submerged. The two waited quietly for a few minutes. “There’s bubbles over there,” reported Willy. “He’s down there all right.” He threw a hooked line in the direction of the bubbles. He dragged back a loose line and tried again. This time the line went tight. “It’s light, though. No fight to it,” Willy remarked.

“You probably got a log or a clump of weed,” Albert observed.

“Okay. Up it comes, whatever it is.”

The older man looked down to click the gun bolt. Willy suddenly shouted and fell backward into the boat upon a couple of dead alligators covered by wet tarps.

“What the—what the hell’s going on, Willy?”

“A face looked up at me in the water!”

“What? You bin drinking hooch again from the bootlegger? Give me the line. You take the gun.… Here, take the gun, god damn it!” He saw a mass of blonde hair floating in the water. He gave a tug, and the head and shoulders of a body broke the surface. “Mary, mother of God,” he yelled, blessing himself.

Willy gaped at the horrid sight. “It’s a woman!” he blurted out hysterically.

“Of course it’s a woman,” Albert said. He put his hand over his mouth as he saw the leeches on the body’s neck. “The swamp’s got at her, too.” He forced himself to look at the blackened face. "She's bin in here awhile."

"God, what'll we do?" Willy's voice was frantic. "The phones don't work in these parts. We can't leave her, but we can't move her either. We're screwed!"

"We signal *them*," Albert said, pointing in the distance. Another boat was crossing an intersecting channel three or four hundred yards away. "Fire a couple of shots in the air, Willy."

Willy pulled the trigger, reloaded, and pulled it again; then he waved the rifle in the air. The boat slowed and then turned abruptly in their direction. It pulled up beside them and cut its engine.

"You boys got trouble?" the driver asked, standing up.

Albert pointed over to the starboard side. "Look what came up from the bottom."

"Jesus!" the driver exclaimed, jumping back.

"We can't move from here. You fellas have to go for help."

"There's a house about ten miles away," the driver said. "Maybe we can call the sheriff from there." The boat started up with a roar and headed east in a hurry.

Albert took off his baseball cap and wiped his brow with his hand. "Okay. Let's get her up."

"What, in the boat?"

"No, Willy. Let's just hoist her up so she's not gator bait."

"I'm not touching her!"

"You don't have to touch her, Willy. Just get a rope around her. Goddamn it!"

Willy managed to get a line under her armpits. The body rose on the winch. Fleshy stumps hung below the torso. "She's got no legs!" Willy yelled. He started to retch over the side.

Albert stumbled backward. "The gators must have got to her. My Christ!"

The two sat there through the sweltering afternoon with the dead alligators and their nightmarish catch suspended on the winch. They eventually calmed down enough to discuss the situation. "Well, there goes the tags for today and likely tomorrow, too," Albert said. "The cops will be swarmin' all over here with drag hooks and questions."

Willy brought himself to look at the body. "I wonder who she was." There were some loud splashes from something in the tall reeds behind him near the shore.

Albert took a long drag on a cigarette. "My bet is she's one of the missing women from around the bayous. The news said the cops have been looking for five of them for a couple of months now."

"I wonder how she got here?"

Albert shook his head. "Could have been murdered and somebody dumped the body here."

Willy looked puzzled. "Whoever did it didn't even try to hide it. There's no signs the body was weighed down or anything."

"He must have figured the gators would get rid of it," Albert surmised.

"Damn!" Willy said. "This is getting freakier all the time. What's holding up the sheriff?"

He'd barely uttered the words when they heard a helicopter beating the air to the south. It soon found them and circled around several times before landing on the water fifty yards away. The engine shut down and a bullhorn called out, “Sheriff’s Department. Is the body fully secured?”

“Yeah, we got a line on her,” Albert replied.

“Okay, sit tight. Patrol boats from the sheriff’s office are on their way.” The helicopter’s engines turned over and revved up. The craft took off, circling low over a wider area.

Within an hour, a small flotilla of fast-moving boats roared up the main channel and surrounded the hunters.

CHAPTER EIGHT

Jack Claye was about to sample his morning coffee when he picked up a call on his office line. It was the St. Paul's Parish Sheriff based in Clairmont, an hour's drive north of New Orleans. The sheriff asked for assistance in the investigation of a body found in the bayous southeast of the town. He reported the body's injuries bore unmistakable resemblance to those of the murder victims in New Orleans. Jack was disturbed yet electrified by the news. After he hung up with the sheriff, he hurried over to Tony's office.

***

Jeremy, Monica, and Tony left for Clairmont that morning for a briefing with the sheriff's team. It was a gorgeous midsummer's day in bayou country, which they fully appreciated after leaving behind the hazy petrochemical factories on the outskirts of New Orleans. The beautiful scenery contrasted starkly with the grim task facing them in Clairmont.

Tony, at the wheel of the van, offered a sober assessment. "With all the women disappearing in the bayous, it was only a matter of time before bodies would start showing up. The murderer's expanding his territory."

Jeremy nodded. "Let's hope he's becoming overconfident; that way, he's more likely to get careless."

Monica sighed. "I hope that's not counterbalanced by the fact that rural crimes can be more difficult to observe. I know we haven't had a credible witness so far in New Orleans, but eventually he's going to be seen doing it there or at least caught on camera. The laws of probability are on our side in the city, but not out here. Maybe the murderer realizes it's safer for him out in the country areas."

"Or it could be the flip side, to show that nobody in Louisiana, city or rural, is safe from him," Tony surmised.

The speculations were still hanging in the air as the van pulled up in front of the sheriff's office. Jeremy took a close look at the place. He saw a fortress-like brick-and-cement building with bars on the windows. Communication towers protruded menacingly from its roof. The stars and stripes hung limply over the building's front door in the still, humid air.

The team met Deputy Ted Deschamps, a ten-year veteran of the department, who ushered them in to meet the sheriff. After accepting an offer of coffee, the three were introduced to Sheriff Roland Petit, a clear misnomer given that he was at least six feet four inches tall and two hundred and fifty pounds. The parish coroner, Dr. Tremblay, was next on the introduction list. He was a diminutive man in his forties, almost a foot shorter than the sheriff. His high forehead and thick, rimless glasses gave him a rather intellectual look.

Sheriff Petit began the briefing. "I don't know how much Jack Claye told you, so I'll take it from the top." He spent the next ten minutes detailing the Baptistes' reports and the grisly scene that confronted the police in the black bayou where the body was found. His voice took on a note of frustration as he reported that, other than the body itself, no relevant evidence was found at the scene. He said that the Baptistes denied spotting any strangers or unusual events in the area recently. Other hunters and fishermen gave identical reports.

"What were your impressions of the Baptistes, Sheriff?" Tony asked.

"I was just getting to that," the sheriff replied. "There were no inconsistencies or anything suspicious in their reports. The pair were clearly in shock when we arrived at the scene. The son, Willy, bordered on hysteria as he described hooking and pulling up the body. The family are well-known hunters in the area. They have no previous contacts with the department."

The sheriff grimaced as he took a drink of thick, black coffee. "Dragging the bayou and probing with sonar also came up with nothing."

"Are there currents in the area, Sheriff?" Jeremy asked.

"Yes, there's a slight westerly current flowing in the direction of the recovery site. You're wondering if the body drifted there from somewhere else in the bloating stage? We anticipated that and spent two days searching upstream, but again, nothing turned up."

"Where does the current originate?"

"Its source is in the Bayou Rouge area, about ten miles to the south east."

"Is Bayou Rouge near anyone's property, Sheriff?"

"Yes, it's adjacent to an old plantation and mansion owned by Charles Vallencourt."

"What's his background?" Jeremy asked.

"He is a reclusive sort of man with business interests in New Orleans. He still lives in the mansion and commutes to the city; his family has owned the property longer than anyone can remember. He has no criminal background but has been involved in some mostly minor property disputes with neighbors. A few have gotten heated and police were called. No charges were laid."

Deputy Deschamps added, "If you want to know more about him and get a feel for the Clairmont area in general, talk to the Boisvert brothers. They're long-time locals who own a fishing and touring business just outside of town."

There was a brief silence. "If there's nothing else," the sheriff said, "we'll let the coroner proceed.... Nothing? Okay, Dr. Tremblay?"

The coroner stood up in front of the group, shuffling his papers. "Very well," he began. "I did an initial examination of the body at the scene and subsequently performed an autopsy and obtained test samples at the morgue. The body was quite decomposed from the high concentration of bacteria in the swamp water. It was also missing its legs, which looked to have been torn off by predators. The body had long, blonde hair and appeared to be that of a young woman. She was wearing matching ruby earrings and necklace."

The coroner paused, clearing his throat. "It's very difficult to estimate how long she was in the water; there's not much reliable forensic science about rates of decomposition in water. But from my experience with other bodies recovered in environments like this, the decomposition suggests she had been there for at least several weeks. She had a crushed larynx, and this appeared to be the cause of death through suffocation. There was no water in the lungs, so she did not drown. It appears she was placed in the water after death."

The coroner frowned. "Now, to the more bizarre findings. There was also a large gash in the lower abdomen, which could not have been inflicted by a predator. It was a precise incision through which the ovaries were removed with surgical skill. It appeared to have been done after death. Because of decomposition, it was impossible to tell if sexual assault had occurred."

He turned to the second page of his report. "There were what appeared to be indigo-colored textile fibers found lodged underneath the body's fingernails. But no other foreign matter was found there. No foreign human DNA was found on the body, but that's to be expected from the body's immersion in swamp water."

The doctor paused for a moment as if reflecting and then went on. "The results of toxicology tests were negative or inconclusive. The state of decomposition may have significantly influenced many test results or limited what could be tested. However, my conclusion is that the overall findings from the examination of the body are consistent with a fatal act of violence inflicted upon it, occurring at least several weeks ago."

"You mention you've seen other bodies from the swamps, Doctor," Jeremy said. "Were you referring to bodies recovered locally?"

"Yes, at least a dozen in the past decade, but these were ruled as suicides or accidental drownings, not foul play…."

"Thank you, Dr. Tremblay," the sheriff interjected. "If there are no other questions, I'll proceed to part two of my report. Okay. The body has been identified from comparisons with dental records and DNA samples from the five recently missing women. There is a match for twenty-nine-year-old Donna Secord, who disappeared about six weeks ago. The jewelry has also been identified by her family. By way of background, she was married, with two young children, to a local fisherman, Don Secord. Their home is located on the bayous, fifteen miles south of Clairmont. She was a life-long resident of the parish and regularly commuted to Clairmont for work as a transcriptionist at the town office."

The sheriff glanced up from his report. "I would see her coming and going from the town office and shopping in town, almost on a daily basis. She disappeared driving home on a small access road leading from Highway 3 to her home. A tree had fallen across the road, blocking it at a sharp bend. The tree had been deliberately cut down. We assume that she was attacked by the murderer as she got out to inspect the scene. The vehicle door was open, and the keys were still in the ignition. The car was found by her husband returning from work a few hours later. No clear tracks of other vehicles were located at the scene."

"Anything suspicious about family or acquaintances?" Tony asked.

"No. The marriage was reportedly happy, and no conflicts were noted with other members of her family, people at work, friends, or others. There appears to be no one who wanted her dead. She had a small life insurance plan with her husband as beneficiary, but they were not in any financial difficulty. Her husband had an alibi in that he was at work with his business partner at the estimated time of her disappearance."

"Is there anyone else in the area known to possess surgical or dissection skills, besides Dr. Tremblay, that is?" Jeremy queried.

"Just the town's doctor, who does some general surgery. The victim had been a patient of his, like ninety-nine percent of the rest of the town. He was working in the local infirmary at the time of the disappearance."

Dr. Tremblay interjected, "I was working at the time, too. But my clients are naturally unable to confirm it." Seeing his attempt at humor fall flat, he added, "However, I do video my sessions in case of court challenge and, naturally, these are open for inspection by the investigating team."

***

The trio debriefed the meeting on the return trip to New Orleans. "I thought the sheriff's team was pretty thorough," remarked Tony as he adjusted the driver's side visor.

"Right, and they need to be," Jeremy replied. "Getting evidence on this guy is like trying to get blood out of the proverbial stone."

"Well, he's being predictable, anyway," Monica added. "The murder is a variation of the same M.O., right down to the indigo fibers."

"Except this time he slipped out of his routine by dumping the body where there was little chance it would be found," Tony countered. "Unlike the city murders, where the bodies are out there for all to see. What's that about?"

"It could just be another level of his sadism," Monica surmised. "Maybe he relished the thought of his victim bloating up and floating around before being torn to pieces by alligators. Desecration and total destruction of the victim. The vanquishing of the enemy."

"Sobering thoughts," remarked Jeremy. "That means this guy's murderous drives are reinforced by each killing and meddling with the body afterward. He'll just keep on going."

The three looked at one another uneasily.

CHAPTER NINE

The three decided to follow up on Deputy Deschamps' suggestion to visit the Boisvert brothers. A week after the sheriff's briefing, they pulled up at Blue Bayou Fishing and Tour Company, about ten miles from Clairmont. Tony negotiated a tangle of mostly dirt roads to get there, complaining that the GPS was completely useless in the area.

The three walked into the main lodge, and Tony rang the bell on top of the roughly hewn, wooden counter. They looked over the place. The lodge's rustic interior was mainly built with cypress and oak planks and logs. On the walls hung photos of the big fish that didn't get away, displayed by proud fishermen. Reproductions of fish species found in the local bayous and streams were also mounted on the walls, identified on brass plates below them. Tony eyed a huge alligator garfish with a two-foot snout. "Holy crap," he said, using one of his rare mild expletives. "Look at the chompers on that! I hope there's none of these things in Lake Pontchartrain. We swim there!"

Jeremy laughed. "I think there are, Tony, but they'd go after other fish, not your toes."

No one answered the bell, so they wandered off to the docks out front. There was an older man bent over in one of the large aluminum boats at the dock, peering into the bowels of a large outboard motor. Another older man, looking tanned and weathered, sat on the dock, serenely rewinding a fishing line on a reel. He looked up. “What can I do for you folks?” he asked with a wide smile.

“The Boisvert brothers?” asked Tony.

“You got ’em.”

“We were sent to see you by Ted Deschamps.”

“Teddy, yeah. I knew him when he was just a squirt. An important man with a badge and gun these days…. You look like police yourselves.”

Tony smiled. “It’s that obvious, is it?” He extended a hand. “Tony Vasquez, NOPD. These are PIs Jeremy Hale and Monica Sauvé.”

“Bud Boisvert,” the man said, shaking Tony’s hand with a strong grip. He turned toward his brother. “Mike, come on up here. We got visitors.”

An equally weathered man in greasy coveralls stepped up on the dock, wiping his hands on a rag.

“The police want to talk to us, Mike.”

Tony noted that Mike didn’t seem surprised. He repeated introductions but did not have to introduce his topic.

“You’re here about the murders, huh?” Mike asked.

“Yes, that’s right.”

“It’s all over the news, and me and my brother know more about the goings-on around here than anybody. I figured you guys would pay a visit, sooner or later. You’re lucky you caught us on our down day.”

Jeremy smiled to himself. Knowing Tony, he knew it wasn’t a matter of luck. Tony had undoubtedly arranged to drop in unexpectedly on their maintenance day. He liked getting off-the-cuff information from people.

“Would you mind answering a few questions, then?” Tony asked.

“No. Fire away,” Mike responded.

Jeremy took over. “Have you noticed anything unusual or different in the town or area over the last couple of months?”

“You mean besides the town being scared shitless with all the trouble around here?”

“But have there been any strangers hanging about lately or locals acting in any unusual ways? Like not in their usual character or routines?”

“Not that I know of,” Mike said. “You, Bud?”

Bud shook his head and kept on rewinding his line.

“Then again,” Mike added, “we got—what’ll I call him—a permanent stranger in these parts.”

“What do you mean?”

“I mean Charles Vallencourt. Why don’t you fill ’em in, Bud?”

Bud didn’t look up from his work. “Charles Vallencourt is from old money,” he began. “Lives in his family’s mansion on Bayou Rouge about five miles from here on the way to Clairmont. You fellows passed it on the way here. It’s an old plantation. Goes back to the French settlers over two hundred years ago. They planted corn and rice for a long time and then made indigo dye. The dye business went bust around 1803, and they got into making sugar after that.”

Bud put his reel down. “The family made their money on the backs of slaves. Worked ’em into the ground. A lot were killed in the steam vats used to make the sugar. Others, called ‘marooners,’ were maimed, tortured, or killed for running away into the swamps. All that stopped when the North took over after the war."

Mike elaborated on the history lesson. "Then the family got into the investment business in New Orleans, and as far as anybody knows, Charles still makes it his living. But he plays his cards close to his chest and keeps pretty well to himself. Nobody in town's seen him for … it must be twenty years. Just sends his help—some think they're bodyguards—into town for things. But his fancy black limo, shaded windows and all, is often seen heading toward New Orleans…. There's something else. Hunters in the bayous near the mansion have seen big plastic bags unloaded at night into his garage area. Nobody knows what's in them, and most don't want to know either."

Bud nodded gravely. "People are afraid of the mansion and its keeper. Some have seen weird lights and heard noises in the bush around there at night."

"Okay, what's all this boiling down to?" Jeremy asked.

Mike stared at him. "We're saying it's no coincidence about the disappearances and the body. People have been saying for two hundred years that bodies were found near the plantation, and not just runaways. Some folks think the commotion at night comes from the souls of murdered people."

Bud added, "But it could be worse. Some think Vallencourt is a rougarou."

"A what?" asked Tony.

Monica smiled. "It's Cajun for '*le loup garou*'—a man that transforms into a wolf."

"A werewolf?" Tony asked, astonished.

"Yeah," Bud replied with a straight face. "It's said the condition runs in Vallencourt's family."

The three investigators smiled at one another.

"Go ahead and laugh," Mike chided, "but it's history. It came across from France with a boatload of settlers in the fall of 1786. One morning, the ship was found adrift off New Orleans. Crews rowed out and boarded her. There wasn't a soul alive. Every man, woman, and child were ripped open like cattle in a slaughterhouse.... Now, listen to this. The bodies didn't match the total on the ship's passenger and crew lists. One person was missing. Two days later, a Frenchman turns up at the registry office in New Orleans asking to register as a settler and the same day bought a large property near what is now Clairmont. That man was an ancestor of Charles Vallencourt."

The afternoon sun was now scorching hot on the dock. Jeremy wiped his forehead with a handkerchief.

Mike was amused. "Why don't you city types come in for something cold before you get heat stroke?"

"We won't trouble you," Tony said, thinking of the cold Cokes in the van's cooler. "But thank you for your time. Here's my card if anything crops up, Mike."

Mike took the card and offered some ominous parting advice. "Keep an eye on the old plantation, folks, and watch your backs while you do it."

The three walked out to the van and promptly raided the cooler. "That was probably the strangest interview I have ever been party to," Tony remarked.

Jeremy laughed. "Well, we've had our taste of Deep South superstition for the day, I think."

"Your right about the superstition," observed Monica. "The rougarou is embedded deeply in the folklore of Louisiana, especially in the small bayou communities. It's equivalent to the bogeyman in other states, meant to scare little children into behaving. Down here, it's also been used to frighten Catholics into observing Lent more conscientiously."

Jeremy smiled. "I haven't kept Lent in decades, but I haven't lost my memory during the full moon yet. Of course, Tony, as a dedicated Catholic, you don't have to worry about that."

Tony appreciated the humor, but Monica continued in a serious vein. "It's interesting how the rougarou gets associated with real murders, though. People resist believing that human beings could possibly carry out terrible murders such as these. So they dehumanize the murderer as an animal or monster. Hence, Vallencourt must be a rougarou."

Tony looked impressed. Jeremy glanced at him as if to ask, "and you were wondering why I hired her?" He then added an insight of his own. "Unfortunately, we don't have to look for rougarous to explain murder. Human beings have enough propensity for violence, including war, already programmed in their genes.... But the key thing about all of this is that the Boisverts and Clairmonters, it seems, are extremely suspicious of Mr. Vallencourt. We need to pursue every lead. Let's find Vallencourt and his ancestors in the town records and see if there are any reports of bodies showing up near his plantation. There's a museum in town as well that may have historical information on the family, such as how they arrived in Louisiana." He grinned. "Who knows? We may even be able to rule out their werewolf origins."

Tony laughed. "That sounds like at least a full day's work," he said. "Why don't we call it for today?"

The others gladly nodded and gravitated toward the cooler.

CHAPTER TEN

The trio returned to Clairmont the following week in an attempt to track down more about the mysterious Charles Vallencourt. They had decided upon a division of labor beforehand. Monica would pore over the town records; Tony volunteered to fraternize with the local barflies, and Jeremy would visit the Clairmont museum.

Jeremy found the old museum next to the town office. It was built in the traditional Louisiana style: brick and stucco etched to look like stone, high first floor, and deep awnings along the walls to help keep out the heat.

The interior was full of antiques and artifacts going back to the early 1700s. Jeremy was struck by the colorful murals on the walls depicting historical places and events in Clairmont. A painting of the old Vallencourt plantation caught his attention, with the mansion surrounded by slave houses, barns, and sugar manufacturing sheds. It brought some life to the Boisvert brothers' accounts. Jeremy noted that the painting referred to the Vaillancourt plantation. The name was obviously anglicized at some point.

"Wonderful paintings, aren't they?" a soft female voice said.

Jeremy turned to find, standing beside him, a pleasant-looking woman with her glasses hanging around her neck. Her nametag announced she was Marlene Chartrand, the Clairmont Museum curator.

"A local artist?" Jeremy asked.

"Was at the time. Maureen Theriault. She has a gallery going now in New Orleans. Is there anything you might be interested in particularly?"

"Yes. The history of the old plantations in the area. The Vaillancourt plantation painting caught my eye."

"Ah, yes. The most famous, if not infamous, family in the area."

"Why infamous?"

"Well, there's quite a dark history to the Vaillancourt family, now called the Vallencourts."

"Not simply small-town folklore?"

"No. There've been documented reports of violence on the old plantation since the slave days. Unfortunately, that was common practice in the slavery era, but the Vallencourts were apparently the most brutal of all."

"So the violence stopped after abolition?"

"No, there have been bodies discovered since, under suspicious circumstances, near the Vallencourt plantation."

"Were these ever investigated?"

The curator sighed. "We're talking about the days when little or no law enforcement existed in the area—at best a rudimentary police force in New Orleans, which took little interest in the rural districts."

"Do you know if the Vallencourts were ever questioned on these matters?"

"Yes, about a body found on the shore of the bayou bordering their plantation, almost ninety years ago. Nothing came of it. The family reportedly had political influence in New Orleans, and some people believed they used it to make the investigation go away."

"You mentioned documented reports about the bodies. Do you know where they are to be found?"

"Unfortunately, most were lost. Back in the 1950s, a New Orleans history teacher, John Meakins, retired in Clairmont and wrote a history book of the area. It included much information on the Vallencourts, such as old reports by people who had discovered the bodies and some reports of the old-time doctors who once practiced here. He bequeathed a copy of the book and its supporting documents to the museum before he died in the 1970s. This is the only copy I'm aware of. Recently, there was a break-in here, and the book and documents were stolen, along with other artifacts related to the Vallencourt family. Nothing else was touched. The sheriff's office was involved, but the theft remains unsolved. It is a great loss to the town."

"Don't you find it odd that only these materials were stolen? There must be other collectible items here."

"I do find it odd, along with many others in the community. Some think it was Vallencourt himself trying to get rid of incriminating evidence about his family. But the sheriff said he didn't have enough to question Vallencourt about it. Political pull, again, some thought."

"So there's nothing at all pertaining to the Vallencourts left in the museum?"

"I didn't say that. There is a diary of one of the witnesses to a body recovery. Whoever took the other material perhaps didn't know about it."

She gently opened the clasp on an old leather and cloth-bound book. The title page was marked *The Journal of Charlene Dupre*. The curator then read aloud the entry of August 18, 1928, "My father and I were fishing in the Bayou Rouge when we spotted what we thought was a bundle of clothes on the shore of the Vallencourt plantation. We rowed over to it and found the body of a young woman. It was horrible—decayed and torn up by gators. I was afraid it was one of the girls from town who went missing over the summer.

"We led Doctor Peterson and the sheriff back to the body. Doc Peterson examined the body but suddenly looked surprised. I overheard him say to the sheriff that something had been taken out of the body and that it wasn't an animal that did it."

The curator then read the entry for August 25, 1928, "Bad news. The body's been named. It was Carrie Dupont, the general store owner's eighteen-year-old daughter, who went missing in July. I knew her to say hello but not much more. It must be so sad for her family and friends. How could such a terrible thing happen in Clairmont?"

***

At six o'clock that evening, the three met in the van to discuss their investigations. Monica presented first. "I sampled the town's records. Of course, there were just too many to read all of them. Most of the references to the Vallencourts were mundane. The family paid their taxes regularly. Town council had to handle several trespassing complaints against the family by their neighbors and disagreements over a stream flowing through their properties and the Vallencourt estate. There were also complaints about disturbing the peace: strange wailing noises around the old plantation at night."

"That's what the Boisverts were saying," Tony remarked.

"Yes, and tensions grew with the neighbors. Eventually, a Vallencourt and a neighbor confronted one another across their property line, holding rifles. No shots were fired, but the town thought this was serious enough to dispatch a council member to mediate. But apparently bad feelings persisted."

Monica shook her head. "This wasn't the worst of it. In the town council meeting of July 15, 1943, mention is made of a shooting death in the bush between the two plantations. One of the neighbor's sons had been out hunting in the common bush area and was found with a fatal gunshot wound. The sheriff's report was attached to the council's minutes. The caliber of the bullet that killed the son did not match John Vallencourt's rifle. The sheriff put it down to a likely incident with a poacher on the property. Some council members expressed suspicion that this wasn't the only gun owned by Vallencourt and that the sheriff got orders to back off by someone influential in New Orleans. There were allegations that other bodies found near the Vallencourt property had been improperly investigated."

"That's the picture I got at the museum, too," added Jeremy. "Except there was an interesting twist. The apparently sole book and its supporting records documenting the history of the Vallencourts and other old families in the area were recently mysteriously stolen, along with other Vallencourt documents and artifacts. Nothing else was missing in the museum. The curator expressed the suspicion of many that Charles Vallencourt himself had stolen the items to remove incriminating evidence about his family. But the thief left behind the diary of a witness to the recovery of a body in Bayou Rouge. I have a photocopy of her account right here. It's very interesting."

Tony took a look at the copy. "So an organ may have been removed from the body. That *is* interesting," he remarked, handing the copy to Monica.

"But with the theft of the history book and its documents, it's doubtful we'll ever lay our hands on the doctor's report," Jeremy added gloomily.

"So how did you do today, Tony?" Monica asked, hoping for better news.

"Well, I hobnobbed with one of Vallencourt's long-term neighbors, who comes into town for beer in the afternoons. At first he complained that the Vallencourts were nothing but trouble and spouted off about similar disagreements and disturbances that you two have mentioned. But as he got more sauced, he started talking about his real concerns. He said bodies have turned up in the bayous around Charles Vallencourt's property. They were ruled as suicides or accidental drownings by successive coroners, but he's convinced some were murdered and Vallencourt arranged to have it all covered up."

"And I'll bet your informant is long on gut feelings and short on facts," Jeremy said.

"No facts, really.... Yet there's an epidemic of suspicions in town against Vallencourt. You have to wonder if there's something to all of this."

"So, what do you think, Tony? Do we surveil the place?"

Tony reached for a piece of his chewing gum. "To be on the safe side, yeah. If we go for limited surveillance, I might be able to sell this to Jack Claye. We'd need a warrant for anything more anyway, and we won't get it now. Everything is either circumstantial or based on rumor. The most we can do now is watch the property entrance and also the mansion from Bayou Rouge."

"Meanwhile," Jeremy said, "we can check the city's corporate records to see what business or businesses Vallencourt owns in New Orleans. Sounds like a good job for you, Monica."

Tony started the van and pulled out onto the main street toward Highway 3. "Well, I feel a little better than when we left the city this morning," he confided. "At least we can tell Jack we have a person of interest in the case."

CHAPTER ELEVEN

It was a late Tuesday night at the office for Jeremy and Monica. The usual business day for the New Orleans office scene had wound down hours before.

"Why don't we call it quits for this evening?" Jeremy suggested.

Monica nodded. "By the way, I won't be able to work late Tuesdays. I've enrolled in a painting class on Tuesday evenings. It's also a chance to meet a few people."

"Personal development, huh? No problem." He thought for a moment. "I don't think I've taken an interest class in ten years. Tony says I'm in danger of becoming a river hermit."

"Are you?"

"Probably. But I could make an exception for a colleague, just for tonight. How would you like to join me for a late dinner? I know a very good café in the Quarter."

"Strictly business?" Monica asked with a smile.

"Strictly," Jeremy said, returning her smile. "I'll sign an affidavit for you if you want."

Monica laughed. "I'll take your word for it."

The two were soon ordering some Louisiana chicken and hot sauce pasta at Leo's Café. They enjoyed a glass of white wine before their meal. A guitarist played and sang a blues number on a low stage in the background.

"This town never stops singing," Jeremy observed. "Blues and jazz are its soul."

Monica nodded. "New Orleans soul, yeah. That's part of the reason I came down here. Maybe to find my own, too."

Jeremy swished his wine around in his glass. "You mentioned your family was from down here?"

"Yes, for many generations. We were settlers from New France in the 1700s."

Jeremy's historical sense was certainly being piqued. "Why don't you tell me about it?"

Monica's face lit up; it wasn't often she had the opportunity to talk about her long and unusual family history. "Well, the family settled into New Orleans. They had business acumen and eventually began importing fine wines, clothing, perfumes, and jewelry from Europe. The business flourished for many decades, and eventually the family opened up a branch in Baton Rouge. Everything was fine until the recession of the 1970s, when the family moved north to Boston and diversified."

Jeremy noticed Monica lightly touching a turquoise pendant she was wearing. "Beautiful pendant. I've seen you wear it before. Is this one of your family's pieces?"

"Not from the business, but it is a family heirloom. The stone has been in my family for almost five hundred years. A distant great-grandfather of mine was apparently a student of a great seer of the time. My ancestor eventually became a noted healer and spiritualist in his own right. It is believed he acquired the stone from the seer. It is said to have magical powers to focus and amplify the wearer's innate spiritual energy. The stone was passed on through the generations to the daughter thought to have the ability to use it most wisely."

"Well, that's quite the story. Do you think you have the ability to use it wisely?"

"I'm open to possibilities. But I wear the stone because it reminds me of my grandmother who gave it to me; she practiced as a psychic in Baton Rouge for many years. She also bequeathed to me a book of spiritual meditations written by this same ancestor. It's a beautifully bound leather book with a red eagle in flight embossed on the cover."

"Have you read it?"

"No, just perused it. I have it in my chest of family mementos."

"What's the red eagle about?"

"My grandmother told me the eagle in flight is a symbol of spirituality and freedom. But she didn't know what the red color signifies. Its meaning has been lost over the centuries."

"She sounds like a colorful person. No pun intended."

"She was. She even used to tell me things about my future and made a prophecy about me once."

"What did she prophesize?"

"I remember her saying that just as the universe is the interaction of opposites, so my life will be a powerful interplay of my rational and spiritual sides. True happiness and wisdom will only come when the two sides are in balance. In fact, there will be a time when my very survival in the world depends on achieving this balance."

"A kind of yin and yang, then? So far, I've met only the logical, scientific side of you: the criminal profiler. Yin but not yang."

Monica smiled at his comment. "I'm not sure I know exactly what the spiritual side is. If it's the side that shows up in church and practices religious rituals, I guess I'm not spiritual. I'm a terrible Catholic who has trouble with all the rules—you know, the dos and don'ts of Catholicism. Worse, I'm only partway to believing in the Trinity. If it's the part of me that is not rational and empirical, then maybe I am. I've always been connected to an intuitive part of myself. In fact, it often got results for the Boston Police Department."

"Sounds like the jury's still out on the spiritual side. But what if your grandmother's prophesy is true?"

Monica laughed. "It does seem dark, doesn't it? If it's true, I'd better start working on that balance—or else.... But tell me, Jeremy, what about you? Are you mister rational/empirical, or is there another side to you?" She looked at him intently.

Jeremy sipped his wine and took refuge in a riddle. "I have a special relationship with ... a kind of mentor that not many people understand. Maybe we can talk about it sometime."

Monica saw an uncomfortable look cross his face, as if he wanted to take back what he'd just said.

Jeremy deployed his signature avoidance tactic. "By the way, how did it go tracking down Vallencourt's business connections? Any hits?"

Monica was caught off guard. "Uh, okay. The elusive Charles Vallencourt is revealed to be a prominent businessman in New Orleans. I checked the business and corporate registries. There's nothing very ominous so far. He runs a financial investment company with a staff of thirty. The office is downtown on Larch Street. A search of court records confirms that there have been no suits or charges against him or his company. He also has a foundation that supports some very well-known charities. He likes to remain private, since there are no photos of him at charity announcements."

"He sounds like businessman of the year," Jeremy commented. "The cynical part of me wants to dig a little deeper into his enterprises. I'll see what we can find out from one of my informants. He's a wheeler and dealer in the money rackets in New Orleans. I'll set up a meeting for us."

***

Jeremy returned to his boat in a gloomy, apprehensive mood, which wasn't helped by the deep fog once again hanging over the river. He mulled anxiously over his revelation to Monica about his special relationship. It wasn't that he gave away much. It was his intention that scared him. He had also barely resisted her invitation to visit her apartment after Leo's. His scared feeling suddenly transformed into a surge of panic.

This wasn't the first time he had experienced such feelings. He flashed back to the worst night of his childhood. He was in bed that terrible night when his mother opened his bedroom door. She came in crying and took his hand. "Mommy is going to have to leave," she said, the words provoking a flood of tears pouring down on him and his blanket.

"Why?" he asked, reaching to hug her and draw her close. "Was I bad?"

“No. It’s because Daddy and I don’t love one another anymore.”

“But can’t you make yourself love him?”

“No. It doesn’t work that way. But don’t be too sad. I’ll be coming back to see you.” She gently unraveled his arms and walked out the door, leaving the room in darkness. He was afraid it would be the last time he would see her.

CHAPTER TWELVE

Jeremy and Monica were driving in his black sedan to a meeting with one of his chief informants, Johnny Gallant.

Aware of Jeremy's list of snitches, Monica asked, "How have you managed to collect so many informants? Pay them?"

"Not if I want to keep my license," Jeremy said. "I have a more powerful incentive: gratitude."

She gave him a puzzled look.

"I've done a lot of work for defence attorneys, which has gotten off quite a few of their clients. Some of the clients, innocent or not, haven't forgotten. They regard my work as a debt to be repaid. So I enroll them in my 'informant program.'" He grinned.

"Brilliant. So is Johnny one of your enrollees?"

"He is. His business partner of the time set him up on an inside trading charge. Now, Johnny is no angel, but he was innocent of the charge. His partner was angling to get him out of the way and take over the business. It looked like Johnny was going down until I uncovered the plot and the charges were dropped."

"Nice. That must have been a good feeling."

"It was, and I got a top-flight informant in the money rackets, too."

The two arrived at the meeting point in a small public park overlooking the river, which sparkled in the strong midmorning sun. They met a slightly built, middle-aged man in a short-sleeved golf shirt.

His horn-rimmed glasses accentuated his rather shifty look.

"Johnny, meet my assistant, Monica Sauvé. Monica, Johnny Gallant."

The three grabbed sausages on buns, smothered in onions and hot sauce, from a steaming vendor's cart. They sat down at one of the park tables in the midst of a flower garden in full bloom.

"So, Jeremy, you've hired an assistant," Johnny said in his Brooklyn accent. "I take it business must be good?"

"Yes, thanks in part to your quality information, Johnny."

Johnny smiled. "I like to keep the money rolling. By the way, before we get down to business, how about we make sure our phones are turned off." He placed his phone on the table. "Just like the old proverb says: 'Trust but verify.'"

The others did likewise. Jeremy thought of a saloon scene from an old Western movie where the card players had emptied their pistols and threw them in a pile on the table before starting to play. The problem was that one of the players had a derringer still strapped to his ankle. Hopefully, Johnny was on the level.

"So, what did you come up with, Johnny?"

Johnny pressed his fingertips together. "This guy Vallencourt is a hard man to track. Any information from his company comes only after a referral and a face-to-face. I've tapped into the grapevine. He's a high-end operator. No mom-and-pop clientele here. He deals mostly in large cap investments for very rich, elite clients. I mean people like Russian oligarchs and Third World dictators. I hear the minimum investment at one time is ten mil."

"Whew," Jeremy said, "they're in the big game."

"Yeah, and these dudes may be laundering their money through Vallencourt. Vallencourt does not appear to have been caught at anything—yet. If he's doing it, he's damn good at covering his tracks, even from the Feds. Big players like this have the money and power to silence inquisitive federal officials."

Johnny looked warily toward the parking lot. "There's one more thing. I may be paying a price for doing this job."

"What do you mean?"

"I mean I think there's someone who's been tailing me since I started looking into Vallencourt. I took the bus today, and then an around-about route walking here. I couldn't have been tailed, but just in case, watch your backs."

"Are you saying you think Vallencourt put someone on you?"

"It's likely. Otherwise, it's quite a coincidence, don't you think?"

Jeremy frowned. "Well, if it's really happening, it could complicate things."

"Yeah. If he makes a connection between you and me, he'll know you're interested in him."

Jeremy took a deep breath and exhaled slowly. "Obviously, in the future we can't be seen together."

"Okay. If I hear anymore, I'll get back to you."

"Thanks, Johnny. This has been helpful. I'd offer you a ride back, but that may not be such a good idea."

"You're right about that," Johnny said, walking toward the main street.

Jeremy and Monica immediately traded their impressions of the meeting. "Do you really trust this guy?" she asked.

"As much as I trust any of my informants," he said. "They all have their limits."

"That's what concerns me. Johnny loves money. I'm not saying it's happening now, but what if Johnny someday gets paid off for telling us something misleading. At what point does greed outweigh gratitude?"

"Yeah, that's a risk we take. We just have to size up what he says. See if it holds water. But you make a good point. A dose of mistrust in human nature is a healthy thing for a PI."

"Right," Monica replied. "And when you size up what Johnny is saying, there are some important holes in what he knows about Vallencourt."

"Exactly. We need to firm up our information, and I know just who we go to next. At any rate, you're thinking and asking questions, and that's how a PI gets the job done and survives. Well done, Monica."

Monica smiled at the compliment. As the two stood up to leave, Jeremy checked his watch. It was almost noon. "Say, Monica, are you interested in lunch at Leo's?" he asked. As soon as he said it, he remembered saying that their last meal at Leo's was going to be a one-off. Was he becoming overinvolved with her?

Monica turned toward him, smiling. "Normally, I would not refuse Leo's, but I already have a luncheon date today."

"Oh?" Jeremy asked.

"Yes, with Daryl Greenwood."

"*Our* Dr. Greenwood?" he asked, puzzled.

"Yes. We both enjoy intellectual discussion, particularly about serial murderers. He was telling me about the workshop he copresented in Washington."

"So, it's strictly cerebral?" Jeremy asked, immediately wishing he could take back the question.

"You got it. I've been meaning to tell you about our conversations."

"Conversations? You've met more than once?" he queried, realizing he had overstepped again.

"Yes. He's interesting and charming in an intellectual way. Very witty. He also knows a fair amount about the history of serial murders in Louisiana, including around Clairmont."

"Did you ask him about his sources?"

"Yes. He says he has a book about the history of the area written by Clairmont's local historian."

"The curator said she thought there was only one copy, and it was stolen."

"I know. Daryl says he's a book collector and came across it at a used book sale recently. So it could either be the stolen book surfacing, or the curator was wrong and there's another copy. It's quite a find, he says. He was planning to raise the matter formally with us, but he's been tied up."

"Well, we're going to have to meet with him sooner rather than later. Meanwhile, have a good lunch. Don't get too stimulated cerebrally."

She laughed. "I'll be careful."

CHAPTER THIRTEEN

Jenny Thibeault, like most seventeen-year-olds in Clairmont, hated the town with a passion. She found it hopelessly boring; anything remotely interesting to her was out of town, mostly in New Orleans. There, she attended T.H. Orley High School, enduring the two-hour round-trip bus ride five days a week. She was attractive, like her mother, and quite popular with the Orley seniors. Indeed, she lived for the adulation of her school friends.

Otherwise, school was just as boring as Clairmont. Though intelligent, she couldn't care less about academics. School was a place to do her time until that twelfth-grade diploma. Then she could do what she really wanted: get out of Clairmont.

Above all, she wanted to escape the fishbowl effect of living in a small town. Everyone knew everyone else's business, which qualified as an adolescent's worst nightmare. But the rumors were the worst. There was unfounded speculation about how far she and her boyfriend Billy had gone in their backseat trysts. Her greatest fear was that this gossip would get back to her father, Louie, a strict, outwardly religious man who would brook no sins of the flesh.

Louie's ire was not reserved just for Jenny. Her mother, Therese, was the other prime target. Her attractiveness was a fact not lost on most of the adult male population in Clairmont. Louie was acutely aware of other men's interest in her and insanely jealous. Jenny often heard her father shouting out his accusations that Therese was having an affair, followed by her mother's quiet, almost obsequious denials. The bedroom door would then slam, muffling the sounds behind it. But Jenny knew what was happening.

Jenny resented her mother never protecting her against her father's rages. But then again, she reminded herself, what could she expect? Her mother could not even protect herself. Jenny also resented being dragged to church for Sunday morning mass at St. Mary's on George Street. She believed her parents were hypocrites, and from what she had heard, the rest of the congregation were no better. She often gazed in church upon the glossy, heavily lacquered statue of Christ upon the cross, suffering for the sins of humanity. He needn't have bothered, she thought.

***

Jenny and Billy were parked on Old Cemetery Road, away from the prying eyes of parents and other adults in their lives. They'd been waiting eagerly all week to be alone in the backseat of Billy's black Lincoln, which he could borrow from his father only on Friday nights.

Old Cemetery Road was aptly named. It ran along the rusted, cast-iron fence of a Cajun cemetery abandoned since the early 1800s. Rumors were that it had been closed after the burial there of victims of a typhoid outbreak. No one came there anymore, except for teens looking for a little privacy and pranksters who would break in on Halloween and destroy a few old tombs. But it was still officially a consecrated Catholic cemetery, as attested to by the cold stone figure of the Virgin Mary at the cemetery gate, staring with blank eyes at the heavens.

Billy was making good progress at undoing Jenny's bra. He took time to savor the experience, since this was likely all he would get tonight. Jenny was careful and forbade touching below the waist. Billy had no such compunctions and always remained hopeful of further attention from his girlfriend.

Jenny suddenly stiffened and sat up. "What was that?"

"What?"

"I heard a noise outside."

"Jenny, there's nobody here but us and the dead people."

"There it is again," she gasped. "Did you hear it?"

"Yeah, something. It's probably some bird or animal." He tried to push her back down on the seat.

"Look! There's a light in the graveyard! Over there, to the right."

Billy peered out the back window. "What the hell? Why would somebody be in the graveyard this time of night? It's been closed forever."

"Let's get out of here!" she screamed. The two threw open the rear doors and jumped into the front seats. Billy started up hurriedly and floored the accelerator, throwing up a cloud of dust in the faint moonlight as he sped off.

***

Deputy Ted Deschamps was on patrol on the backroads around Clairmont. A call from the dispatcher at the sheriff's office came in over the radio. "Deputy. Received a call from Gus Moreau on Old Cemetery Road. You'll recall he recently lodged a complaint about a break-in on his property. He reports that a few minutes ago he saw lights in the old cemetery and is concerned there are vandals there."

The deputy frowned. "Okay, Dispatch. Proceeding to the cemetery." It was against his better judgment—not that he was superstitious, but there could be difficulties spotting snakes in the dark overgrowth of the cemetery. He had made the mistake of stepping on a copperhead as a kid and almost died from the experience. He turned off on a connector road and soon arrived at the cemetery gate.

The cemetery was deeply shadowed and silent. He shone his flashlight into the darkness. A clutter of old monuments, overgrown to varying degrees by grass and low bushes, showed up in its beam. There were no signs of disturbance that he could see from the road. He got out of his vehicle and checked the rusty lock and chain on the main gate. They were fully intact. No one had entered that way.

He sighed and walked along one side of the fence. A musty, earthy smell filled the humid air. A section of the fence had fallen in, and he stepped through it into the cemetery. He played the light on the ground in front of him, being careful where he stepped. Just more gray-green, crumbling monuments with their faded inscriptions. A village of the dead, he thought.

He noticed that the muddy ground near the fallen fence had no footprints in it. Nobody had come in that way either. A rustling came from a nearby tangle of bushes. He quickly shone the light on it but could see nothing unusual. He reminded himself uneasily that the cemetery was not far from the swamp, albeit on higher ground; there was always the possibility of an alligator lurking around. As he panned the light on a cluster of tombs to his right, he thought he saw a dark lump on top of one of them. He drew out his sidearm and approached it. He inhaled sharply as the light clarified the mass. It was the body of a woman lying face up, legs spread, on the monument. His heartbeat quickened. She was definitely dead—probably within the last few hours. He quickly checked out the immediate area around him with his light and then called the dispatcher. "Female found deceased in St. Michael's Cemetery. Request immediate backup."

***

The town's rumor mill was in full production the next morning. Clairmonters awakened to the news flashes that the body of a woman had been found in the old cemetery. They heard the police were treating the death as "suspicious." No further details were released, leaving the gossipers to fill in the blanks. Some thought it was one of the women reported missing in the bayous. Others believed she was probably a fresh victim from Clairmont. So far, no one had been reported missing from the town, but it was still early. Regardless, it had to be the work of the same killer as in the New Orleans murders. It was only a matter of time before another body would turn up, maybe right in town.

Betty Moreau, Gus's wife, brought her produce into the farmers' market that morning. She said it was a good thing Gus noticed the lights in the cemetery, or no one would have known about the body—at least no one but the killer. It was no accident, she added, that the body was found next to the back quarter of the Vallencourt property.

The locals' fears were magnified by the fact that almost no crime happened in the little town, other than the odd drunken brawl at Landry's Bar on the weekends or some teens shoplifting on a dare. Most of the drunks spent the night in the parish cooler and were let off with a warning the next morning. The store owners, ever conscious of business, never laid charges against the teen shoplifters. The kids were driven home to face family court with their parents. Indeed, crime was so rare, the townspeople never bothered to lock their doors at night, and they were proud of the fact. But many said they were locking up tonight.

Jenny barely restrained herself from telling her friends she had seen some strange goings-on at the cemetery, but she would have had to reveal why she was there, and that might get back to her father. So, in a hushed voice, she confided her feelings to Billy over a Coke at a back table in Dewer's Restaurant.

"What if it was the murderer right there at the cemetery, Billy? You didn't listen to me right away. We could have been next!"

Billy shook his head. "You're paranoid. The cops said it just was suspicious, that's it."

Jenny looked him straight in the eye. "That's code for murder. They just don't want to tell us yet."

"You watch too many crime programs."

"Just wait, Billy. It'll be one of those women they're looking for, murdered like the ones in New Orleans."

Billy sipped his Coke in silence, reluctant to push the issue further. He was not going to risk ticking off a girl with a body like hers, even if she was uptight about sex.

"It scared the hell out of me, Billy! Last night I had a nightmare that we were trapped in the back seat of the car at the cemetery, and something was coming for us in the dark. Then I woke up all sweaty."

"Yeah, you and the whole town are freaked out. My dad says there's been a run on shotgun shells and pepper spray at the hardware."

"My old man is one of them. Thinks Vallencourt did it and blabs it all over town."

"Your old man hates him anyway. I hear he says Vallencourt is some kind of sinner for all the inbreeding in the family."

"So you're not freaked out?"

"No. Let's find out what happened first. Maybe it was a suicide in the cemetery, for all we know. I found an awesome parking spot we can try out. Are we on for Friday night?"

Jenny's eyes opened wide. "Are you crazy?"

Billy laughed. "No, just horny like always."

"That figures. It won't be with me for a while, buddy." As her voice raised, a cascade of giggling arose from a group of preteen girls within earshot.

Jenny did not tell her boyfriend everything. She'd had a feeling for a week that she was being followed by someone. But if she told Billy, he would only call her paranoid again. He would ask her how someone could possibly follow her in a small town like Clairmont and get away with it. But she'd had the feeling in New Orleans, too, when she would leave school to smoke pot at noon hours. Puzzling, she thought, but maybe Billy was right and her imagination was getting away on her.

CHAPTER FOURTEEN

Less than a month after the body was discovered in the bayou, Jeremy, Monica, and Tony attended another dismal briefing at the sheriff's office.

Sheriff Petit began his grim presentation. "So, here we are again," he said with an undertone of frustration. "This time it concerns a body found by Deputy Deschamps in St. Michael's Cemetery two nights ago. I understand you've already been filled in by Jack Claye about the circumstances surrounding the discovery of the body. Here are shots of the crime scene," he said, displaying the photos on a screen. "As with most of the other murders, the body's been posed, naked below the waist, legs open. As you can see, it was placed on its back on top of an old monument."

"Any reason it was that particular monument, Sheriff?" Tony asked.

"Not that we can see. It belongs to a teenage boy from the Robitaille family who died of typhoid in the early 1800s, just before the graveyard was abandoned. We researched what historical records are available. The Robitailles were everyday farming people who did not appear to play a prominent role in the area. There were no red flags attached to the family such as criminal history or conflicts with other locals, debts, etc."

"So the placement of the body was random, then?" Monica queried.

"Maybe. But the tomb is closest to the cemetery's boundary with Vallencourt's back quarter. The fence in that section has collapsed." He pointed to a photo. "It's been down for many years."

"Is there evidence the body was brought into the cemetery through the gap?"

"It could have been," the sheriff said. "As the photos show, the area is long grass. Though you can't see it well in the images, the grass has been displaced to form a faint trail to the Vallencourt property, which then disappears. Mind you, this is not far from the bayou, and large animals, like gators, might have made their way into the cemetery through the gap. There are two other downed sections. One, proximate to the bayou, showed no footprints in the muddy gap. A second, facing a country lane on the other side, might have been an entry point. However, the ground is more elevated there. It's hard and dry and would have shown no prints anyway. Entry was definitely not through the front gate, which was chained and locked that night."

The sheriff paused and looked around expectantly. "If there are no further questions, I'll turn the briefing over to our coroner.... Okay, you have the floor, Dr. Tremblay."

"I'm sorry to have to meet with you all again under these tragic circumstances," the coroner began. "I have examined the body and sent tissue and blood samples to New Orleans for testing. As the test results are not yet back, my report today is preliminary. However, there are sufficient findings to provide initial insight into what happened with the body. The body bore the same injury patterns found on the other female victims: signs of sexual assault, torture, removal of the ovaries, and crushed larynx, which appears to be the ultimate cause of death. The estimated time of death is about two hours prior to the body being found by Deputy Deschamps."

The investigators looked at one another uneasily. They had expected to hear it was the same M.O., but the words of confirmation from the coroner weighed heavily on them. The depressed mood in the room was almost palpable.

Doctor Tremblay continued with his sobering report. "No DNA was discovered in or on the body, which might relate to an attacker. Indigo cotton fibers were found on the body, as was the case with all previous victims. There is one very unusual finding, however."

The others looked at him curiously.

"Some plant material, specifically seeds and leaves, was found on the clothing of the victim, as if the body had lain in or been dragged through this material at some point. Though I am not a botanist, I have never seen this plant material before on other bodies or locally in general. It appears exotic and not native to Louisiana. I've sent samples to be analyzed. That's about it, so far."

"Thank you, Doctor," the sheriff said. "As you are all aware, the body's been identified as Marlene Chartrand, forty years old, who lived in Clairmont with her husband Ed, thirty-nine, and her two children. Marlene was a well-liked, active member of the community and a churchgoer. A background check reveals no discernible reasons why she would be targeted for murder. She had no known enemies, got along well with people, and apparently had a happy marriage and satisfying work as the curator of the local museum."

Sheriff Petit frowned, lines of tension spreading across his forehead. "Unfortunately, her work routine may have made her vulnerable. The murder was on a Friday evening. Every Friday evening, she worked late at the museum and left near sunset. The rear driveway offered opportunity for an attack. It's out of the way and not visible from the street. At that time, there would be very little traffic or pedestrian movement near the museum. Not surprisingly, there were no witnesses."

The furrows in the sheriff's forehead deepened. "There's evidence that she was abducted as she tried to enter her vehicle in the parking lot of the museum. Her car door was open. She may have attempted to access the panic button on her keys; the keys were crushed on the ground near the vehicle, as if they had been stepped on with considerable force. As you can see from the photos, there were other signs of a struggle, with some blood spatter. We believe it's hers, but it's being tested. Her side-view mirror on the driver's side was practically knocked off."

Sheriff Petit pointed again to the screen. "Her purse was found on the driver's seat of the vehicle and did not appear to have been disturbed. Therefore, robbery was probably not a motive. If Marlene closed up on schedule, whoever abducted and killed her and dumped the body in the graveyard didn't waste much time. He or they were ruthlessly efficient at it…."

Jeremy seized the moment to inform the group of his contact with Marlene Chartrand at the museum. "I was there following the discovery of the bayou body, doing a background check on the Vallencourts and on the history of the plantations in the area. What are the odds that several weeks later she shows up murdered? Although there were no others present at the time I talked with her, I could well have been seen entering the museum, and this was on the same afternoon as my colleagues were doing background checks on Vallencourt in town. Someone may have concluded I was doing the same at the museum."

"It's a small town," the sheriff said. "People notice things like that."

"Yes, and I think we should keep in mind that the curator was one of the most knowledgeable people about the history of the Vallencourts, aside from the Boisvert brothers. As you know, the main history reference for the area was mysteriously stolen from the museum, but the curator had read it. She also directed me to an entry in an old diary, which documented finding a body with a part missing from it in 1928, on the Bayou Rouge next to the Vallencourt property. We don't know if the curator may have subsequently told others of my contact with her."

Sheriff Petit listened closely to Jeremy's words. "So are you saying that your contact with Marlene may have come to the attention of Vallencourt, who then targeted her?"

"I'd say I have questions on my mind about that, Sheriff. It will be interesting to find out where that plant material on her body came from locally. That may tell us where she was at one point the night of the murder, perhaps the site of the murder itself."

"This could be one of the big breaks in the investigation," Tony added. "When would you expect the results to be in, Doctor?"

"In about two weeks' time."

"There's another big question," Tony said. "Why would the body have been dumped in a local cemetery not used for two hundred years?"

"I think to panic the townspeople even more," the sheriff replied. "Remember, this was on the heels of another local woman's body being found in the bayous."

"Agreed," Monica said. "Let's remember that the murderer seems to get pleasure out of the pain of others. Clairmonters are predominantly Catholic. Their horror is undoubtedly magnified by the desecration of a Catholic cemetery. Placing the body on a typhoid victim's monument may not be random after all. It would bring to mind the terrible typhoid epidemic that struck the town in the early 1800s."

"That makes sense," responded Jeremy. "But there's also a good chance that a body placed at the remotest section of the cemetery wouldn't have been discovered before being destroyed by scavengers."

"You would think so," said Sheriff Petit. "But the place is a favorite parking spot for teens, who might notice any lights or unusual sounds in the area. Neighbors were also on alert after a recent break-in at Gus Moreau's. Gus himself spotted the light in the cemetery and informed us. So the chances of the cemetery being investigated that night were better than they would seem at first glance. By the way, have you had a look for yourselves at the crime scenes, yet?"

"No, we're heading out to them right after the conference, Sheriff," Tony said.

The sheriff nodded. "You know, I'm concerned about the atmosphere of paranoia that's growing in town about all of this. A few rabble-rousers are channeling it into anger."

Jeremy remarked, "My grandfather had a saying: 'The fearful man is the one to keep an eye on.'"

"Well, I'll be taking his advice into account," Sheriff Petit replied. "We'll be monitoring the situation in the streets pretty closely. As far as the instigators are concerned, I have a mind to warn them that they could be charged with attempting to incite public violence."

CHAPTER FIFTEEN

It was a dark, drizzly Sunday, befitting Jeremy and Monica's visit to Clairmont to attend the funeral of Marlene Chartrand. Officially, the two came to the funeral to represent the investigation team. Unofficially, Jeremy was there out of a nagging sense of guilt over Marlene's murder. Part of him felt he had been careless in so openly visiting Marlene at the museum some weeks before her death—that he didn't consider the murderer or an informant might have been watching his moves that day. Rationally, of course, he knew it wasn't his fault. She might have been targeted for other, unknown reasons. He did not own a crystal ball, he told himself. Even if his visit somehow played a role in her death, he could not have foreseen that.

He had been tempted to confide his feelings to Monica during their drive to Clairmont, but he'd thought better of it. He was still wrestling with his feelings as they pulled into the congested parking lot of the Church of the Divine Rapture.

On the outside, it was a typical country church, a whitewashed, stone-facade building with a high, peaked roof capped by a traditional wooden steeple. Upon the steeple was mounted an ornate, horn-blowing angel. The bright lights inside the church lit up the long, narrow, stained-glass windows punctuating the church's walls.

As the two walked toward the church, they noticed the cemetery to their left, jammed full of tombs of various shapes and sizes. An open one solemnly awaited the conclusion of today's ceremony.

As they ascended the steps to the front door, they were met by the mournful strains of organ music. A thin, gray-haired usher greeted them in the foyer, leading them to the few remaining places in the last pew.

Jeremy and Monica recognized a few people in the crowd. Sheriff Petit and Deputy Deschamps had come to pay their respects. Marlene's considerable extended family occupied the first several rows. The closed casket, bedecked with myriads of colorful flowers, rested in front of the family, at the foot of the alter.

Jeremy looked around at the church walls, which were anything but typical. A series of large murals depicted dramatic, seminal Old Testament scenes; many were battles against enemies of the Israelites. It struck Jeremy as odd that there were no scenes of the New Testament and the coming of Christ.

The organ music suddenly stopped, and the throng rose as the pastor entered and mounted the pulpit. Jeremy and Monica exchanged surprised looks. It was Dr. Tremblay. They had heard that the doctor was a part-time pastor for a small church but were unaware that he was presiding at Marlene's funeral.

Dr. Tremblay smiled and motioned for everyone to be seated. There was a long pause, interrupted only by some coughing in the audience. The pastor looked out into the crowd, appearing to gather his thoughts. At last, he spoke. "We are here today to celebrate the life of Marlene Chartrand…."

For the next half hour, Jeremy and Monica listened attentively to the doctor's oration about what he believed defined Marlene's life and personhood. Jeremy became reflective. How do we attach value to another human being's life? Dr. Tremblay has his viewpoint about Marlene. Her friends and acquaintances have theirs. Her family has its perspective. But if Marlene was a witness to the eulogy today, would she agree with this evaluation? He projected ahead to his own deathbed. Would he value his own life at the end? Would he say it had been well lived?

The doctor paused at the end of the eulogy, and everyone waited for a comforting prayer or perhaps an inspiring hymn. But the service took an unexpected turn. "As we all know," he began, "the circumstances of Marlene's passing were not natural. In fact, these were dark and sinister. I am sure that this matter is on everyone's mind today and must be spoken out loud.... The beast has walked among us once again. From the shadows, it cruelly and senselessly struck down one of our flock. With all due respect for the feelings of the family, I wish to say that it is easy to succumb to anger and despondency—even to lose faith over this profound loss. We may not stop to think that in doing so, we merely give the beast what it wants: to sow fear and hatred, to close our hearts to God and to one another, and to rob ourselves of the spiritual source of meaning in our lives. And so we must, in dark moments like this, consciously work to reinvigorate our faith and reconfirm we are on the path of goodness. As Peter (5:8-9) said, 'Be alert and sober-minded. Your enemy, the devil, prowls around like a roaring lion looking for someone to devour. Resist him, standing firm in the faith….'"

Jeremy listened closely to the pastor's words. He flashed back to his childhood abandonment and then to the rape of his sister. He had lost faith in God, then, and had never regained it.

***

The ceremony at the graveside concluded in the mid-afternoon. The weather was still abysmal. The forlorn mourners made their way under a canopy of black umbrellas back to the protection of their vehicles.

Jeremy and Monica talked as they walked across the soaked, short-cropped grass to his car. "I didn't realize that Dr. Tremblay was so eloquent," Monica remarked.

"Some of his imagery was pretty powerful," Jeremy agreed. "The 'beast' sums up this murderer very well. He's a ruthless predator."

"And if we take the religious message out of his words, then some of his advice applies to us," Monica added. "Don't lose faith in our ability to solve these crimes. Don't give over to anger and despondency. We will win out against this killer in the end."

Jeremy replied with a slight nod, clearly not as inspired as his colleague at that moment.

Monica looked over at him, silently, for a few moments.

"What's on your mind?" Jeremy asked.

Monica hesitated but then said, "I had an unusual experience in the church today and at the graveside, too."

Jeremy cast a curious glance in her direction.

"I … I had the strangest feeling that Marlene was there watching the proceedings."

"Well, that's not unusual for people to experience."

"It is for me. I've been to many funerals, but this has happened to me only once before, at my grandmother's funeral. You know the one who gave me the pendant?"

"Yes, but I heard that people often sense the presence of someone, or even a beloved pet, for quite some time after the death. Some even report visions of the person. Mostly it happens to those who are close to the deceased and are in mourning."

"That's what makes this even more bizarre. Marlene is someone I've never met before—only heard of. A stranger."

"What do you make of it?" Jeremy asked.

"I'm not sure. I know we can be victims of wishful thinking in cases like this. We want to believe in survival after death. So, when confronted by death, the subconscious creates feelings and perceptions that seem to fulfill our wish."

"Yeah, that makes sense to me," Jeremy agreed.

There was a long pause. Then Monica said, "But yet I wonder if there was something more to this. The feelings were so strong and persistent today."

"Maybe your spiritual side is finally surfacing?"

"Yes. Well, maybe," she replied, looking a little unnerved. "If so, I'm not entirely sure I'm ready for it."

The two finally reached the car and got into its comfortable interior, relieved to get out of the cold rain. Jeremy started up and selected a piece from his country and western collection. A loud song about a cheating lover came on, mercifully drowning out their thoughts.

***

Monica returned to her apartment that evening in a somber, unsettled mood. She made dinner, which she barely touched, and distractedly watched a movie. She turned it off halfway through and went to bed early.

Her sleep was restless and dream-filled. At 3:00 a.m., she awoke with a start, realizing she had just come out of a dream—or was it a nightmare? Vivid memories of the dream flooded into her consciousness. She was a fourteen-year-old again at her grandmother's funeral. Her grandmother lay in an open casket, cold and lifeless—a touched-up version of her former self. Monica was heartbroken and frightened by her grandmother's death and by the fact that she, too, would someday become a shell in a box.

As she viewed the casket, she felt a hand cupping hers, and she looked up, expecting to see her mother. But it was not her mother beside her; it was her grandmother, looking as vital and alive as she had always been. Monica was no longer frightened as she looked into her grandmother's kind, wise eyes and felt the warmth of her smile.

"What were you afraid of, Missy?" her grandmother asked, using a name she used to call her. "What we call death is only a transformation of life. From where did you originally come? Before your mother's physical womb? Was not your conception another act of transformation from something prior? Beginnings and endings, like conception and death, are but convenient illusions.

"Do not be afraid to reach out to the world beyond logic, beyond your senses. There are other ways of understanding reality. Do not be frightened by these ways. Find them. Embrace them. Their roots already lie within you." Her grandmother enveloped her in a cocoon of deep love and hope as the dream ended.

Monica lay fully awake, thinking about the dream. She remembered the "real" funeral where, as a fourteen-year-old, she had sensed her grandmother's presence watching the proceedings, just like at Marlene's funeral; she had been frightened by both experiences. But her grandmother had been much more in the dream. She was an incarnated presence capable of love, touch, and kindness—a wise mentor.

Monica knew that the dream spoke to both the fourteen-year-old child within her and the mature adult that she now was. But what were the other ways of apprehending reality that her grandmother had alluded to in the dream, whose roots were apparently already within her? She felt an impulse to reach over to her night table and touch the pendant upon it. She wanted to feel the cool, smooth surface of the turquoise stone. It was an irrational impulse, perhaps, but she did not hold back.

As she touched the stone, more questions flooded into her mind. Who, on a deeper level, was the first ancestor who had passed on the turquoise stone? What knowledge did he possess? Was his legacy pure superstition, or was it a valid insight into another kind of reality?

CHAPTER SIXTEEN

Sheriff Petit was settling into his favorite armchair to watch the football game. He'd barely cracked his first beer when his wife came in. "Roland, there's a call for you from Ted Deschamps." He got up, grumbling, and took the phone in the hallway.

"Yes, Ted."

"Sorry to disturb you, Sheriff," his deputy said, "but there's something you need to know. We've got a missing kid."

"Who?"

"Jenny Thibeault."

"Louie's kid?"

"Yeah. He just called. She's not been seen since last evening. She said she was going to Dewer's but didn't arrive there. He checked with her friends today after school, but apparently none have seen her."

"Damn," the sheriff said. "With all the paranoia in town about the murders, you'd think he would have called earlier."

"He didn't report it till now because she can take off once in a while to a friend's overnight, after a family fight. There was one last night. He figured she had just gone to school in the morning."

"So where are things at now, Ted?"

"I'm informing all the deputies to keep an eye out for her. They already have a description and a recent photo. We'll be checking out her usual haunts and friends."

"She has a boyfriend, doesn't she?"

"Yeah, the LaPlante kid. He's still in town and on our priority list."

"Okay. I'll be at the station in twenty minutes."

***

Tony, Monica, and Jeremy drove back to Clairmont the next day upon Sheriff Petit's request. Eight hours earlier, the sheriff had officially declared Jenny a missing child. As procedure demanded, he informed the state and New Orleans Police and sent out bulletins to the missing persons registry and media. He also asked Jack Claye for help in determining if there were possible links between Jenny's disappearance and the other disappearances near Clairmont.

Based on the sheriff's information, the trio decided to start by questioning Billy LaPlante. They were met at the door of the LaPlante home by the father, Theo. He ushered them into the living room, where Billy and his mother, Margarite, sat on the sofa. After introductions, Tony thanked the family for seeing them on such short notice and requested to see Billy alone.

Billy was a tall, wiry kid, with plentiful acne and reddish hair shaved at the sides. He wore a rather surly look.

"We'd like to ask you a few questions about Jenny," Tony began. "She *is* your girlfriend, right?"

Billy nodded.

"You two been going out long?"

"About a year and a half."

"That's a long time. How would you describe your relationship with Jenny?"

"We have our ups and downs."

"Has it been more up or more down, lately?"

"I'd say down."

"What's been happening, Billy?"

"She hasn't been herself since the body was found at the cemetery."

"Like how?"

"She's been scared, like the rest of the town, I guess. Real paranoid. She even said she thought she was being followed in town and in New Orleans, too, at lunchtime."

"Did she spot someone in particular?"

"No. I told her it was all in her head, but now I'm not so sure."

"Are you saying someone could have been following her?"

"Yeah. She wouldn't have just taken off on her own. She would have told me and maybe some of her friends what she was up to."

Jeremy took over. "Going back to how Jenny was scared, did that cause any problems with you two?"

"Yeah, I think she was mad at me because I called her paranoid, and she stopped going parking with me, too."

"How did you feel about that, Billy?"

"How do you think I felt? It bugged me, but I didn't argue with her. She's got a temper like her old man's when she gets going."

"Tell us about the father."

"The dude's a bully. Roughs up Jenny and her mom whenever he feels like it."

"What has Jenny told you about that?"

"She's really choked about it, and it's been getting worse lately. He's a religious nut. Thinks she's loose and tries to beat it out of her. If he only knew."

Jeremy looked at Billy questioningly.

"That she doesn't put out much," Billy clarified.

"How do you feel about that?"

"Like I said, I'm bugged, but I'd never lay a hand on her, if that's what you're getting at."

"Has Jenny mentioned other problems?"

"No. She gets along with pretty much everybody."

"When was the last time you saw her, Billy?"

"The day before last, on the bus from the city."

"How did she seem?"

"Okay, I guess. I was going to meet her at Dewer's, but she didn't make it."

"Were you two getting along that day?"

"Yeah. Fine. Listen, I didn't do nothing here. You guys are wasting your time. Why don't you get out there and find the low-life that did this?"

"That's what we're going to do, Billy," Jeremy said. The three realized that they had gone as far as they were going to get with Billy at the moment and stood up to leave.

Tony thought it was a waste of breath, but just in case, he asked, "If you remember anything else that might help find her, let us know, okay?" He held out his card.

Billy gave him his best sulky look but took the card.

***

"So, what do you think?" Tony asked as he tried to avoid the potholes while driving to Jenny's parents' home.

Monica sighed. “I was tempted to do the Heimlich maneuver to get him to cough up more information.”

Jeremy smiled. “He wasn’t exactly forthcoming, but he had a few interesting things to say. He seemed to believe there was no way she would have run without his knowing about it. Also, his statement that Jenny suspected she was being followed fits into our killer’s M.O. Her movements in the evening were predictable in that she regularly visited Dewer’s after dinner.”

“True,” Monica remarked. “There’s one puzzling thing about Billy, though. Did you notice he didn’t show any sign of distress about his girlfriend’s disappearance, despite his apparently close relationship with her? The only emotion he showed was anger.”

“That’s true,” Tony remarked.

Jeremy responded. “Well, their relationship has been rocky lately. Maybe he’s been turned off on her.”

“Turned off enough to do some damage to her?” Monica asked.

“We would have been tipped off by the sheriff’s office about any violence in Billy’s background,” Jeremy said. “But we’ll check that with them.” He noticed that Monica seemed lost in thought and gave her a quizzical look.

She replied to his unspoken question. “There’s something else about this kid I can’t put my finger on.... I think we should keep an eye on him when he’s in the city.”

“I’ll ask Jack,” Tony said. “He’ll complain about scraping the bottom of the resource barrel, but

I think he'll okay it for a while." Tony braked and pulled over to the curb at Jenny's house. As they walked up to the entrance, Monica noticed someone looking out an upstairs window.

Louie met them at the door and led them to the comfortable leather chair and sofa in his den. Behind his desk was a brick fireplace that looked as if it was rarely used. Above its thick cypress mantle hung a picture of the crucifixion. A large gold cross with rosary beads was propped on the mantle. On each side of the fireplace were several old muskets and swords mounted on the walls.

An odd mix, Jeremy thought.

As Louie sat down at his desk, Tony asked, "Will your wife not be joining us?"

"She's really upset at what's happened and feels she can't talk about it. She did enough already with Deputy Deschamps."

"I'm sorry to hear that," Tony said, "but we must speak with her anyway. This is a serious police matter."

Louie paused and then got up to get his wife; they heard him climbing the stairs adjoining the living room.

"Are we getting some resistance from the mother?" Monica asked.

Tony shrugged. "I guess we'll find out."

Louie reappeared with Therese in tow. She looked as if she had been crying. She was heavily masked with foundation cream around one eye. The cream was partially washed off, revealing a dark shadow underneath.

“We’re sorry to disturb you, Mrs. Thibeault,” Tony said, “but it is in the interest of your daughter that you speak with us.”

Tony turned to Louie. “But let’s start with you, Mr. Thibeault. What can you tell us about your daughter’s disappearance?”

“There’s not much to tell,” Louie said. “Two nights ago, after dinner, she said she was going to Dewer’s Restaurant, which she usually does at that time. It’s a kids’ hangout. She didn’t come back that night, but she can do that if she’s upset. She always comes back in time for school in the morning, but she didn’t come back this morning. We thought she’d gone to school directly from a friend’s. But when she didn’t return at the usual time from school, we became concerned. We phoned her friends, but none had seen her since the previous day. I called the sheriff right away.”

Therese began to sob in the background, revealing more of the shadow under her eye.

“Was she upset the night she left?” Jeremy asked.

“Yes, we had an argument.”

“What about?”

Louie’s jaw muscles visibly tightened. “What it’s always about: that boy she’s been seeing. She’s too young to date, but she sneaks out anyway. The boy is trying to take advantage of her, and I think she lets him. The bible demands chastity from unmarried girls. I’m saving her from sin.”

“How do you try to save her, Louie?”

Therese’s sobbing grew louder.

“She receives punishment by the belt.”

“You belt her? That’s defined as abuse, Louie.”

"Call it what you will. It is discipline to correct her, as condoned by the bible."

"Is this why she runs to friends overnight periodically?" Jeremy queried.

"That is testimony to how she fears righteous punishment."

"You think she just decided to run, period, this time?" Jeremy queried.

"I don't know," replied Louie, glaring at Jeremy.

"How about you, Mrs. Thibeault?" Monica asked. "What do you know about your daughter's disappearance?"

Therese gave her husband a wary glance. "It happened just like my husband told you. She gave no sign that she was running. Her things are all there. Even things that mean a lot to her. Her account is untouched; she has no money. She didn't tell her friends anything…. You're on a false trail trying to blame Louie for it all! No! She's been taken! This is not helping her, so look for the monster who did it. You don't have to look far. He lives fifteen miles down the road in that mansion. That's where she is."

Louie jumped up behind his desk. "I'll kill him!" he shouted. "'You will pursue your enemies, and they will fall by the sword before you, sayeth Leviticus.'"

The investigators looked at one another in amazement. Tony stood up to his full height, facing Louie. "Stay away from Vallencourt!" he warned. "Interfering with him will only make things a lot worse for you and your family."

That quieted Louie, who sat down again behind his desk.

Monica took advantage of the silence to resume questioning Therese. “What’s all the cream around your right eye about, Therese?”

Therese turned her face away.

Monica glared at Louie. “Is this more righteous punishment?”

Louie was silent, and Monica spoke to Therese again. “You do know that abuse is a crime, and Louie can be charged. That’s an option open to you.” Monica got up, walked over to the sobbing woman, and took her hand. “Come, Therese, show me your daughter’s room and the special things that she left behind.” Therese stood up and led Monica out.

There was a stony silence in the den. Then Louie’s anger boiled over. “She had no right to question my discipline in my own home. Just like in the bible, I am the family patriarch. The state has no business interfering with God’s rules.”

Jeremy spoke up. “There’s a great deal of difference between discipline and abuse, Louie. I don’t think you make that distinction. In the modern world, that gives the state the right to intervene.”

Before Louie could reply, Monica returned. “I think I found out what I needed to know,” she said. That was the cue for the three leaving the unhappy houschold.

They walked to the van and stood beside it, discussing the rocky meeting with the Thibeaults. “I can sure see why the kid would want to run,” Tony commented.

"He's a violent religious fanatic," Jeremy said. "That was obviously a black eye the wife had. By the way, Monica, it was a good thing you weren't around for Louie's commentary on your interventions."

"Oh? What did he say?"

"Let's put it this way: he wasn't complimentary."

Tony laughed and changed the topic. "So, Monica, what did you find in Jenny's room?"

"Just like the mother said, she evidently didn't take any of her things, including things of sentimental value to her. Her cell phone was gone, but that's to be expected. Kids go nowhere without their phones."

"So we could still be left with a sudden impulsive decision to run with what she had on her," Jeremy said.

"Or somebody nabbed her on the way to Dewer's," Tony added.

Tony's phone rang. It was Sheriff Petit. Tony put the phone on speaker and the three leaned into the open side door of the van to listen in.

"We've got a developing situation downtown," the sheriff said. "The town's riled up about the disappearance, and an armed mob is gathering in the town square. They're blaming Vallencourt and working themselves up to confront him on his estate. I've contacted state police, who are on their way. We could do with a hand trying to manage this until the state boys get here. I could deputize Monica and Jeremy, if they agree."

Tony looked at his colleagues. They nodded. "We'll be right over," Tony said.

CHAPTER SEVENTEEN

The team arrived a few minutes later to find a chaotic scene in the normally placid town square. The sheriff's description wasn't quite accurate. There wasn't a mob there, but rather a cluster of mobs—small groups of angry men waving rifles and shotguns. They egged one another on with shouts of vengeance against their perceived enemy, Charles Vallencourt. Two hundred years of dark suspicion and repressed hatred were finally surfacing, Jeremy mused. If the sheriff didn't handle this right, the day could end very badly.

Sheriff Petit, flanked by his deputies, stood on the stone fountain at the base of an old statue of General Robert E. Lee. All the debate over removing Confederate symbols from public places had somehow bypassed Clairmont, Jeremy thought. Did the sheriff realize he was standing in front of the perfect symbol for an uprising?

Through his bullhorn, the sheriff alternately pleaded with and threatened the crowd, which had by now coalesced into one angry mass governed increasingly by thc capricious forces of mob psychology.

"Folks," the bullhorn blared, "you have gathered here today for an unlawful purpose: to take the law into your own hands. You must disband immediately. The state police are on their way in force, and they will guarantee that you disband. Make no mistake about it. We don't want anyone to get hurt. So go home to your families."

The sheriff paused to assess the effects of his words on the crowd. Unfortunately, the decibel level had only gone up. “You cannot be judge and jury on this matter,” he continued. “That is the mentality of a lynch mob. We have a hard-won justice system to handle situations like this.”

A man shouted from the crowd. “The law has covered up for the Vallencourts for two centuries. That will end today!”

“There is no proof that Charles Vallencourt or anyone else did anything illegal. This investigation is still ongoing, and we have brought in the best people from New Orleans to look at it. The fact is that we only know she is missing. We do not yet know why.”

Another from the crowd yelled, “And what about the bodies in the bayous and graveyard, and the missing women? What don’t we know about them? Bodies have been found around the Vallencourts since the slavery days. The family has not been brought to justice yet.”

“You do not serve justice by blaming this man for murders he has not been charged with. I know all of you. You are peaceful, good people. Family men. The salt of the community. Do not commit a crime that will stain the rest of your lives. Go home. Your families will thank you for it.”

A third man yelled out, “We’re here for our families! They need protection from a monster who kills women and children!”

A huge roar of approval went up from the crowd, which in a convulsive mass movement made for their vehicles, clearly intent on heading out to Vallencourt’s.

The sheriff had lost the verbal skirmish with the mob. He stepped down from the fountain looking disconsolate and alarmed at the same time. “You know what you’re up against,” he said to the trio. “Eight of us facing ten times as many.” He deputized the two PIs and passed out shotguns and body armor to his three reinforcements. “God help us until the state police arrive.”

The small police force tramped on their accelerators, trying to catch up with the cloud of dust in the distance to the south. They passed the stragglers at the end of the column of vehicles but were forced to slow by other cars zigzagging into the passing lane to impede them.

The sheriff saw a shotgun aimed at them from one of the obstructing cars. He turned his steering wheel hard to violently push the offending vehicle off the road. It careened down an embankment into a bayou, where it came to rest, its radiator steaming. The sheriff glanced at his side-view mirror. “They look all right,” he said. “But they won’t be if they don’t get out of there fast. These roadside ponds are crawling with gators.”

Arriving at the estate’s entrance, the sheriff saw it was already too late. The property’s steel gate had been battered in with an old, two-ton farm truck, which was parked, disabled, on the side of the road.

The police rushed by the angry caravan pushing up the long driveway. The mob had already gathered in front of the mansion. Three of Vallencourt’s bodyguards stood between them and the mansion, twelve-gauge shotguns raised. A shadowy figure looked out from a second-floor window of the old building.

The sheriff's vehicles roared up to form a line between the opposing camps. The deputies jumped out of their cars and immediately disarmed the bodyguards. Jeremy, Monica, and Tony positioned themselves behind the police vehicles, shotguns in hand. Jeremy thought it was incredibly ironic that they were putting their lives at risk to protect one of their main suspects.

The police ducked as the mob launched a hail of stones at the cars, accompanied by a torrent of verbal abuse. The bodyguards jumped behind the mansion's pillars, although one was not quick enough and sustained a wound to the head. To the cheers of the crowd, he quit the battlefield and was let in the front door of the mansion, his head bleeding.

A well-aimed rock smashed the second-story window where the figure watched the melee; the figure disappeared. The crowd jeered. "Coward! You're only brave with women and children," one shouted.

On the right flank, a man threw a rope and noose over a sturdy branch of a large cypress tree and placed a lawn chair underneath it, making an impromptu gallows. Another cheer rose up from the crowd. "Hang the bastard!" someone yelled.

Another hail of projectiles hit the police line and smashed all the first-floor windows of the mansion. Then a flaming object was thrown from the crowd onto the mansion's porch. It was a Molotov cocktail, which exploded into flames. The remaining bodyguards scrambled from behind the pillars to extinguish the fire. The crowd mocked their frantic efforts to beat down the flames.

Jeremy looked over anxiously at the sheriff, fervently hoping he would now seize the advantage. Otherwise, lead projectiles would likely be coming their way next.

Jeremy's anxiety rose several more notches when he spotted Louie Thibeault in the mob, holding a shotgun. His face was contorted by pure rage and hatred. If there was anyone there who could start a shooting war right now, it was Louie. Here was Louie's chance to take down the walls of a modern-day Jericho.

The sheriff did not disappoint. He grabbed his bullhorn and maxed the volume. "Any of you who raise their weapons will be going home in body bags tonight," he threatened. "Think hard about that. Think about your families burying you a couple of days from now. Would they think all this was worth it?"

The volume of the jeering lessened. In the distance, the sound of a helicopter beating the air announced the imminent arrival of the first forces from the state police. The helicopter soon hovered over the mansion, several hundred feet up in the darkening sky, outside of shotgun range. Its brilliant spotlight blinded the crowd. The barrels of high-powered sniper rifles poked out from the open bay.

The sheriff blared out another sobering message. "You're now in the crosshairs of expert marksmen in that helicopter. Drop your weapons and disband."

To the relief of the police, some began to throw down their guns and shuffle back through the crowd toward the main road.

The sheriff spotted someone he believed to be one of the leaders in front of the crowd. He recognized him as Jerry Couteau, a retired town councilman. The sheriff called out to him over the bullhorn. “Jerry, you were an elected official, entrusted with the welfare and safety of Clairmonters. It is your duty to be a responsible example to the men around you. Drop your weapon and lead your people out of here. Now!”

Jerry hung his head and threw his rifle on the ground. “Let’s go, boys,” he said. The rest slowly began to drop their guns, with one exception: Louie Thibeault, in tears of frustration, was left standing alone. As his last act of defiance, he took his shotgun and smashed it against a tree. Then he stomped off, trailing the others.

At that moment, dozens of state police vehicles, their lights flashing, pulled up and surrounded the retreating crowd. The sheriff and his diminutive force had carried the day.

Jeremy looked over at Monica next to him, still clutching her shotgun tightly. He was proud of her. She had stood her ground with the rest of them in the face of mortal danger. He remembered his initial concern that someday she might not have his back. She was starting to prove him wrong.

Tony unloaded his shotgun and leaned it against the police car. He turned toward Jeremy, wiping the sweat from his forehead. “That could have gone either way,” he said hoarsely. “Did you see Thibeault out there? The crazed look on his face? I thought he would take a pot shot for sure, and that would have been it. That helicopter tipped the scales for us. Remind me to attend prayers this Sunday."

Jeremy smiled. He reminded himself it was soon time for another communion with the river.

***

The river air was fresh and invigorating the next evening, scrubbed clean by the rain, which was just now subsiding. The *Mississippi Dream* drifted southward with the currents once again.

The river runs eternal, Jeremy thought—a striking sentence, even if its grammar needed improvement. He contrasted the river to his own life. After the close call yesterday at the old Vallencourt place, the precariousness of life was on his mind.

He looked as the last drops of rain struck the surface of the river. Each initially created a tiny, chaotic splash, which spread out in orderly, concentric circles. They grew ever larger and weaker, finally disappearing as they merged with the water. Was not life like that: a bundle of energy, which in its time dissipates into the flow of the universe? A single bullet from that mad mob yesterday could have ended the expanding circles of his own life or someone else's—or could it have?

He remembered a book he read recently that drew parallels between modern physics and Eastern philosophy. The author's theme was that the universe, from macro to micro, is integrated and holistic in nature. This led Jeremy to an interesting question: What did life or death really mean if they cannot truly be separated from one another?

But it was time to let go of his thoughts. He imagined them falling into the river just as the raindrops had, merging with it. He began to contact the subconscious level of his mind.

CHAPTER EIGHTEEN

Jeremy, Monica, and Tony met with Jack in his office for an update on the investigation. Jack broke into one of his rare smiles and then walked around to shake their hands. "I want to commend all of you for backing up the sheriff at Vallencourt's."

"I think we now know what it was like to be at Custer's last stand," Tony remarked.

"No doubt," Jack replied, "except nobody came to rescue poor Custer. I hear it was touch-and-go with you guys until the helicopter arrived. That was quite an act of bravery; some might say it was beyond the call of duty. I'm going to recommend to the chief that you three receive the mayor's commendation."

"Does that mean we get the honorary keys to the city?" Jeremy quipped, grinning at Tony and Monica.

The joke seemed to go by Jack. "We've got multiple investigations going on, and I want to tie up some loose ends," he said in a serious tone. "Vallencourt has unfortunately been making headlines, so we'll start with him. We've had cameras surveilling his property and the parkade at his office building. Most of it's pretty routine. He keeps regular business hours and heads home to the mansion in the early evenings. We haven't noticed anything suspicious yet, with one possible exception." Jack turned his laptop toward the others and tapped the mouse. A video came on screen. "This was shot a few days ago from our camera on a small island on the bayou near the mansion. He has a delivery truck bring in large crates and full plastic bags to the mansion regularly. If that is not unusual enough, it's always at night."

"His bodyguards are keeping a pretty close eye on the unloading," Tony observed.

"Yes. Take a look at the guy on the left. He's watching the surroundings closely, especially the only publicly accessible area, the bayou. It's as if they don't want to be observed."

"The locals are also suspicious about the cargo, according to the Boisvert brothers," Jeremy added.

"We'd all like to know what's in those crates," Jack responded, "but right now, we would not get a warrant to examine them or the delivery company's manifests."

"There's new information that he may have something to hide regarding his business affairs," Jeremy added. "A second informant told me he may be laundering money for shady, big-league clients and paying off federal officials to cover it up—a federal offence. Evidence from two informants might be enough for the FBI to get a warrant to examine his business records and, if we're lucky, that may shed some light on the crates."

Jack nodded. "Good thinking, Jeremy. We'll keep your idea in our back pocket for now. If the lab results come back positive for Marlene's blood in the cocoa grove, we'll have enough to get a warrant on Vallencourt ourselves. If not, we'll involve the FBI along the lines you've proposed. Either way, we just might clear up the crate mystery."

Jack sighed and reoriented his laptop. “Then we’ve got the Jenny Thibeault matter. It’s just as murky. I received an update from Sheriff Petit. They’ve combed through the electronics of Jenny’s friends and her boyfriend. Before she disappeared, Jenny had been telling her friends online she’s been depressed, mostly about family and Billy, but unfortunately, she hasn’t been very specific about what. She also said she’s been upset because she believed she had been followed in town and in the city. She felt Billy didn’t believe her, and that upset her more.”

“So she could have run without telling Billy,” Jeremy added.

“You would think,” replied Jack. “Unfortunately, there have been no calls, texts, or emails from her phone since she disappeared, or any transactions on her bank account or credit card. Zero. So, if she’s run, what’s she living on?”

“Not much,” Tony said. “Anything show up on Billy’s electronics?”

“There’s been no communication from her on his electronics, either. He tried to contact her a couple of times, but she hasn’t responded. Prior records indicate a lot of communication with Billy. They run hot and cold. Sometimes they’re arguing, other times they’re best buddies. Sexual issues are usually at the forefront. The sheriff also mentioned that, despite their conflicts, there are no indications that Billy was ever physical with her. He does have a temper, however, and is known to get into fights if crossed. But so far he’s avoided run-ins with the law.”

"If Billy is behind this in some way," Monica said, "he could have deliberately sent out a few calls to her to throw us off—to show us he had nothing to do with her disappearance. What do we know of Billy's behavior in the city?"

"We've gone ahead and tailed him during his noon hours and free periods at Orley High School. He hangs with friends at school who say they know nothing about her disappearance. Also, he occasionally goes downtown to smoke weed. Jenny has not put in an appearance downtown when he's there."

"So far, this does not appear to be a situation where Billy conspired with her, aiding her to run," Jeremy said. "Unless they've been very clever about covering their tracks."

"And that's possible," Monica interjected. "They're both reasonably intelligent kids, so we can't rule out they planned this together to help her get away from Louie."

Jeremy shook his head. "If so, she's doing it the hard way. Unless she's with friends from New Orleans, she's completely isolated. That's not like her."

"Her friends at school also say they haven't seen her," responded Jack. "I suppose they could be covering for her. After all, we cops aren't exactly high on the adolescent popularity scale."

"Anything about changes in her behavior at school before she disappeared?" Monica queried.

"Yes. Her teachers and friends note she had been withdrawn and irritable and seemed less interested in school for some weeks prior to her disappearing. She hadn't apparently confided why to anyone. Interestingly, she hadn't left the school grounds, either, and that's unusual for her."

"Part of a pattern of withdrawal?" Jeremy asked.

"Or was she afraid of being followed?" Tony countered.

"Whatever was going on with her, if Jenny's run, she can't last long without financial support," Jack surmised. "I'd give her a couple of weeks. Otherwise, we'd better start looking for a body."

The others looked at Jack in grim silence.

***

Jeremy and Monica were driving back to the office after the conference with Jack. Jeremy was fighting the downtown rush-hour traffic.

"Remember the team looked into the Museum of Torture and the Morbid a month ago?" Monica asked out of the blue.

"Yes, and I recall there were no significant leads picked up. I knew investigating the place was a long shot."

"The investigators must have thought so too," Monica commented. "They didn't check it out as thoroughly as they could have."

Jeremy gave her a curious look.

"They checked out the two partners in the museum and their staff for criminal records and a few background details, and nothing came up. They didn't look at close relatives. The female co-partner was listed in Louisiana corporate records as a 'secret partner,' and that stayed in my mind."

Jeremy shrugged. "I understand she's an official in the department of health. I'd imagine she doesn't want to be associated publicly with a business like that."

"Sure, but what if there's more to it? Out of curiosity, I checked Orleans Parish marriage records, and she has a male partner, one James Madera. I looked into him further. He owns a medical equipment company selling to clinics and hospitals."

"And so?"

"Well, the museum is known for one of the best collections of old medical instruments in the world. I also checked out his past business history, and over twenty years ago he owned a small antique store on Frank Street, long before he got into his current business. Guess what his specialty was?"

"Don't tell me. Old medical instruments."

"Right, and don't forget torture apparatus."

"You're thinking this guy is an undisclosed partner in the museum?"

Monica nodded. "Otherwise, all of this is quite coincidental, isn't it?"

Jeremy's face hardened. "I believe the partners and staff would have been asked if anyone else was involved in the business. I'll check that out. But if so, they likely lied about this guy. I've got an informant who might be able to provide more information on him. Good work, Monica."

***

A week later, the two met in Jeremy's office to discuss the suspected undisclosed partner again. "I got one of my informants to check this guy out some more," Jeremy said. "Bingo! People have heard of him in the S & M club scene off Bourbon. He hangs around at a club called Spaghetti &

Meatballs and picks up playmates there. Apparently he's a shady character known as the Black Marquis. His trademark is a black cloak he wears to the club."

"A sadistic link," Monica mused.

"Right, and there's more. The informant says he's involved in smuggling unknown goods through the port of New Orleans."

"Obviously, then, there are no records connecting him to the goods."

"Yes, and to add to our suspicions, the informant tailed him and found that the same night some goods were smuggled in, our suspect delivered crates through the freight entrance of the museum after hours."

"The plot thickens," Monica remarked.

"Thicker than meets the eye," Jeremy replied. "I also found out that the investigating detectives had indeed asked the museum staff and partners if anyone else was involved. They denied it. Thus, they very likely lied to cover for this guy."

"I take it you don't want to confront the museum about this yet?"

"Exactly. That would only alert him that we have him in our sights. I think we should begin with a visit to the museum as curiosity-seekers. Let's see for ourselves what this exhibition is about and what it might reveal about the guy who likely had a hand in creating it."

***

That evening, Monica returned home feeling exhausted from the investigation and its glacial pace. She badly needed a diversion. Her questions about her mystical ancestor and the strange dream of her grandmother lingered in the back of her mind.

After dinner, she went into her closet and opened up her family chest. She took out the old leather book of spiritual meditations and looked at the cover for a few moments, admiring the dynamic beauty of the red eagle in flight; its colors were still rich despite the centuries that had passed. She traced the outline of the eagle with her fingertip, marveling over the obvious care that had gone into the book's construction.

She carefully opened the book and read the introduction. The French of the period was daunting but mostly decipherable. The text referred to a single consciousness that pervades the universe, to which human consciousness is inextricably joined. All mystical powers, the writer asserted, stem from the ability of the mind to directly apprehend the one consciousness. It went on to say that this ability is present in young children, but is lost as the child grows older and his mind becomes structured with concepts. But the mind can be taught to reconnect with the one consciousness again. This, the author said, is the purpose of the book's meditations and prescriptions.

Monica put the book down. She was mystified and startled by the description of a reality much different from her own concepts. Yet she was curious. Perhaps its meaning would become clear through actually experiencing the meditations. She picked up the book again and turned to the first meditative exercise.

CHAPTER NINETEEN

Jeremy, Tony, and Monica sat sipping their coffees in Jack's office, waiting for their team leader. They did not yet know what was on the agenda, but Jack wouldn't call a briefing unless it was important.

Jeremy noticed Jack walk in wearing his usual impassive face, no doubt from learning never to give anything away that he didn't intend to. Good advice for cops, politicians, and poker players.

Jack sat informally on the corner of his desk. "I've got some good news on the Marlene Chartrand investigation," he said.

The others looked up expectantly.

"Roland Petit called today. We've got the test results for that plant material found on Marlene's body." Jack had the total attention of the others. "The material is cocoa leaves and seeds."

"Cocoa?" Jeremy questioned. "It's grown only near the equator, isn't it?"

"That's right," Jack replied, "and the botanist was surprised that the material was local. He thinks it's a hybrid designed to survive during the cold snaps that can happen in Louisiana. But he said the plant materials don't look healthy. They're atrophied."

"So where did it come from?" Tony asked.

"This is interesting, too. The sheriff talked to a retired botanist in Clairmont and showed him the materials. He says they are indeed local—on the Vallencourt property, no less."

The others gave Jack a puzzled look, mixed with a glimmer of hope.

"Apparently, about one hundred years ago, one of the Vallencourts hoped to introduce commercial cocoa to Louisiana. He planned to sell cocoa beans to the chocolate industry in New Orleans. The fellow knew something about breeding plants. He developed a hybrid just like the department's botanist said, hoping to make it survivable in the cold periods here. Although the plants grew, the cold stunted them, and they couldn't be used commercially. There are patches of them still around on Vallencourt's property."

"Then Marlene's body must have been in one of those patches at some point," Tony said.

"Exactly. Vallencourt is going to have a hard time explaining this. I've secured a search warrant to investigate his property as a potential crime scene. Tony, you can take a team of techs out there, as soon as possible. It's been a few weeks. If the cocoa patch is a crime scene, we don't want it to degrade any further before we get to it."

Jeremy, Monica, and Tony stood up and gleefully shook hands. They included a few pats on the back for Jack, who kept his sober composure.

Jack punched in something on his keyboard. "The sheriff has emailed another report to us. It's the background investigation of Charles Vallencourt we have been waiting for. He says it wasn't easy to put together because the family is so secretive and reclusive. Not much is publicly known about Charles over and above rumor. But apparently, Roland managed to track down an ex-staff member of Vallencourt's who retired and lives in Clairmont.

She was a nanny for Charles and later the head maid in the household staff. So she knows quite a lot about him. She was very reluctant to talk when contacted. She seemed worried about repercussions from Vallencourt. But she finally relented when anonymity was promised by the sheriff."

"His own nanny is afraid of him," Tony observed. "That tells us something."

"Apparently. The nanny said Charles was an only child and because of ostracism by the townsfolk, he never had playmates at the mansion. She also described the parents as a cold, critical pair, quite detached from their son. The mother did attempt to parent him in his younger years but for some reason found him too much to handle and left him largely to the full-time care of the nanny. From then on, the mother was only involved when she felt discipline was needed. She was quite strict and believed in corporal punishment."

"Poor bonding with the parents and early abandonment by an overly punitive mother," Monica summarized.

"It looks that way," Jack said. "The nanny remembers Charles as an angry, sullen child. Much of his negativity was directed toward his mother, and he rebelled against her. But his rebellion seemed to eventually generalize to female authority figures. He was tutored privately, and the female tutors found him disobedient and unmanageable. His parents sent him to private school in New Orleans, where he continued the same pattern with female teachers."

"And so he's on his way to being a woman-hater," Tony said.

“So it would seem, Tony,” Jack said. “He was reclusive with other children, and when he did socialize, he spent his time teasing and fighting, especially with girls. In turn, he was severely teased by the girls, especially for what seemed to be some very noticeable OCD behaviors. He was eventually expelled from the private school.”

“It could be that he associates being humiliated and degraded with females,” Jeremy said. “We’ve thought that degrading females is a motive of the serial killer.”

Jack nodded and continued with the report. “It’s interesting that he settled down when he was placed in the public-school system in New Orleans. A male biology teacher in high school recognized his skills in anatomy and dissection and became a kind of mentor to him. His grades greatly improved, and he went on to major in biology in university, where he further developed his anatomical and dissection skills. I needn’t point out the potential significance of that.”

Jack looked around at the others. The excitement in the room was almost palpable. “It was in university that he developed an interest in paleontology. He planned to go on to graduate school in the subject, but his father insisted that he quit school and become a partner in his finance business in New Orleans. He had no interest in finance, but he could not resist his controlling father and gave up his academic ambitions to become a junior partner. Nevertheless, he was intelligent enough to eventually run the business successfully, after his father retired. But he harbored much resentment toward him and toward his mother, who had not supported him on the issue."

"Now we see a potentially very important element in Vallencourt's development," Monica said. "He never had much control in his life. Indeed, his early rebellion may have been an unsuccessful attempt to have some control in his family."

"Which means we may have an individual with a pathological need for control as an adult," Jeremy added.

"And this, too, can be a trait of serial murderers," added Monica.

"Well," Jack said, "you two psychoanalysts will have a chance to analyze him first-hand if we find that he really does have this cocoa grove."

Jeremy and Monica thought they saw a rare look of amusement cross Jack's face.

***

The New Orleans investigating team arrived at the front gate of the Vallencourt estate at 7:30 a.m. the next morning. Sheriff Petit, Deputy Deschamps, and the botanist from Clairmont were already there, waiting impatiently. The rendezvous had been timed to arrive slightly earlier than Vallencourt's routine departure time to go to work at his New Orleans' company. At eight sharp, the gate opened and a shiny black limo appeared.

"Right on time," the sheriff said. He walked over to the darkened rear window of the limo, which opened to reveal the owner of the estate. "Morning, Mr. Vallencourt," the sheriff said. "We have a warrant to search the grounds of your property."

"Whatever for, Sheriff?" Vallencourt asked. His voice was calm, but there was a certain wary look in his eyes.

"You can ascertain that for yourself," the sheriff replied, handing over the warrant.

Vallencourt perused the document and nodded. "I've been expecting something like this. It was only a matter of time before the mad murder theories of some of the locals would be acted upon. You can't be serious, Sheriff, that I had anything to do with these terrible murders?"

"We have our job to do, Mr. Vallencourt. You know you can't prevent us from searching the property."

"Yes, I do, and neither would I try. I've got nothing to hide. I presume I'm free to go? I've got a full day ahead of me."

The sheriff nodded and waved him through. The limo's window closed, once again shadowing the businessman. The limo rolled slowly forward, turning south at the intersection toward New Orleans. The sheriff had the feeling that its passenger was watching them the whole time.

The small caravan of police vehicles made its way through the open gate to a point about a quarter mile up the driveway. From there, they were guided by Dr. Ouellette, the botanist who had been designated an official consultant by the sheriff's office. They made their way on foot into the thick bush to the south toward Bayou Rouge.

Jeremy walked beside the botanist and struck up a conversation, partly to relieve the tediousness of the walk. "I'm curious, Doctor. How did you find out about the cocoa patch here?"

The botanist smiled. “Illicitly, I’m afraid. I know Vallencourt’s gardener, who lives in town. Sharing an interest in horticulture, we became friends. He told me about the cocoa plants and their unusual history. One day, when Vallencourt and his bodyguards were away, he let me in to see the plants. It was all very fascinating—from a botanist’s point of view, of course.”

After twenty minutes of trekking through the bush, the expedition reached a small cluster of trees, which stood out from the usual cypresses, pines, and oaks. Dr. Ouellette paused and smiled. “Feast your eyes on the only known wild cocoa trees in Louisiana,” he said.

The group stared at the dozen or so trees. They were nothing much to look at. The trees were quite small compared with others in the area. Their trunks and branches contained a few green, oval-shaped seed pods, from which cocoa beans were derived. Some pods lay smashed open on the ground beneath the trees amongst scattered cocoa leaves.

The techs began their work meticulously documenting the scene as the rest of the group kept its distance. Jeremy marveled at how methodical they were. First, they took broad photos of the scene and its surroundings. Then they did a general walk-through of the immediate area, careful not to disturb anything. This was followed by a series of walk-throughs, focusing on details. The techs gathered and bagged samples of the leaves and pods, taking close-up photos. They earned every penny of their pay, Jeremy thought.

The others were allowed into the area only after the techs had finished. Jeremy took a look beyond the periphery of the cocoa patch. It was pretty thick bush all the way around, but east and west, there were some trails in the direction of Bayou Rouge and toward a fallen-down section of the graveyard fence, which was not far off.

Jeremy saw one of the techs come up to Tony and show him a clear sample bag. "We've got blood on some of the leaves," the tech said. "We were lucky. It was underneath the canopy of the tree and had some protection from the elements. Naturally, we won't know if it is human or animal until it is tested. But we should be able to get some good DNA from it."

Tony walked over to Jeremy. "If that blood sample is from Marlene, we'll be able to get a warrant to search the mansion and the rest of the property. Vallencourt's not going to be happy about that."

"No," Jeremy said, "and it'll be interesting to see exactly how he reacts when we show up at his door."

CHAPTER TWENTY

The testing of the blood samples from the cocoa grove was expedited and, to the relief of the investigators, it revealed that the blood matched Marlene Chartrand's DNA. Jack Claye was able to secure a badly needed search warrant for the mansion and the remainder of the property.

The investigation team arrived early the next morning at Vallencourt's front gate and buzzed the mansion. The low voice of one of his bodyguards answered.

"Police," announced Sheriff Petit. "Open the gate." There was a whirring of electric motors as the newly replaced gate slid across its rails.

The police vehicles once again made their way up the lengthy drive, which was flanked by tall, majestic oaks, creating a tunnel effect overhead. The sheriff was soon ringing the mansion's doorbell, and the low voice answered again on the intercom. Sheriff Petit bent down to speak into it. "Have Charles Vallencourt meet us at the front door," he ordered.

In a few moments the team saw, for the first time, the full person of Charlcs Vallencourt standing before them in the open doorway. Jeremy studied him closely. Vallencourt had a commanding presence. He was tall—almost as tall as the sheriff—and well built, suggesting he worked out. He had medium-length gray hair, which was immaculately styled. His features were refined, but Jeremy was distracted from them by the stern, cynical expression on his face.

“I gather you’ve found something of interest?” Vallencourt asked in a haughty tone.

“Enough to get a search warrant for your house and property,” the sheriff replied curtly. He handed the warrant to Vallencourt, who declined to take it.

“I’ve sent for my lawyers who will read it shortly,” he announced. “But do come in, and do what you need to do. I realize I don’t have to answer any questions, but I choose to do so with my lawyers present, if that’s part of your plan. I already told you I have nothing to hide. As Shakespeare once said, ‘The truth will out’. And I’m sure it will be in my favor. I do have a question, though. Am I being charged with something?”

“No, not yet,” the sheriff said. “Right now, you are a person of interest in the investigation into the murder of Marlene Chartrand.”

Jeremy thought that Vallencourt seemed nonplussed as the police troop pushed by him into the foyer. It took grit to quote Shakespeare in these circumstances. Was the man really as confident as he seemed? Or was it a façade, a tactic, perhaps?

Monica was struck by the classic décor of the foyer. A curving oak staircase ascended to the second floor. The walls were a shade of medium blue; the floor was tightly fitted, oak boards sprinkled with bright, intricately patterned Persian rugs. She surmised that most of the old wood probably came originally from the property itself.

As the tech team dispersed, the rest of the team walked observantly down the long hallway, carefully not touching anything. Vallencourt trailed after them, clearly discomforted by his unaccustomed role as a follower.

The group entered through a towering doorway into what had been a spacious old ballroom, now renovated into a luxurious salon and dining area. Elegant eighteenth-century French furniture was tastefully placed throughout the room, overhung by old, crystal chandeliers on the ornately decorated plaster ceiling.

Vallencourt saw an opportunity to take charge and invited the investigators to sit at the main dining table. He noticed Jeremy staring at the collection of old portraits lining the walls. "I see you're interested in the Vallencourt portraits," he remarked. "They cover our lineage back to the 1700s, when Louisiana was still a French colony." He sighed. "Unfortunately, though, I am the last of the line. As you probably already know, I am unmarried and have no one to carry on the name."

There was a long silence as the investigators just looked at him. The silence was broken by a bodyguard knocking at the salon door. "Excuse me, sir. Your attorneys are here."

"Very well, Davis. Show them in," Vallencourt instructed.

In a few moments, two men in three-piece suits, carrying leather briefcases, walked in and introduced themselves. They sat down at the table, taking out their laptops. "Your warrant, please," one said to the sheriff. The two of them huddled over the warrant for a minute and then the older, presumably more senior lawyer said, "It seems in order." He turned to face his client. "You know, Mr. Vallencourt, that you're not required to answer any questions here today under the Fifth Amendment. In fact, we recommend that you don't—even with us present."

"To me, those who are guilty hide behind the Fifth Amendment," Vallencourt said. "I bear no responsibility whatsoever in this matter. Why should I be afraid?"

"Because sometimes innocent people are railroaded into confessing or at least into giving information that can be twisted against them," the attorney responded. "The police are here on a very serious matter."

Vallencourt nodded. "Well, that's what you two can do then. Stop me if you feel I'm too talkative."

The senior lawyer shook his head disapprovingly and made a note on his laptop.

Sheriff Petit opened the questioning. "Do you know anything about the murder of Marlene Chartrand?"

"No, nothing," Vallencourt replied. "Other than she was found dead in the cemetery, and everyone in town knows that. It's a terrible tragedy."

"Did you know her?"

"I knew of her. It is common knowledge she was the museum's curator; that's all I know about her."

Jeremy piped up. "Were you concerned that she had special knowledge of this area? Knowledge that could throw a negative light on your family?"

"Don't answer that," interjected the older lawyer. "It's suggestive."

His client ignored him. "I was not aware of what she knew," Vallencourt replied to Jeremy. "Besides, it would be very difficult for her to add much to the mountain of silly, superstitious suspicions about me and my family that the town has entertained for two hundred years, wouldn't it?"

The lawyer rebuked Jeremy. "I believe you're trying to antagonize my client. You must desist with that type of questioning."

"No," Vallencourt said. "Let him question away. After all, we are after the truth here, aren't we?" He looked pointedly at the investigators.

Jeremy continued. "There was a book, a history of this area, that was stolen from the museum recently. Were you aware of this book?"

"Yes, but not of its contents."

"So you're saying you didn't know the book documents a string of bodies turning up around the Vallencourt property for the past two centuries?"

"That's right. As I said, I didn't know of its contents. I am aware of the rumors about bodies. Many are outright concoctions by the townspeople; others that actually happened were coincidences. Why, the locals even think my family are rougarous—werewolves that savagely murder people. So what stock should anyone put in their suspicions? I hope you're not going to check if there was a full moon the night of the curator's murder."

"Mr. Vallencourt," the lawyer said in a pleading voice.

Jeremy kept pushing. "Evidence has been found placing Marlene Chartrand on your property on the night of her murder. What's your response to that?"

"You're now trying to intimidate my client," the lawyer protested. "Don't answer, Mr. Vallencourt."

Vallencourt ignored his lawyer again. "That is shocking," he replied to Jeremy. "I have no idea why she would have been there, unless the murderer brought her there for whatever reason. Perhaps to frame me."

"Why would he do that?"

Vallencourt replied before his lawyer could object. "Because I have many enemies in town," he said. "They've been trying to hang a Vallencourt for two hundred years. You yourself witnessed the last attempt: the mob in my front yard not long ago.... By the way, I have not thanked all of you for the stand you made—very courageous. But it's ironic, don't you think, that now you're trying to hang me in your own way."

"Mr. Vallencourt," the lawyer cautioned again, wiping his forehead with a handkerchief.

Vallencourt waved him off. "You know," he said to Jeremy, "I recall something the night of the murder. One of my bodyguards thought he saw a light in the bush on my property. The staff investigated but found nothing. Ask them and they'll tell you. That could have been your murderer or murderers."

Jeremy looked him straight in the eye. "You mention you've got many enemies. Could it be you were giving some payback for all the trouble they've caused you?"

"You're implying by murdering a few?"

The lawyer reproved Jeremy. "You've asked a speculative, leading question."

Tony interjected. "This is not a courtroom right now."

Vallencourt gestured for quiet around the table. "I'll answer the question. No. I am not a violent man and would not stoop so low to physically seek revenge on someone. Unlike the mob at my doorstep."

"Not even to Louie Thibeault?"

"Who? Oh, the clothing store owner."

"Yeah, the last one standing after the mob retreated that day. I'm sure you saw him."

"What are you driving at?"

Jeremy ignored the question. "I'm also sure you're aware that his daughter disappeared recently."

"I follow the news. Another tragedy, I'm afraid."

"Is Louie Thibeault one of your prime enemies in town?"

The lawyer interrupted again. "I would not answer that, either."

Vallencourt glared at Jeremy. "If you're insinuating I abducted his daughter to get even with him for disparaging me, it's a ridiculous notion."

"Where were you the night of her disappearance?" Jeremy asked.

"I'm sure you would know, as you've got the place under surveillance. My chief of security is an ex-military intelligence man who knows about such things."

"So answer the question."

"I was here all that evening. You can verify that with my staff."

"And how about the evening of the murder of Marlene Chartrand?"

"It was the same. Home for the entire evening."

"Are you carrying your cell phone?" Tony asked.

"Yes."

"You can hand that over right now," Tony said. Vallencourt placed his phone on the table.

"There's another matter," Tony said. "What are all those boxes that are delivered here in the evenings?"

"I knew that would be coming up," Vallencourt said. "You and I both know the locals believe human bodies are shipped here for some malign purpose."

"Well, are they?" Tony asked.

Vallencourt produced a thin smile. "There's some truth to it, but not for malign purposes."

The lawyers gasped audibly, and the investigators looked at one another, astonished.

Vallencourt spent a few moments savoring the reactions around the table. "Come with me," he said. "I'll show you what I mean."

He led the mystified group down a long hallway to a heavy, stainless-steel door, which contrasted starkly with the old décor of the mansion. A computer scanned his iris, and the door slid open. "You're some of the privileged few to view this in its entirety," he announced.

The group entered and stared in awe at an immense room built of white stone and marble in the classical Greek style. Towering, ornate pillars supported the domed glass ceiling, which formed a broad skylight—one of the few modern aspects of the room's construction. On pedestals were numerous fossils, from the remains of ancient sea creatures to the skeletons of dinosaurs and extinct mammals.

Jeremy had never seen anything like this since his visits to the Smithsonian and the British

Museum. This was indeed a first-class museum of natural history—a privately owned one, which must have cost a fortune. The fine stone and imported marble alone must have cost millions.

"As you can see," Vallencourt said proudly, "my interests are in paleontology. I have one of the finest collections of fossils west of the Mississippi. But to get to the point of why I brought you here." He led the group over to several glassed-in cases, each containing a small collection of skulls and other bones. "These are my prize specimens: the human bodies I was talking about." He pointed to a partial skull. "This was found in the Rift Valley of East Africa in the 1960s. It's a female Homo sapiens, one hundred and ninety thousand years old. I call her Charlotte." He paused to relish the moment. "So, as you can plainly see, my interest in human bodies is purely academic, an intellectual hobby." He gestured toward the great room. "All this is what's been shipped in boxes to the mansion. I hope you aren't too disappointed."

The two lawyers looked profoundly relieved. Although Tony and Monica tried to put on a straight face, Jeremy could tell they were deflated by the discovery that Vallencourt's human bodies were hardly victims of murder—at least of the modern-day variety.

Jeremy tried to gain the upper hand with their suspect. "These fossils appear as good or better than any I've seen in national museums," he said. "How did you possibly come to acquire them for a private collection?"

Vallencourt smiled. “There’s a market for fossils out there,” he said. “And I assure you it’s completely legitimate.”

Jeremy was just about to reply when the lead tech came to the door. “We’re done with the upstairs,” he said to the sheriff. “You’re free to inspect the area.”

Sheriff Petit nodded and turned toward Vallencourt. “You and the attorneys remain here until further notice,” he said sternly.

As the investigators left, Jeremy glanced back at Vallencourt. Round one of the questioning was over, he thought, and he wasn’t at all certain if anyone had won.

***

As the three drove back to New Orleans, they shared their impressions of the wily Charles Vallencourt.

“At no point was he even close to cracking,” Tony observed.

“He was a cool customer, all right,” Jeremy said. “A skill probably honed by his long-term business experience facing down or outwitting competitors and—who knows—maybe regulatory bodies as well. At any rate, he had all the right answers.”

Adjusting her legroom in a rear seat, Monica added, “I think he is quite intelligent, too, which undoubtedly helped him today.”

Tony reached down to turn up the air conditioning. “His self-confidence was amazing. Would any of us be able to stand our ground if we were told evidence from a murder investigation was found on our property? And then to have the guts to go on the counterattack? That was really something!"

"Let's add to that refusing advice from his lawyers, after helicoptering them in, no less," Monica said.

Tony laughed. "Yeah, he really gave them a hard time! I thought the senior guy was going to have an anxiety attack."

Jeremy took out his phone to make some notes. "Yes, it's either the mark of a man who knows he's innocent or the tactic of a guilty man trying to persuade us he's innocent."

"The latter would be very cunning," Monica said. "You know, some of the qualities we've been talking about here fit with the murderer's likely profile. How do we know that Vallencourt showing us the fossilized bodies wasn't a clever ruse to deflect from the possibility some of those crates may have contained modern-day murder victims, too?"

"Then our techs should come up with DNA from those crates," Tony offered.

"If the crates haven't been burned," Jeremy cautioned, "and I wouldn't put it past him."

"Yeah, maybe," Tony replied. "The techs are also going to search the property further for signs of any disturbed ground. It'll be interesting to see if they come up with anything from the mansion, too."

"There was one thing that was perfectly clear about him," Monica asserted. "He's certainly feeling persecuted by the townspeople. There was a lot of anger about that. And he transferred some of that to us. Witness his statement about our trying to hang him, too, only in our own way. I'm not so sure that he's above revenge, as he says."

Jeremy shrugged. "I don't know. It's true he was especially angry about the mob on his property. He mentioned that twice. And frankly, I can't blame him. I've never seen a spectacle like that. It was like the townspeople in some Gothic novel storming the castle of a dark villain."

"Just maybe it's well deserved," Tony said. "Private museum or not, we have not gotten to the bottom of this yet with Vallencourt. Not by a long shot."

Monica picked up on the theme. "We saw what hundreds of years of anger and fear can do to a peaceful little town. The Vallencourts are likely just the other side of the same coin—made angry and fearful by years of persecution and harassment. Repressed feelings find their way to the surface somehow. Clairmonters became the mob. What have the Vallencourts become?"

Tony and Jeremy had no reply to that. The three drove on in solemn silence.

CHAPTER TWENTY-ONE

A few days later, the trio furthered their investigation into their other potential suspects. They visited the Museum of Torture and the Morbid near the French Quarter on Armand Street to view first-hand what the Maderas were involved in.

The front of the sizable two-story building was a façade of an old castle. The large windows facing the street were draped in black; medieval-looking stone statues stood guard at the entrance. As the three entered the spacious hallway, they noticed that huge paintings of Dante's Inferno and other depictions of torture hung on the walls.

"Somebody has a flair for the dramatic," Jeremy remarked.

They joined a curious group that sat on old, wooden benches, which looked like pews possibly rescued from a torn-down church. A young guide, who introduced herself as a graduate student in history, provided a solemn presentation on the history of torture and on some of the grimmer aspects of old-time medical treatment. They were then turned loosc to wander through the exhibits.

The investigators decided to view the displays of old medical instruments first, suspecting James Madera had a particular hand in setting them up. On the way, Jeremy commented, "I was surprised that torture has such a long history. All the way back to ancient Persia."

"Unfortunately, as the guide said, torture is not just history," Monica responded. "It's still being used today. The guide put it well. We like to think of ourselves as an enlightened society, morally superior to those who used torture in the past, say in the Middle Ages. The sad fact is we've only become more secretive and adept at doing it."

"Waterboarding with terrorist suspects, for instance?" Jeremy asked.

"Yes," replied Monica. "And what else should we call solitary confinement in prisons? I've studied it. If it's used for punishment for long periods of time, that's torture. People exposed to that can suffer long-term psychological and physical harm."

Tony was taken aback. "I never thought of solitary confinement as torture, but yes, it fits the bill." He shook his head slowly. "Maybe there's a cruel streak in human nature that we don't even notice sometimes."

"I'm more of an optimist, Tony," Monica said. "I wonder if there really is such a thing as 'human nature.' I think we are what we learn. We start off as a tabula rasa—a blank slate that our experience fills in.... By the way, there is one thing that struck me as odd in the guide's presentation today."

"What's that?" Tony asked.

"Her spiel mentioned nothing about sadism, deliberately inflicting pain for one's own pleasure. This is a major motivation behind torture. Even when somebody asked a question about it, she barely touched on the topic."

"That's interesting," Jeremy said. "Are you suggesting that maybe she intentionally omitted sadistic motivations in her presentation?"

"Yes, and if so, why might that be?"

"Has she been told not to bring too much attention to the darker, sadistic nature of this exhibition?" Jeremy asked. Before anyone could answer, they arrived at a mock-up of a seventeen-century surgeon's operating area.

Tony read from the plaque underneath a set of instruments encased in an old wood and glass cabinet. "Patients upon which these instruments were used were often in excruciating pain during operations, as anesthesia was unknown at this time period. If they did not die upon the surgery table, they often did so from infections afterwards. There was no sterilization of instruments. In fact, rich physicians of the time took pride in their expensive, ornate surgical instruments. Note the artistic swirls and designs on the amputation saw above, a perfect breeding ground for bacteria."

"And those were the days long before antibiotics were known," Jeremy mused out loud. "You know the saying 'the treatment is worse than the disease'? I think I know now where it comes from."

"Remind me to check out my dentist's drill next time," Tony said, a little alarmed.

The medical devices of the 1800s and early 1900s were no more reassuring. Jeremy spotted a display of antimasturbation devices used on patients in some psychiatric institutions of the day. He read out loud, "It was widely believed that masturbation was not only unhealthy but also caused mental illness. Devices were fitted to the genitals of both men and women patients, which would cause pain upon masturbation, such as electric shocks."

“Who would want to collect things like this?” Tony asked.

“How about someone fascinated by cruelty, who scours the Internet to get them? Maybe travels the world to find them,” Monica surmised.

“Well, I’m sure we’ll find something for every sadist in this place,” Jeremy remarked.

The three quickly moved on but encountered further horrendous “treatment” devices. They cringed as they saw the Mark II Electrotherapeutic Chair, used to treat World War One soldiers with battle fatigue (PTSD). The soldiers were strapped in and given strong, general electrical shocks to the body in the hope this would cure their disorder.

“I wonder if this or the electric execution chair came first?” Tony asked glumly.

Monica said, “I think the latter, Tony, and it’s not used anymore. But some pretty invasive electrical treatments are still around today, like ECT for clinical depression that doesn’t respond to other treatments.”

“And does it work?” Tony asked.

“Apparently for most, but the effects can be temporary and the patient may need booster sessions or other treatments to maintain improvement.”

“Well, there’s never a free lunch,” remarked Tony. “Anything else on the downside?”

“Yes, some report serious side effects like permanent memory loss and feelings that their personality has changed.”

Jeremy frowned. “So, with ECT we have a chance of getting better, but we can lose parts of ourselves in the process. Kind of a mind-boggling proposition."

They continued on trepidatiously to the most horrific displays in the museum: the instruments of torture. The first room they entered was theatrically decorated as a medieval-like dungeon cell, dramatically lit in red and bordered by deep shadows. The first pain-dispensing device they saw was the Judas Cradle, used for interrogation by the Spanish Inquisition in the sixteenth century. It was a high stool coming to a sharp point on top. The victim was gradually lowered to a sitting position on the point to increase pain, as required. Since the device was rarely cleaned, many victims died later of infections.

"I gather they got the point," Tony said in an attempt at dark humor to break the tension.

The other two stared at him. "That's terrible, Tony," Monica admonished.

Next to the "Cradle" was an even more fearsome interrogation device, the Iron Chair. The victim was bound in the chair, which had sharp spikes protruding from it. A hole in the seat conveyed flames from a fire underneath, which would burn the victim's bottom without being lethal. The device was so frightening that it was often not necessary to use it; the accused would apparently confess or implicate others after merely viewing it.

Monica broke the investigators' stunned silence. "The ironic thing about these contraptions is that they were often useless in obtaining any credible information. The victim would say anything they thought their interrogator wanted to hear."

"So it was all for nothing," Tony remarked.

"That's about it," Monica replied, "except maybe when they were used publicly. Whole towns used to turn out for the torturing and execution of victims. The spectacle would terrorize the population into obeying the authorities."

"It looks like victims were also psychologically tortured through public humiliation," Jeremy said. He pointed to a heavy looking flute-like device that some were forced to wear around their necks in public for being "bad musicians." He also gestured toward a female mannikin with its legs pinned in the stocks, its tongue in wooden clamps. "This was a punishment for overly talkative women in colonial America."

"That, too, is ironic," Monica said. "I remember my psych courses saying punishment never really gets rid of a behavior anyway. It just suppresses it temporarily."

Tony couldn't resist another quip. "I could find a use for the clamps for some people I know. Present company excluded, of course."

The three had had enough and turned toward the entrance. Along the way, they noticed very different reactions from their own in some of the other visitors: what seemed to be amusement and fascination. Were these the reactions of the sadistically inclined among the museum crowd? And how deeply did sadism reach into the mind of James Madera, likely a prime investor in this gruesomely cruel exhibition? Deeply enough to kill, perhaps? They began to hatch a plan to find out.

CHAPTER TWENTY-TWO

The plan was hatched. Monica and Jeremy would go undercover to the favorite hangout of the Black Marquis, a BDSM club in the French Quarter. To Tony's huge amusement, the two were to go disguised as an S & M couple on the make, hopefully to glean more information about their suspect.

It wasn't easy getting to that point. Jeremy encountered a surprising prudish streak in Monica. She finally acquiesced when he reminded her of why she had come to New Orleans in the first place. "You wanted to get field experience, didn't you?" he asked. "And to be some place earthy. Here's your chance."

They concentrated seriously on the details of the operation after that: devising aliases and identities and studying S & M, including a dictionary of BDSM terms.

On the day of the operation, the two were at the office, finalizing their preparations.

"What did you say the club was called again?" Monica asked.

Jeremy smiled. "Spaghetti & Meatballs."

"It sounds more like a restaurant than a club. Why would it be called that?"

Jeremy's smile broadened. "The name stands for S & M, but that's not the only reason."

"Well?"

"Let's put it this way. You'd better look it up yourself."

She gave him a somewhat disapproving look. "I thought we were being open about all of this?"

"Yes, but I've got my limits with a female colleague."

Curious, Monica asked her phone to define the term. Her eyes widened. "That *is* gross!"

"Right," Jeremy said. "We're not attending church tonight. This is another example of how we're not up on everything yet. We're bound to get something wrong. So let's keep in mind our cover story: we're a couple growing bored with our sexual relationship and are new to the BDSM scene."

"I'm with you."

"Good. This also reminds me of my number-one rule of PI undercover work: don't get caught. The reasons are obvious, but not the least of them is that people get angry if they find you out, and that can be dangerous with some, particularly if they're carrying."

"Got it."

"Okay. Meet you in front of Spaghetti & Meatballs at ten tonight."

"What about Tony's request to see us in disguise before we go?" she asked with a grin.

Jeremy laughed. "No way. We would never live it down."

***

Jeremy arrived at a few minutes to ten at Spaghetti & Meatballs. Couples and singles were already streaming through the front door. He smiled as he saw Monica approaching. She wore tight black leather pants, a matching open jacket, and knee-high spiked boots. Her blouse displayed a naughty saying: I like the top. She also wore the

BDSM symbol, the triskele, around her neck. He thought she looked downright gorgeous in a dark, erotic sort of way, but he quickly banished the idea from his mind.

"You look pretty convincing, Anne," he said as she walked up to him.

She looked at his equally form-fitting leather outfit and his steel-toed cowboy boots. His half-open shirt revealed his bountiful chest hair and the chain collar around his neck. She smiled broadly. "You look convincing yourself, Andre."

He took her hand. "Shall Mr. and Mrs. Colbert get this over with?"

The two were met by a doorman and ticket person, who charged a hefty entrance fee. They were informed that a club membership was available for another considerable fee. They declined but took a list of club rules.

The place was practically filled with couples seated at tables in skin-tight outfits made of just about everything but cloth. Their ornaments, hanging paraphernalia, or their t-shirts made it generally easy to spot which of the BDSM letters applied to each, but some were more generic. The singles sat at the glistening stainless steel and glass bar.

Over to the right, watched by the crowd, was a stage in which pairs or trios of members played out their scenes for each of the various genres, although there were crossovers. Each pair had specialized equipment upon which one was draped or suspended in various vulnerable positions. To the side, were a number of private rooms, for which tickets could be bought at the bar. Appropriate recorded theme music by some of New Orleans' favorite S & M bands titillated the crowd.

Jeremy and Monica sat down at the last available table.

"Quite the savory place," Monica commented sarcastically.

Jeremy did not reply. He was surprised Monica's moralistic side was surfacing again. He'd thought they'd moved beyond that.

"I'm curious," Monica said. "What's on the list of rules?"

Jeremy looked down at the list. "It starts off with the usual: adults only, no drugs allowed, impaired people will not be admitted.... Here's something different. No more than two drinks will be allowed per patron."

Monica scanned the alcohol list. "Is this why drinks cost twenty-five dollars apiece? They're making their money on that and the door fees."

"Don't forget the private rooms. Seventy dollars per half hour for two couples, thirty dollars for one, according to the sign at the bar."

"Who can afford that?"

"Obviously only the well-heeled." He looked to see if she recognized the pun, but it went by her. "Let's see.... There's also no sex in the public play space. Patrons will wear at least underwear at all times."

"I gather there's no mention of what goes on in the private rooms."

"No, except that no more than four people at a time can occupy a room."

"It sounds unduly restrictive to me," Monica deadpanned.

Jeremy grinned. "I just had an interesting thought. To appear more genuine, we should consider making a show of going into a private room for a while."

"Dream on," Monica said. "Remember, under all this leather, I'm armed."

Jeremy was about to quip something back when Monica announced, "We're getting some interest from the couple behind you."

Jeremy didn't look back. "Okay, let's draw them into the spider's web, shall we?"

Monica flashed her best smile toward the couple, and in a few moments they appeared beside them, uncomfortably close to their table.

Jeremy looked up at the slender columns of leather and latex next to him to spot the beaming faces of a middle-aged man and woman looking down at them.

"May we join you?" the woman asked in a surprisingly husky voice.

She seems to be the dominant one, Jeremy thought. Oops, I mean the one on top.

Monica gestured the couple to their seats. Their garb was so tight, she half expected them to squeak as they sat down.

"We're Rosie and Henry," the woman said.

The undercover agents shook their hands. "Anne and Andre," Monica replied.

"So, we haven't seen you around here," Rosie commented.

"Yes, we're new to the BDSM scene," Monica informed her. "We heard this was the best club in town."

"Mostly," Rosie replied, seeming to leave something unsaid.

"It's an expensive place," Monica remarked.

"Yeah," the woman said, eyeing Jeremy as she sipped her drink. "But it's worth it if you meet the right couple." Rosie got down to the core of the matter. "Are you two interested in some action?"

"It depends," Monica replied.

Jeremy stifled a smile with his hand.

"Depends on what?" Rosie asked.

"We're into edge play," Monica declared.

"Whoa," the woman said. "That's pretty heavy for a couple new to the game. Have you tried risky play before?"

"We're working up to it."

Rosie looked at her partner. The bottom half finally spoke up. "I notice you're wearing the triskele. You know that tells us the three rules we have in the club."

Monica feigned ignorance. "What's that?"

"Safety, sanity, and consent. We don't do anything that's dangerous. We do it only with sane people, and we honor consent in our play at all times. In fact, before we do anything, we use a contract with our playmates. Rosie's got one in her pocket, if you'd like to see it."

Jeremy cleared his throat, barely stifling another laugh. "Well, I don't know about dangerous, but we're at least sane and consensual. Aren't we, Anne dear?"

"So, what's your kink?" Monica asked the couple.

Jeremy smiled to himself again. She was really getting into the role now.

“We’re mainly into S & M, but we’re flexible. Sex is a big part of it for us, but we’re into it for dominance and submission, too. We do it to bond with one another. We carry top-bottom roles into our regular home life, but it’s often hard to pull off.”

“We’re more into sex and pain,” Monica stated, “and, like I say, we want to go hard edge.”

Monica reached into her coat pocket for a mini camera hidden in a package of cigarettes. She deftly placed the package on the table facing the bar and activated the camera by pulling out a cigarette. Their suspect had just arrived.

“Well, you seem like a nice couple,” Jeremy offered, “but we’re really interested in a guy called the Marquis.”

Rosie’s eyebrows shot up. “The Black Marquis? You know the rules we just talked about? He breaks all of them. He’s dangerous!”

“Why do you say that?” Jeremy asked.

“Because he picks people up here. Only the new ones who don’t know any better. He’s sent more than a few of them to hospital, and maybe that’s not all of it. At first, we gave him the benefit of the doubt that he accidently slipped into edge play that got away on him. But it happened too often to be just accidental.”

“So if this guy’s breaking the club rules, why is he allowed in here?” Jeremy queried.

Rosie looked around uneasily and lowered her voice. “One big reason is that he’s well off, and we think he’s bribed the club owner to look the other way.”

She gestured toward the bar. "See that woman on the second last seat on the right? She was nearly killed by that jerk and reported it to the owner. He did nothing and told her not to give a bad rep to the club through unsubstantiated accusations."

"Maybe we need to talk to her about this guy," Monica said.

"If she'll talk to you, and that's a big if," Rosie warned.

"What's her name?" Jeremy asked.

"She goes by Emma," Rosie replied as she and Henry got up to leave the table in disappointment.

Jeremy looked over at the bar. "She's alone, nursing a drink. There's nothing like the direct approach. Why don't you go and invite her over?"

Monica headed for the empty bar stool next to the hoped-for informant. Jeremy took a deep breath as he watched her walk away. He was almost mesmerized by her slinky form. He would actually be relieved when they got out of these erotic outfits.

He sipped his drink as he watched the two start up a conversation. He knew Monica was making progress when the woman turned to look at him.

In a few moments, Emma and Monica joined him at the table. "We won't beat around the bush, Emma," Monica said. "We've been thinking of some edge play with the Marquis, but we've been told you had a bad experience with him."

"That's the understatement of the year," Emma said. She cast a wary eye around her. "I'll talk to you about him just to save your skins—but not here. Join me outside. I'll go first. Follow me in a few minutes."

The three soon gathered on the nearby street corner. Emma's cigarette suggested they were on a smoke break. "I just passed the bastard at the bar," she announced.

"You don't seem rattled," Monica observed, taking out a cigarette from her pack in her breast pocket.

"No, and I'll tell you why in a minute.... It all happened about a year ago. I was new to the club and got swept off my feet by the Marquis. He's a charmer at first, but get alone with him and it's hell on earth. The Marquis went to the restroom before we left the club, and someone next to me got up and left a note on the bar near my hand. The note warned me not to go with him, but I brushed it off as some kind of practical joke. I left with the Marquis for a hotel room. Big mistake."

Emma took a deep drag on her cigarette. "He bound me up on St. Andy's cross frontwards, and he immediately began to beat on me. I knew it wasn't going to work, but out of desperation, I used the password agreed upon to withdraw from the scene. He ignored it and kept at me for the longest time. He raped me twice. The last time he choked me till I blacked out. When I awoke, I was untied and on the floor. Thankfully, he had left. It was through the grace of God I survived. I had flashbacks and nightmares for months after."

Monica shook her head. "That's horrible," she said. "Did you report him to the police, Emma?"

"No."

"Why was that?"

"Because of shame, really. I was already ashamed that I was kinky, and then I stupidly allowed myself to get into a bad position with a total stranger. When I did eventually complain at the club, I got shut down by the owner."

"So how can you stand to be in the same room as this perpetrator?"

"I saw a therapist for nearly six months, who helped me shake off the symptoms. So now I can actually see the guy without freaking out."

"Yeah, but why do it?" Jeremy asked. "Why not just go to another club?"

"Because there are not many, and they are super seedy. Except for the Marquis, this is the best place in town to meet playmates." She stubbed out the remainder of her cigarette and began to stroll back toward the club. "My advice to you two is stay away from the Marquis. You'll live longer."

Jeremy made sure Emma was out of earshot and turned toward Monica. "Well, we appear to have met a survivor of the Black Marquis."

"Yes, and she seemed to give a pretty convincing account of a near-death experience at his hands."

Jeremy frowned. "Black certainly seems to be an appropriate adjective for this guy. If her report is true, he's going to kill someone during his 'play,' accidentally or on purpose—if he already hasn't. Sadism and violence are a bad combination. Our killer is testimony to that. How about we go back and keep an eye on him."

The Marquis was still at the bar as Jeremy and Monica re-entered the club. He was engaged in what looked like flirtatious conversation with a young woman, who appeared to be a single.

As the two PIs sat down at another table, Monica positioned her concealed camera to video the Marquis and his female friend. "Something's going to happen here," she said.

"I just hope she doesn't take off with him," Jeremy added.

The couple got up and walked over to the ticket area at the end of the bar.

"Well, it looks like it's in-house," Jeremy said. "At least we don't have to worry about him doing her in."

The couple soon disappeared into one of the private rooms. Monica kept her camera focused on the door. "We'll soon know how she reacts to the Marquis," she said.

"Yeah, and with Emma's report, we should have enough to get warrants on this guy and set up surveillance," Jeremy replied.

Monica nodded. "We seem to be making some progress."

"I hope Jack thinks so, too. Tony tells me he's been complaining about the resources being put into the case."

"There can't be half-measures," Monica retorted. "We're in this the whole way or not. Jack has to accept that."

"I really think he does," Jeremy said. "But he's got people he's accountable to."

The door to the private room suddenly swung open, and the Marquis strode out, quickly heading for the front door.

"He wasn't in there long," Jeremy remarked.

The two PIs waited expectantly for the Marquis' playmate to emerge, but several minutes went by without an appearance. "This doesn't look good," Jeremy remarked.

"Here she comes now," Monica said, aiming the camera.

The woman stepped out of the doorway, dabbing her eyes with a tissue and appearing flushed and disheveled. Looking straight ahead, she walked rapidly to the club's front entrance.

Jeremy and Monica stood up to follow her. As they crossed the floor, Jeremy noticed the indifference of the crowd to the plight of the fleeing woman. They're all silent conspirators in this rotten, dangerous business with the Marquis, he thought. No less guilty than he.

Jeremy and Monica caught up with the woman a few hundred feet down the dark street. "Miss! Miss!" Jeremy called out. "Hold up a bit."

The woman continued forward at a brisk pace, apparently paying no attention to him.

"Please let us help," Jeremy beseeched her.

The woman stopped and turned toward them. "You can help by leaving me alone. Hit the road."

"Look," Jeremy said, "we know the kind of man he is and what he might have tried to do."

"Tried? He started to choke me hard and threatened to kill me if I didn't cooperate. I fought him off, and he ran for it. What the hell kind of club is this that allows a creep like that in there?"

"We think the same thing," Monica said. "Why don't you let us call 911? Tell the police about it."

"What planet are you from? You should know cops don't take S & M people seriously. They think we're perverts and we're to blame for getting ourselves into dangerous situations and wasting their time. And if I inform on this guy, he's likely crazy enough to come after me. So go be good Samaritans with somebody else." She turned her back on the investigators and walked away.

"Did you record that?" Jeremy asked.

"Yeah," Monica said, reaching in her jacket to turn off the mini camera.

"Good, let's get it over to Tony and Jack."

They were just about to turn away when they heard a low growl from a powerful engine nearby. A black sports car rolled slowly by on the other side of the street. Jeremy wasn't able to identify the make but thought it might be a high-end European job.

The car stopped under a street light as the woman walked by. "What's that all about?" Jeremy asked.

Monica didn't answer, but she took out her camera and focused it on the sports car, getting a close-up photo of the license plate and make.

The woman turned toward the car and gave the driver the finger. The sports car gunned its motor, screeching its tires violently as it sped off and disappeared in the distance.

"The Marquis?" Jeremy asked. "If so, what's he trying to do? Harass her? Stalk her?"

"I wouldn't put it past him," Monica said. "Domination through fear is a characteristic behavior of these guys."

Jeremy nodded. "We may have a very promising suspect for the murders. Tony and Jack will find these recordings really interesting."

CHAPTER TWENTY-THREE

The next morning, Jeremy, Monica, and Tony met in Jack's office to debrief the undercover operation at Spaghetti & Meatballs. Jack was delayed, giving the others opportunity for some small talk.

This was the first meeting with Tony since the operation. Jeremy noticed Tony's wide grin and knew he was in for some razzing. "Okay, Tony," he said, "let's have it."

"Have what?" Tony asked innocently.

"I'm sure you've got at least half a dozen choice comments for me."

"Well, now that you mention it, I was disappointed when I didn't see you two in your evening costumes."

Jeremy cast an I-told-you-so look at Monica. "Sorry to disappoint, Tony, but we had an important date at the club."

Tony's grin grew wider. "At Spaghetti & Meatballs, no less. I looked that up. Do you know what it means?"

Jeremy rolled his eyes. "I do, and we don't want to hear about it again. Right, Monica?"

"Yeah, I think we're finished with that one," Monica said.

Tony was readying a truly devastating follow-up quip when Jack spoiled things by entering the office. He looked quizzically at the others. "Am I interrupting a private joke or something?"

"Yes, you are, and thank God," Jeremy said.

Characteristically, Jack immediately got down to business. "Okay, what do you have on this Spaghetti & Meatballs operation?" The others attempted to stifle a collective laugh.

Jeremy cleared his throat. "Sorry, Jack. Just a little comedic relief. As you recall, Monica and I went undercover into a local S & M club whose name I won't repeat." Tony and Monica giggled again, eliciting a disapproving glance from Jack.

"The objective was to gather information on a forty-two-year-old man by the name of James Madera, who frequents the club. He was known to our informant and at the club as the Black Marquis—rumored to be a violent, sadistic predator. Monica twigged into him initially through a computer search of corporate registrations. He's the spouse of a secret partner at the Museum of Torture and the Morbid here in New Orleans. We think that he may be involved as a hidden buyer for the museum. The initial investigation into the museum had not uncovered this possibility, and we decided to look into him."

Jeremy went on. "We have direct reports, covertly recorded, from two women at the club who claim to have been physically or sexually assaulted by him—one in a sadistic manner. He also apparently made death threats to the other when she didn't cooperate in edge play."

Monica gave Jack the camera, which he plugged into his laptop. "There's the suspect, James Madera," Monica said, pointing to the screen. "He's sitting at the bar on the far left—black cloak and all."

"And with his reputation for extreme sadism," Jeremy remarked, "it's no wonder he's called the Black Marquis." Noting Tony's puzzled look, he added, "You know, Tony.... The Marquis de Sade?"

The three spent the next half hour viewing and reviewing the videos. Jack asked about the sports car that had pulled up near the second woman.

"We ran the plate," Tony said. "It was Madera's."

"So what was he up to?" Jack asked. "Intimidation? Stalking? Worse?"

"All of the above would be in line with his allegedly aggressive behavior," Monica observed.

"Whatever it was, I doubt he was offering her a friendly ride home," Tony replied.

"What do you think of the women's accounts?" Jack asked.

"There's little doubt they were telling the truth," Jeremy said. He looked at Monica, who nodded. "The woman from the private room definitely showed signs of distress after her encounter with Madera."

Monica added, "The other, Emma, gave her report despite taking a risk that she might get thrown out of the club if found out. From this point of view, I can't imagine why she would exaggerate or falsify her report."

"There were also no signs from the videos that either was lying," Tony said.

"It looks that way to me, too," Jack agreed. "But without the willingness of either of them to make a formal complaint to us, we don't have enough to bring any charges against Madera—even if he is a dangerous man. The best we can do is get search warrants on him to gather more evidence that might incriminate him directly in some violent act. Maybe he's vain enough to video himself doing something, for example. At the very least, we might scare him off from any further crimes."

"Right," Tony said. "We've also done a background check on the guy, which will support a warrant on him."

"What have you got, Tony?"

"It's more what *we* have got. Monica and I put this report together. I'll give her first crack at this."

Monica was surprised by Tony deferring to her. Perhaps he wanted to give her some experience at taking the lead in a case presentation. She quickly stepped in. "Well, sir, we have his student records from university. He was a medical student in Louisiana in the late nineties. He had top grades in medical school, especially in anatomy and dissection."

"Well, well," Jack said.

"Yes, and hear this. Despite his good grades, he was bounced from the school in his second year after complaints from female students and a female professor. Apparently, he made frequent sexual comments and other negative remarks about women."

"Misogyny?" Jack asked.

"It appears to be. And they complained about being ogled by him too."

Jack nodded. "So how did the school handle it?"

"The school gave him a chance to reform. He was enrolled in counselling and gender sensitivity training, but the complaints got worse. Rather than have to deal with a formal sexual harassment process, the school decided to can him."

"In my day, we called it getting the dean's vacation," Jeremy quipped.

"Except it was a permanent vacation," Tony said.

"Yes, and he angrily denied all the accusations and blamed the female complainants and the school for the problems," Monica added.

"But I can see his anger at the school," Jeremy pointed out. "He seems to have been denied due process."

"He appears to have felt that way, too," Monica added. "In a rage on his last day at school, he confronted the dean of medicine in the hallway, loudly accusing him of railroading him out of the program."

"So he leaves school with a serious chip on his shoulder," Jack said.

"Very likely," Monica agreed. "But he had a long history of anger before that. We have some family background on him from social service records, and it's not good. James and his family were seen by social services when he was nine years old. Neighbors had reported that the Madera children were neglected and abused by their mother. A social worker indicated that the abuse was on and off, but it went on for quite a few years. All the children were adversely affected by it, especially James. He was described as an angry, moody child, prone to getting into fights and rebelling against authority. He also used taunting and verbal abuse, mostly with the girls, and seemed to enjoy this."

Monica paused and looked at Tony, wondering if she was taking up too much airtime for a junior member.

Tony picked up on her cue. “The Maderas were well-to-do and lived in an upscale neighborhood here in the city. The father, Max, was alcoholic and stressed trying to keep his electrical supply business afloat. He wasn’t home much, and when he was, he was often drunk and abusive toward the mother. She then apparently took this out on the children. The father knew about the abuse but did nothing to stop it. The children also witnessed the parents fighting and the abuse toward the mother.”

Jeremy sighed. “Not a great start for the kids.”

“No, but there was something positive. The family went into counselling and seemed to improve. There were no more complaints from the neighbors, and the case was closed after about a year.”

“So, what’s your assessment of all this?” Jack asked.

“There’s no great leap of imagination here,” Monica said. “Our report concludes that his considerable animosity toward females in his background is doubtlessly based originally on negative feelings toward his mother. Furthermore, he may have modeled his father’s abusive behavior toward the mother, generalizing it to other females. Also, he likely has marked self-esteem issues, which would not have been helped by the fact that his father apparently failed to protect him from the mother’s abuse.”

“Another reason to be angry,” Jeremy observed.

“Okay, I’ve heard more than enough,” Jack said. “Tony, let’s get search warrants on him.”

“I’ll have the paperwork submitted to Judge Abellard by the end of the day,” Tony said with a smile.

“By the way,” Jack added, “I’m disturbed by the fact that a violent person like Madera is allowed in the S & M club, as well as by the allegation that he’s tolerated because he’s paid off the owner. Once we have executed the warrants, we should warn the owner that he must throw this guy out and tighten up background checks on his club members. We’ll tell him if he doesn’t, he’ll be getting a visit from the morality squad. There must be some old morality law on the books we can leverage.”

***

That evening, Monica turned on a relaxing piece of music from her classical collection. She used the sonata as background music for her now regular meditations.

She sat down on a large cushion, which she had placed on the floor near her window overlooking Bourbon Street. Across from her was a small stand on a low, rustic table, which displayed her venerable ancestor’s meditation book. She contemplated for a while the majestic red eagle on the book’s cover. Then she turned to the next meditation exercise, one of a series promising to develop in the aspirant ever higher levels of spiritual awareness.

After only a few weeks of practice, she had found it easier to calm and center herself. She also had some success at quieting the streams of thought that ordinarily filled her mind. She was even noticing some interesting effects in her everyday life. She spent less time focusing on the past and future and more on the present moment, which seemed more real and important. She also found herself observing things instead of thinking about them so much. She even felt that her intuitive side was strengthening, although she had no hard evidence of this yet.

Monica finished her meditation, returning to ordinary awareness. She stretched and was about to get up when she suddenly flashed back to Marlene Chartrand's funeral. She remembered feeling that Marlene had been there observing her own funeral. There had been several reoccurrences of the memory, and she had reflected a great deal on this. Perhaps the feeling was a reminder that she had yet to face up to her own mortality. Or perhaps Marlene was symbolic of the shocking unpredictability of life. Marlene had been a living, productive human being one day and then brutally murdered by a serial killer the next—like a bolt from the blue.

Monica shook her head. She would get no further in understanding the feeling this time, either. "Let it go," she said to herself as she walked toward her collection of travelogue DVDs.

Late that night, Monica experienced a strange nightmare. She was standing alone at night, barefoot and in her pajamas, on the dewy lawn of the Church of the Divine Rapture, the site of Marlene's funeral. She faced the church, which stood empty and dark. The cemetery holding Marlene's mortal remains was on her left. The clutter of tombs was illuminated by a brilliant, starry sky and an intense full moon.

Suddenly, a great black cloud covered the sky, and the scene fell into darkness. A violent wind arose, billowing her pajamas and chilling her body. A bolt of white-blue lightning struck the church steeple, blowing up the angel on its peak into tiny pieces and starting the steeple on fire.

She fled from the church into the dark cemetery. Panicked, she blindly stumbled through the maze of tombs, colliding with several of them, bloodying her nose. Another bolt of lightning hit the tomb next to her, breaking it into pieces and throwing her to the ground. She looked up at the shattered tomb. There, in front of her, stood a corpse in its burial clothes. Its eyes were two dark hollows in its decayed face. One of the corpse's hands pressed against a bloody gash in its abdomen; another was held beseechingly out toward Monica. She shrieked in terror as she recognized the corpse of Marlene Chartrand.

Monica awoke with a start. Her heart was racing, and her hands were shaking. She got up out of bed and grabbed her housecoat on the way to the kitchen. She heated up a mug of hot milk and sat down at the kitchen table, cupping it in her hands, which were now steadying.

What did the dream mean? Was it just dramatically symbolizing some of the thoughts she'd had about Marlene, or was it some kind of paranormal image? Or maybe it was just her brain processing memories during sleep that caused the bizarre experience. There were no clear answers.

***

The next day, she called the Clairmont Fire Department without daring to introduce herself.

"Have you had any calls for a fire at the Church of the Divine Rapture?" she asked a man who identified himself as the chief.

"No," said the chief. "Are you reporting a fire?"

"No," Monica said. "Have there ever been any fires there?"

"Not to my knowledge," the chief said. "Who is this, anyway?"

Monica evaded the question. "It's probably nothing. Thanks for your time, Chief."

She became reflective. The call ruled out something real that happened or was happening. So it was either just a vivid dream or a premonition. She'd keep track of the news in Clairmont. She laughed to herself that the chief probably thought she was either unhinged or a pyromaniac planning a fire.

CHAPTER TWENTY-FOUR

The trio arrived with their search warrants at the opulent Madera home in Lebeau Gardens, an upper-class district in Northwest New Orleans. A pair of techs accompanied them to gather electronic and other potential evidence.

They were met at the front door by Ava Madera, the suspect's wife and secret partner at the Museum of Torture and the Morbid. She stared in stunned silence at the troop gathered on her front porch.

"Mrs. Madera?" Tony asked.

"Yes?"

"I am Tony Vasquez, New Orleans Police Department." He flashed his badge at her. "We'd like to speak to your husband."

"What's this about?" the wife asked, the pitch of her voice rising.

"I'm sorry, Mrs. Madera. We need to speak with your husband privately."

In a few moments, James Madera stood before them in the doorway. Jeremy noted that without his cloak, his physical appearance was much more evident. He was heavyset and muscular, of medium height, with dark hair, graying at the temples. He had a prominent aquiline nose embedded in his hard, sharp-edged features. His poker face revealed nothing of what was going on behind it—neither did his narrow, unblinking eyes. How much cruelty was behind that undecipherable mask?

"What can I do for you?" Madera asked in an even tone.

Tony introduced himself again and served the warrants to his suspect.

The burly man in the doorway spent a minute reading the documents, keeping his straight face all the while.

This guy's a polygrapher's nightmare, Jeremy thought.

"Assault reports by two women?" Madera asked.

"That's right," Tony replied, "and we've got plenty of questions for you, too."

"I know my rights," Madera retorted, "and I don't have to answer any of your questions. So either arrest me or shut up about it and do your search."

Tony ignored the hostile response. "You're right. You don't have to answer any questions. But don't you think it would be smart to tell your side of the story about these allegations? You might persuade us you're innocent. Unless you really are guilty and afraid of giving yourself away."

"Maybe I should get a lawyer."

"You have that right, too, or if you're not guilty, you might straighten out this whole matter right now—face-to-face, man-to-man."

Jeremy gave Tony an admiring look. Tony had sensed James Madera would not turn down a challenge or a test of wills.

Their suspect appeared to think for a moment. "I'll go with that. But the second I want to stop answering questions, I want that respected."

"Agreed," Tony said.

The team was ushered into the hallway. A tech immediately confiscated Madera's cell phone and asked about the location of other electronic devices in the home. The techs dispersed to find them.

"They're seizing the computers?" Madera asked. "They won't find anything incriminating on them."

"We'll see what they come up with," Tony responded.

"Let's get this over with," Madera said as he led the three into his study and gestured toward an opulent leather couch in front of his desk. A tech was already there, bagging his computer.

Jeremy took the lead. "Have you ever assaulted a woman in any way, Mr. Madera?"

"No, absolutely not."

"Have you ever threatened a female with physical harm or threatened her life?"

"Never."

"Have you engaged in torturing a woman?"

"No, of course not. That's ridiculous. Why would you even ask a question like that?"

Jeremy ignored the question. "Do you engage in sadistic sexual practices for pleasure or domination?"

Madera smiled. "Yes, I belong to the S & M scene. Controlled sadism for pleasure and domination is a normal part of that. But there are limits. All the playmates must agree to a code that this is strictly consensual and does not involve harm or coercion."

"Do you practice this code?"

"Yes. All my relationships are consensual."

"Well, there are people in the S & M scene who say otherwise."

"Mere rumors. I know of people who are into edge play, but I'm not one of them. I'm into pretty normal S & M."

"What's normal S & M to you?" Jeremy asked.

"A lot of bondage, some light flagellation, and boss talk."

"And light flagellation means?"

"I mean low-level whipping."

"Are there injuries?" Jeremy asked.

"Not if it's done right, and I do it right."

"Is choking a part of this?"

"No. That's for those who are into edge play. As I said, I don't do that."

Jeremy gave him a skeptical look. "That's not what we've heard. The two women who say they were assaulted state you choked them."

"I don't know who you're talking about, but I would never do something like that. They're clearly lying."

"Why would they lie about that?"

"The old motive of revenge, for starters. I have many partners, and who knows, some may resent the fact and become jealous. Jealousy is a powerful feeling. It could lead to making false accusations."

Monica interjected. "I notice you left out the sexual parts in your description. What goes on therc?"

Madera smiled coldly. "Yeah, sex is a normal part of S & M and, of course, goes together with pain and domination."

"And does that include rape?"

"Utterly ridiculous! The answer is no. As I said before, I go by the code. No harm to others. Period."

"Yet one said you raped her."

"Whoever it is you're talking about, it's well known in the S & M scene that some people, particularly the inexperienced, may not be totally accepting of their S & M tendencies. After allowing themselves to be dominated sexually, they can have a major guilt trip. They may try to blame the whole thing on their playmate, perhaps even accusing him of rape."

Tony piped up. "We understand that your wife is a partner in the Museum of Torture and the Morbid."

"Yeah, so what?"

"Do you have any direct connection yourself to the museum?"

"Nothing on my own. I do help her set up some of the exhibits, that's all. Is there something illegal about that?"

Tony left the question unanswered. "So, do you have any personal interest in the topic of torture?"

"No. What are you getting at? That I use torture with my playmates?"

"Well, do you?"

"That's absurd. It's one thing to help out at the museum, but it's another to actually torture people. I can tell you I wouldn't last long in the S & M scene if I did that."

"Unless you use threats to get your playmates to cover up your assaults," Tony countered. "Does that happen?"

"No. That in itself would be coercive, wouldn't it?"

Tony ignored the challenge. "One of the female complainants said that you threatened her when she refused to cooperate."

"Again, I don't know who you are talking about. But some playmates new to the scene can misinterpret domination or boss talk as threatening. They get the wrong idea."

"You seem to be a pretty misunderstood guy, all right," Jeremy said sarcastically. "By the way, you've mentioned inexperienced playmates twice now. Do you somehow prefer this group?"

"Not particularly, but I can find their innocence appealing, at times."

"Meaning?"

"Meaning I like to introduce them to new experiences."

"Does that imply leading naïve people into risky situations?"

"That sounds pretty diabolical. I can assure you I'm not the dark villain of the S & M scene. And not knowing the identities of these two makes it impossible for me to get specific."

Tony jumped into the dialogue. "Well, if your memory comes back to you, I'd advise you to stay away from them."

"Is that a threat, Detective?"

"No, it's a health tip," Tony fired back.

"What do you think I am? Some mobster who gets rid of the prosecution's witnesses before trial?"

Tony shrugged, saying nothing. It was clear that they would get little more from the Black Marquis today.

***

"What did you make of Madera?" Tony asked as they drove away from the Madera residence.

Jeremy shook his head slowly. "He certainly tried hard to discredit the women with all that psychobabble. Although it was creative, I must admit."

"Maybe he's missed his calling as a psychologist," Monica quipped.

"It may not be too late," Tony said. "I hear a lot of prisons have good college outreach programs."

Jeremy laughed. "There's only the small matter of convicting him of something first, Tony."

"I think he's convicting himself," Monica observed. "There were all sorts of signs that he wasn't on the level with us. He was far too cool and straight-faced, for instance."

"Yeah," Tony said, "and like you noticed, he conveniently left out the sexual parts of his S & M affairs and probably downplayed what he did report."

"I'll wager, too," Jeremy said, "that he's into the museum much more than he alluded to. If our informer was right, he's at least a shady buyer for the place. We still have to look into that…. And I don't believe his denial that he has no personal interest in torture, either. What about his former antique store, which specialized in old medical and torture instruments? He owned this well before he met his wife. I think he's been attracted to torture for a long time and using it with his playmates."

"And I wonder with his wife, too," Monica commented. "Is she another playmate?"

"If not, Madera must be catching hell from her right now," Jeremy commented.

"I wonder how much she knows about his night life?" Tony asked.

"I think it's likely she's aware of his affairs," Monica replied. "But does she know about the extent of his violence? She seemed pretty shocked to see us at the door today."

"Unless it was an act," Jeremy said. "We have to consider the possibility that she may somehow be complicit in all of this, perhaps an enabler who lives vicariously through his behaviors."

Tony maneuvered the van into a narrow parking spot in front of his colleagues' office. "Well, he seems to fit the profile of the serial murderer, all right. But has he actually crossed the red line and murdered? It'll be interesting to see what the techs find. If we're lucky, there may be some videos or photos in his electronics, or maybe some trophies that tie him to the victims."

CHAPTER TWENTY-FIVE

The day after the warrants had been served to their suspect, Tony called Jeremy with some news. "Ava Madera called me this morning. She wants to see us about something but wouldn't say what. She says it's important. I said I would arrange an appointment with the three of us at headquarters."

"We can come in this afternoon. I'm curious about this."

"So am I. We have to keep in mind she may have been sent by her husband to fish for information."

"Got it. Mrs. Madera does all the talking, right?"

"Right."

***

Jeremy and Monica sat at the cold metal table bolted to the floor in the cramped interview room at NOPD headquarters. The harsh, flickering, neon lights reflected off the stainless-steel tabletop and the whitewashed concrete walls.

Jeremy shifted uncomfortably on his hard, straight-backed chair. "I can see someone confessing just to get out of here."

Monica laughed and turned back to her phone, trying to distract herself from the surroundings.

Tony escorted Ava Madera into the room. "Have a seat, Mrs. Madera. Can I get you some coffee?"

"No, I'm fine—about the coffee, anyway."

Monica and Jeremy stood up and introduced themselves. It was Monica's first opportunity to take a close look at their suspect's wife. She was slightly built, appearing to be in her early forties. Her features were quite refined, needing only light makeup for enhancement. Only her bloodshot eyes and flushed cheeks detracted from her good looks.

Monica noticed that she wore a stylish black business suit, likely purchased from a high-end clothing shop. A black pearl necklace hung around her neck, contrasting with her white blouse. She stared down at her hands clasped together on the table.

"What can we do for you, Mrs. Madera?" Tony asked.

Her eyes rose to meet his. "I'm not here to spy for my husband, if that's what you think," she began. "I want you to know I've been aware of his affairs for many years. It wasn't always this way. Early in our marriage, he tried to draw me into S & M sex at home, which I tolerated to keep the marriage together. But he grew ever more sadistic, and I refused him. It was at that point, about five or six years ago, he started going to the clubs." She paused as if to gauge the reactions of the investigators.

She went on. "I knew he'd started to practice edge play out there, but I hadn't known until yesterday—or perhaps didn't want to know—that he'd gone beyond that. He told me about the assault accusations, saying they were gross exaggerations by insecure women, but I knew he was lying about how violent he had become." Her eyes teared up. "I know that's practically incriminating him, but yesterday was the final straw. I can't turn a blind eye toward him any longer—not when he's harming people. I'd be enabling him, and that's probably what I've done all along.… I mean, I work for the state, the Department of Health, for god's sake, and I'm living with a husband who runs around assaulting people? Jesus!" She paused to blow her nose.

"Where are you going with all of this, Mrs. Madera?" Tony asked.

"Where I'm going is divorce court," she said. "I'm leaving him. I make a good salary as a department head, and I can afford a decent place for me and the children."

"How does that involve us?"

"I know him. He's not going to react well to my leaving, especially taking the children with me. He's got a terrible temper, and I know he's going to come after me. He's got a hatred toward women to begin with. His mother, Karen, was neglectful and abusive. He's never resolved his anger and feelings of abandonment toward her. He's going to view me as another abandoning female. It's not that males escaped his anger, either. I heard from his brother that he used to be the neighborhood bully and beat up on kids, male and female, that he thought didn't like him."

"What do you think he's capable of doing now?"

"I think he's capable of killing me."

"And what about the children?"

"He loves them too much to harm them physically. He could kidnap them, though. He lost his love for me a long time ago—if he had any to begin with.... How does this involve you? I'm asking you to give me and the children protection when I leave. Have my apartment watched, at least for the time being. I want a restraining order, too, though I doubt it's enough to keep him away from us."

Tony nodded. "We'll give serious thought to your protection request and let you know very soon. As for a restraining order, that's up to a judge to decide, not us. You can pick up an application form from the court clerk's office or online. It has to be submitted back to the court clerk. I know it sounds bureaucratic, but I'm afraid that's the way it is."

Monica jumped in. "You mentioned he'd lost his love for you. Will you tell us what the relationship was like?"

"He could be violent toward me early in the marriage, but that stopped when the children came along. He was mostly cold and detached and verbally abusive to me after that, but he made sure the children wouldn't hear him. The only thing that would connect us was the children. We were parents only, not partners. I had my life, for what it was, and he had his."

"So what kept you in such a loveless relationship?" Monica asked.

"It's simple, really. The children. As I said, he loves them, and they love him. I couldn't bear to deprive them of their father. My own father died when I was seven years old, and I grew up in a single-parent home. I know what it's like to be without a father." She dabbed her eyes with a tissue. "But how can I allow him to be around the children now? What kind of role model is he? He's no more than a criminal. I have to draw the line."

Jeremy leaned toward her. "I'd like to ask you about the museum, if you don't mind?"

"That's fine."

"Will you tell us how exactly you're involved there?"

"Yes. I'm invested as a secret partner."

"Do you have any personal interest in the subject matter?"

She produced a wry smile. "None. It was strictly James's idea that I get involved. He has an obsession about sadism and torture, and he relishes buying and displaying these exhibits; he even hangs around the exhibits as he takes pleasure in people's shocked or horrified reactions to them, particularly the women. He fantasizes about his displays, too, and tried to bring his fantasies into our sexual relations. I said no.... So, you see I'm just a paper front for him at the museum. He makes the decisions and handles the money—all in the background."

"If it's entirely his idea, why are you even involved? Isn't it a little risky for you, given your government job? Secret partner or not, you're still registered in the public corporate records."

"I know. I'm involved because I wanted to keep my marriage together, such as it is," she said with a sheepish look. "I've sacrificed too much for it, haven't I? As soon as I leave him, I'm getting out of the museum."

"You mentioned he's a buyer. How does he get his pieces?" Jeremy continued.

"He's never revealed that part, and I haven't asked. Another thing I turned a blind eye to, I guess."

"Is there anything else that you would like to say?" Tony asked.

"Yes. Is there some reason you make this room so uncomfortable?"

Tony smiled knowingly. "We'll be in touch with you soon, Mrs. Madera. Thanks for coming in."

Ava Madera stood up, smoothed out her suit, and gave a final dab to her eyes on her way out. As soon as the door closed, the debriefing was on.

"I don't think she was playing us, do you?" Tony asked.

"No," Jeremy said. "She seemed genuinely fed up with the guy and afraid of him, too. Her description of him, in general, adds weight to our profile on Madera as a potentially violent man toward women."

"Also," Monica said, "she's carrying a lot of guilt and embarrassment about overstaying in the marriage and enabling this guy in many ways. She seems to have finally decided to stand up for herself and the children."

"Yes, and how's Madera going to take it?" Jeremy asked.

Monica sighed deeply. "It's a concern. People with his background of abandonment and violence can sometimes snap and go off the deep end with their families."

"Yes," Jeremy responded, "and if he is the murderer, will his wife leaving him set off further killings?"

“Well, we’ve got a tracking device on his car and a tail on him,” Tony said. “It’s going to be tough for him to pull anything off right now.”

“Unless he manages to dodge us,” Jeremy replied. “We know he’s quite intelligent.... So, are you going to ask Jack for protection for Mrs. Madera?”

“Yeah. He won’t like it, but we’ll likely get a patrol car in her neighborhood.”

As the three got up to leave, Jeremy became reflective. It was ironic that in investigating the murders and trying to prevent more, they had potentially set the stage for another murder. Now, they had to tie up resources to prevent that. The whole thing seemed maddeningly never-ending.

CHAPTER TWENTY-SIX

It was Jeremy's monthly get-together with his sister, Kathy, and her family. After a deviled crab dinner on Kathy's patio, Jeremy played with his nephews, Thomas and Sonny, for a while. Their total fascination with games never ceased to amuse him. They were happy kids, he thought. That's the way kids should be—without a care in their world. If only he and his sister had grown up in such a world.

Kathy's husband, John, eventually coaxed the children into the car for a ride to a playground near the river. This was one of the rare times Jeremy and his sister could be alone.

"You'd make a great father," Kathy remarked.

"Maybe," Jeremy said, "but not a great husband."

"You just think you won't," she replied. "You haven't met the right person yet. That's all. When you do, you'll forget all about your hang-ups."

"You're a born optimist. I think I'll need a bit more than that."

Kathy let his statement pass by. "I saw Mom last week. She was asking about you. She always asks about you." She noticed the usual glaze coming over Jeremy's eyes whenever the topic of his mother was raised.

"I know what you're going to tell me. She worries about me."

"Well, she does. All alone out there on the river. No girlfriend. A boozer for a buddy."

"Tony cracks a few, but he's no boozer.... Besides, she should have been doing her worrying about me—and you—thirty years ago."

"You're still carrying around a lot of anger toward her, Jeremy."

"Still? Does that imply that I shouldn't be?"

Kathy avoided the question. "There is such a thing as forgiveness."

"Have you forgiven her, Kathy? She did the same thing to you."

"Yes. I think I have."

"Well, I'm happy for you—really I am—that you were able to find that within yourself. But I can't."

"Can't or won't?"

"How could I feel otherwise? She said she was coming back, and she never did. It's like I ceased to matter to her. How do you deal with it when you suddenly don't matter to a parent? Someone who meant the world to you."

"I know. I felt the same way for a long time, too, until she reached out to me and I had a chance to talk with her, to understand her."

"You mean hear all the rationalizations and excuses she came up with to justify what she did?"

"No, I mean to finally see where she was coming from as a human being when she left and didn't contact us for all that time. I've tried to tell you many times what I learned, but you didn't want to hear it. You wanted to shut me out. Are you going to do that again?"

Jeremy said nothing.

"Not to play the psychotherapist, Jeremy, but I think you want to hold on to your anger. It's easier than facing your sadness; it's easier than facing her sadness."

"Maybe I'm simply not interested in her sadness. Maybe she deserves it."

"The anger speaking again. I sometimes think, too, you use that anger to toughen yourself up. You draw on it as a force to help you deal with life."

"What's wrong with that?"

"Nothing, for a while. But don't you see? As a thirty-eight-year-old man, you can find better ways to be strong and tough in your life. You don't need that anger anymore."

"You sound to me like a psychotherapist."

She laughed. "I went through a lot of therapy about the assault. I still hear my therapist's voice in my head."

"And did you forgive that sexual predator too?"

"No. I came to terms with that. I decided to stop being a victim."

"Surely you don't mean accepting any responsibility for what happened?"

"No, I accepted responsibility for my feelings about what had happened. I refused to be embittered by it any longer and to feel low about myself because of it. I refused to allow what happened to control my life."

"Yes, and that is good, too. Forgiveness has its limits, doesn't it?"

"I knew *that* was coming," she retorted. "I sometimes think you're too clever for your own good!"

Jeremy laughed.

"But there's one thing you seem to have missed."

“What’s that?”

“That you have frozen yourself in time over Mom’s leaving. You have not allowed the abandoned little boy inside to grow up. He’s still there in a man’s mind and body, limiting your life, making you less than you could be.”

Jeremy was taken aback by her blunt characterization of him. There was no more to be said, but deep down, he began to weigh her words.

***

As Jeremy drove home that evening, his thoughts returned to his sister and their childhood together. He remembered fondly how close they had been for many years after his mother left. He was a kind of surrogate parent to her, reading her children’s stories and, later on, helping her with her homework. He was also very protective, taking care of more than one bully who had tried to harass her. Then, there were the many mornings he’d get her off to school while his father slept after his night shifts at the docks.

Jeremy recalled the rough downtown neighborhood where they had grown up. Unemployment was high, single-parent families were the norm, and crime was an ever-present danger. There were two cardinal rules he and his sister were told to observe faithfully: never talk to strangers, and be careful about some of the adults they did know. His father believed that these simple strictures had street-proofed them—right up to that terrible day that proved him wrong.

Kathy, then nine years old, broke the first rule. She stopped on the way home from school to talk to a strange man. She was grabbed and then raped in the back of a van.

After that, the joy of life seemed to drain away from her. She was never again the boisterous kid he had known. Jeremy learned that rape was not only a violation of the body, but also a crime against the soul.

He remembered, sadly, how his sister had drifted away from him after that. He sometimes wondered if she had blamed him for not protecting her that day. He certainly blamed himself for not being there with her.

He recalled his anger when the family could not afford the therapy she needed and how she had languished in depression and withdrawal for so many years. There was not even the satisfaction of justice being brought to the perpetrator, who was never caught. Jeremy had felt his sister was just a case number in the NOPD file and that little real effort had gone into the investigation.

He had made two vows to himself. The first was that he would become an investigator someday and bring justice to the forgotten victims like his sister. The second was that he would find the money to pay for good therapy for his sister. Eventually, he accomplished both—and more. He not only offered services to the well-off, but part of his practice was dedicated to pro bono work for those who could not afford his fees.

Jeremy reflected on his sister's long road to recovery. She had succeeded not by seeking to punish the perpetrator, or forgiving him, for that matter. Her words came to mind: "I accepted responsibility for my feelings about what had happened."

He thought deeply about those words. Kathy had made a choice. She could have gone on being the victim, blaming the perpetrator for ruining her life, but chose instead to free herself from the trauma. Jeremy recalled a famous quote from Jean-Paul Sartre, a thinker he had much admired in his university days: "Freedom is what you do with what others have done to you." The existentialist philosopher's words in *Being and Nothingness* reverberated in his mind as he turned into the Bay Bayou Marina.

He boarded his boat. It was still another hour to sunset, and the river beckoned to him. He went up to the bridge and turned over the engine, which responded with a low growl. After a check of his instruments, he cast off, steering upstream. The powerful diesel pushed the boat easily into the current.

It was a beautiful evening on the river, its waters reflecting the golden-orange and red colors of the lowering sun. Traffic was light tonight. Only the swishing sounds of the bow breaking the current could be heard above the muffled beat of the engine. He soon reached his turning point and swung his craft around in the direction of the current. As he cut the engine, the boat seemed to relax into the water, taken by the currents like a piece of driftwood. Jeremy took a deep breath and let it out slowly as he contemplated the beauty around him. He imagined his thoughts falling into the river and merging with it, sweeping his mind clear of the flotsam and jetsam of his intellect. He no longer thought about the river and the sky. Instead, he experienced them as felt parts of himself as he moved inward toward a deeper self—perhaps to deeper truths.

CHAPTER TWENTY-SEVEN

The serial murder case had been occupying much of Jeremy and Monica's time, and they found themselves working at the office on a sunny Saturday to clear up the backlog of other cases. After a few hours at his desk, Jeremy was gratified to see the stack of papers in his inbox diminishing.

His phone rang. He was glad to see it was Tony, whom he had not heard from in several days. "What's up, buddy?" he asked cheerily.

"You seem in a good mood this morning," Tony remarked. "It must be a beautiful day on the river."

"Actually, I'm toiling in the office today. No rest for the diligent, you know."

"If you're working on the case, I wouldn't get my hopes up for any overtime. Jack's been complaining about money again."

"It's good Monica and I are working on something else, then. We're in no danger of Jack's ire."

"Working on a Saturday," Tony chastised. "You two had better get a life out there."

"I'll be sure to pass on your advice to her, Tony."

Tony paused in advance of some ominous news. "Listen, Jeremy. Something's up with James Madera. The tracker on his car's gone dead, and we lost him. I alerted his wife and bumped up patrols in the vicinity of her apartment."

"Those trackers are pretty reliable. He's likely found and disabled it."

"Yeah, we think so, too. Anyway, he's on the loose right now. I don't have to tell you two to keep your eyes open for him. He may have an axe to grind with us over his wife and kids leaving him."

After hanging up with Tony, Jeremy reached for his coffee mug. Suddenly feeling queasy in his stomach, he changed his mind about the coffee and headed to Monica's office down the hall. He found her at her desk, concentrating on her computer screen. "I have some bad news," he announced.

She looked up from her work.

"Madera's tracker stopped transmitting. We lost him."

Monica tensed. "Great. He's up to something. Likely, he's going to make a move on his wife."

"Yeah, probably. But Tony's warned us to be alert for him, too."

Monica nodded. "It's true some guys like Madera believe that others are responsible for their problems and go after them out of revenge."

"So we need to be especially careful, right?" He noticed her worried look. "This is when the going gets hard," he commented. "But there is a bright side to this. If Madera is stressed out, he'll make mistakes, and then we'll get him."

***

The week went by with no news of Madera. It was a Friday evening, and the two PIs were working late at the office again. Jeremy rubbed his eyes and stood up from his desk to stretch. He walked over to the expansive east-facing window. The downtown was especially beautiful at night. From his third-floor office, he could see the multicolored lights of the city reflecting in the river, blending with the lights of the freighters and barges slowing moving north. He smiled as he recalled himself as a child visiting his father at the docks during his nightshifts as a security guard. He would share his dad's ham and rye sandwiches and walk with him along the docks on his rounds. This was his introduction to the beauty and peacefulness of the river.

Jeremy returned to his paperwork, which had overflowed from the in-box to his desk. This was the part of the job he hated most, and he took every opportunity to procrastinate about it. He thought he heard a noise in the hallway. It's probably the janitor, he thought, but he noticed the main door was unlocked. Looking for another reason to put off the paperwork, he stood up to go to the door. As he made his way, the doorknob turned, and the door swung open.

The stocky figure of James Madera stood in the doorway. Jeremy's heart raced as he flashed back to Tony's warning about their suspect. He backed away toward his gun in his desk drawer and tried to put on a brave face. "What brings you here, Mr. Madera?" he asked, struggling to keep his voice even.

The visitor stood in ominous silence, with his typical poker face, staring at Jeremy. After what seemed to Jeremy an eon, he finally spoke in a low, gravelly voice, which sounded more like an animal's growl than human speech. "Do you have a wife and children, Hale?"

"No."

“Neither do I now. At least they no longer live with me.”

“Yes, I know.”

“But you don’t know what it feels like to have your family ripped away like that. To have your heart ripped out.”

Jeremy did know but said nothing. He kept on slowly backing away. Maybe, he thought, he could use the desk for cover, if he needed to. He felt a rush of adrenalin when he noticed Madera had one hand behind his back.

“Everything was all right until you three delivered that warrant. The next day, she left me and took the kids. I’m sure you offered her protection from me, too.” Madera lost his poker face as his lips curled into a kind of snarl and his bloodshot eyes bulged.

He stepped forward. “It’s your fault, you bastards!” he shouted. “I’ll show you what it’s like to have your heart ripped out.” The hidden hand emerged with a six-inch knife in it. He rushed at Jeremy, holding the knife high. Jeremy grabbed his wrist, desperately trying to keep the knife from slashing down at him. But he felt the hot, sharp slice of the blade several times on his upper arm. The two tumbled over onto the floor, locked in combat, knocking over the desk and sending the papers flying.

Jeremy heard a shout on his right. “Drop the weapon! Now!” Monica stood just outside her office doorway, aiming her handgun with both hands at Jeremy’s assailant.

Madera rolled off Jeremy and dropped his knife, reaching into his pocket. He pulled out a gun and fired twice at Monica but was wide. Monica returned fire. One shot missed, but the other hit him in the shoulder.

Madera was back on his feet and ran for the door. He covered himself with two more wild shots in Monica's direction.

Jeremy, on his hands and knees, finally retrieved his handgun and ran after Monica, who had pursued Madera out the door. He heard two more shots in the hallway. He reached the door, fearing the shots had not been from Monica. Expecting the worst, he was relieved to find her still standing, her smoking gun raised. Two bullet holes punctured the fire exit door, through which Madera had escaped. Spots of blood led to the exit.

Monica lowered her gun and felt Jeremy's hand on her arm. "Are you all right?" he asked frantically.

Monica found herself hugging him, and he hugged her back with his good arm. The intensity of their embrace surprised both of them.

"I'm okay, but you aren't," she said.

Jeremy looked over at his bloodied arm. "I think it looks worse than it is," he reassured her, and perhaps himself too. "The cuts don't seem too deep."

"Let's get you into the office and stop the bleeding." She led him back to his office chair and helped him get his shirt off. "You've got several gashes on the upper arm. They're still bleeding." She took a pair of scissors to his shirt to make a tourniquet, which she tightened on his arm. "That should help," she announced.

She phoned 911. He objected, but she completed the call anyway. She then called Tony, putting on the speaker as he answered. “Tony, you better get down to Jeremy’s office right away.”

“Why, what’s happening?”

“Jeremy’s been stabbed.”

“What?”

“Don’t worry. I think he’s all right. Some stab wounds to the upper arm. The bleeding’s controlled, and the paramedics are on their way.”

“It’s Madera, right?”

“Yeah.”

“I knew it. Are you okay?”

“I’m okay, but Madera isn’t. I winged him in the shoulder, but he got away after a firefight.”

“My god! I’ll be right down. I’ll warn the patrolling officers in his wife’s neighborhood and have the dispatcher send out an all-points bulletin on Madera.” Tony clicked off.

Jeremy and Monica hugged one another again in silence. They heard the wails of approaching sirens.

CHAPTER TWENTY-EIGHT

Monica walked briskly down the hallway in the recovery area of St. John's Hospital. She encountered a burly, uniformed police officer outside Jeremy's door, who promptly relieved her of her handgun. She wouldn't at all mind the reassuring presence of a police guard for herself, but she knew that was pure wishful thinking.

She knocked gently on Jeremy's door and was rewarded by the sound of his voice. "Come in," he said, "unless you're an assassin."

She smiled as she opened the door. If his sense of humor was intact, she thought, he was okay. He was bundled up in the bed, his bandaged arm in a sling. She went over to give him a hug, mindful of the injured arm. "So, how's the arm?"

"It's in one piece again," he said. "They had to do quite a bit of stitching, but it should be okay in about a week. The wound's close to a major blood vessel, though, and they decided to keep me in overnight for observation. It could have been a lot worse."

"Yeah," Monica agreed. The bizarre scene of Madera on top of Jeremy trying to knife him flashed in her mind. She could have lost him right then and there. "Are you in one piece emotionally, too?"

"I think so," he said.

"You're sure? You're not giving me some macho denial crap, are you? You came pretty close to meeting your maker last night, Jeremy."

He smiled. "But I didn't," he said. "The key thing is that I was fighting to make sure I didn't, and it worked long enough for you to get there."

"You know, Jeremy, you're no less of a man if you acknowledge your fear."

"Yeah, I can acknowledge I had it," he said. "It helped me deal with the situation, and that's that. Why dwell on it further?"

Monica thought about what the psychopathology course she took in college had to say about the causes of trauma. She remembered one theory that trauma comes from the feeling of helplessness to deal with a life-threatening situation. Helplessness becomes "frozen" in the person. What Jeremy was saying made sense in a way. He was never totally helpless with Madera. But she would keep an eye on him, nevertheless.

"And what about you?" he asked. "How are you doing?"

She paused for a moment and then said, "I've been on edge since it happened. I was down here with Tony waiting until 3:00 a.m., when the doctors told us you were stable. I went home, but it did no good. What little sleep I had was riddled with nightmares. I thought it was worry about how you were doing, but it was more than that. I was thinking we both could have been killed last night, and what if Madera is crazy enough to come after us again?"

"Yeah, I understand that," Jeremy said. "It's perfectly normal to feel that way. I don't think it's trauma, from what I know about it. But you got a good scare put into you. The important thing is to learn from this experience. We were careless and let ourselves be vulnerable in the office last night. We have to be more security-conscious and alert from now on."

"I already notice that I'm more vigilant about what's going on around me."

"Well, that's good."

"Yes, within limits. I can't be going around feeling paranoid, either."

"There's a difference between vigilance and paranoia," Jeremy reassured her. "You'll find your balance. Your mind is in protective mode right now. Just go with it."

She nodded, reflecting on his words.

Jeremy was silent for a few moments and then said, "You know, I've been shot at before but never had a madman attack me with a knife. Believe me, it's a strange experience. The will to survive kicks in. It's like my mind stepped out of the way, and my body did the fighting for me, and I was watching it… But I wonder if it was losing." He gave her a grateful look. "I think you saved my butt last night."

"I was lucky," she said. "He was a worse shot than I was."

"But you stood your ground," Jeremy protested. "You shot it out with him."

Monica frowned. "It's as if you didn't expect I'd have your back in a showdown. Is it because I'm a woman? What is it with you guys and the myth that only a man can face up to danger?"

Jeremy felt his face flush. "I admit the thought has crossed my mind, but after the standoff at the Vallencourt place, I knew I was ninety-nine percent wrong."

"What about the other one percent?"

"I found that last night. You were absolutely courageous and not such a bad shot, either. You winged him and scared him off. That's what counted. Then you practically scorched his tail end going out the exit door."

"Okay. Stop before you make me into some kind of storybook heroine."

The two looked at one another silently for a few moments, declaring an unspoken truce. They had almost lost their lives last night. Both realized that life (and perhaps love?) were far too precious to waste in conflict with one another.

CHAPTER TWENTY-NINE

A week after the shoot-out with Madera, Jeremy, Tony, and Monica received an urgent early-morning call from Jack to meet him at headquarters. The sun had not yet risen as the four gathered in Jack's office. Jeremy arrived with his right arm in a sling.

"How's the arm?" Jack asked.

"Sore. The doctor advised I keep it immobilized for a few weeks."

"So the wounds were deeper than first thought?"

"Yeah, but nothing critical. Just as long as I don't have to arm wrestle with anyone."

Jack missed Jeremy's humorous note, as usual. "About why I called you here at this ungodly hour," he said. "The killer has been at work again. A security guard found the body of a young woman in a downtown alley behind a commercial building. She's been identified as a nineteen-year-old college student, Elena Martinez. She was likely walking home from a late-evening class and dragged into the alley. The crime has all the earmarks of the serial killer we're looking for: apparent sexual assault, mutilation, and torture, followed by murder, likely through choking. Samples from the scene have not yet been analyzed, but the techs tell me they'd be surprised if any DNA material from the murderer was recovered. We've got indigo fibers on the body again." Jack sighed. "There were no witnesses or camera recordings. It's the same deal."

"Damn," Jeremy said. "This happens despite all the newsflashes about the murders and warnings to young women not to go out alone in secluded areas at night."

Monica shook her head. "Young people rarely think about their mortality. Nothing can touch them."

"Any leads on Madera, Jack?" Tony asked.

"Nothing. He's sunk into the slime somewhere. Not even any reports from the hospitals or clinics concerning a gunshot wound. The FBI just emailed to inform us that he's been put on their most wanted list. They'll be out looking for him in force—a big boost to our search efforts."

"I'm a little surprised he made the list," Jeremy said. "What's that about?"

"Well, they've been concerned about all his red flags for some time. His attempting to murder you and Monica really raised his profile with the Feds. That this serial murder happened only a week later, while he's been on the run, put him over the line as a suspect."

"But what about his shoulder? How could he have managed another murder so soon after getting shot?" Jeremy asked.

"Monica may have just grazed him. There wasn't a lot of his blood at the scene in your office. Most of the blood was yours. As I say, no reports from the hospitals or clinics regarding gunshot wounds have been received. He may have been fit to carry on."

"I would have thought he'd go for his wife first," Tony commented.

"Normally, that'd be my first guess, too," Jack replied. "But recently her security has been ramped up, and I'm sure he was aware of that. Maybe he went for an easier target. By the way, results from the searches of Madera's home, business, and vehicles have come in."

The others looked at him expectantly.

"On the negative side, we've found nothing, so far, linking him directly with any of the murders. No images of his victims on his electronics. No trophies or DNA material from the victims or fibers from their clothing. No dissection tools or instruction materials on dissection. The techs took a look, too, at his wife's jewelry, just in case he may have given her jewelry taken from a victim, as serial murderers will sometimes do. Unfortunately, nothing was found."

"In a way, I'm not surprised," Monica remarked. "He's probably intelligent enough to sanitize his usual surroundings of any evidence. Just like his crime scenes."

"Sometimes criminals are not so smart about their computers," Jeremy said. "Has he been on any sites featuring sadistic sex and violence?"

"Yes. They had been deleted, but our techs recovered them. He's downloaded from sites showing young female victims being tortured, raped, and murdered. We don't know if it's real or simply being acted. But it's awfully sick stuff."

"He was probably using it as material for sexual fantasies," Jeremy said. "It fits in well with what his wife said about his becoming increasingly sadistic in their sexual relationship. He probably tried to get her role-playing the victim."

"I recently read a criminology journal article on the role of fantasy in serial murders," Monica added. "The connection between violence and sexuality is often formed early in adolescence, from exposure to sadistic reading or video materials or other experiences about which the individual fantasizes during masturbation. The connection between aggressive/sadistic fantasies and sex becomes reinforced with repetition. Each murder is an attempt to express the fantasy in ever more sadistic and realistic ways. After a while, murdering becomes practically compulsive."

"So they go on until they die or get caught," Tony said.

"That was the conclusion of the article," Monica replied.

Jack's face darkened. "Well, we can't afford to wait till the killer croaks," he said acidly. "So let's get on with finding him, before his 'compulsion' kicks in again. I would normally call a full case conference today, but our FBI consultants, Professor Greenwood and Lara Trahan, have been at FBI headquarters in Washington for the past few days, presenting a workshop. They're back tomorrow, so I've scheduled a conference then at 1:00 p.m. sharp."

***

That evening, Monica began another meditation; it would be a welcome relief from the frustration of the investigation. She turned to the next meditation in her spiritual manual. The topic was the gathering of information beyond the five senses. She imagined this was the equivalent of the modern term "extrasensory perception."

She began her meditation in the usual way. She visualized her thoughts flowing through her mind and disappearing. Her consciousness focused gradually to a point deeply inside of her mind, like a pinpoint of light in a dark room. She stayed with the experience, fully accepting it. She was simply being in the moment. It was a state of non-thought, no expectations, and little sense of the passage of time.

She began to follow the extrasensory prescriptions. She imagined herself reaching out to the world outside of the dark room, receptive to it, accepting anything that would come. The book had evoked the image of a flower orienting itself to the sun, absorbing the sun's light fully. She focused on this image for a while, not thinking about it but simply experiencing it.

She felt a slight shift within herself. Something was forming in the dark room of her mind. A group of wavy lines emerged, which she perceived rather than visualized. It formed into a pattern of interconnected rectangles, with a gap between two of them that had some depth. There was a bright flash of light from the gap. The pattern also had an orange tint to it, with white-gray lines between the rectangles. She paid attention to the image until it dissipated spontaneously.

Monica brought herself back to normal awareness and opened her eyes. She was puzzled. What had she just perceived? It seemed vaguely familiar, but yet she could not place it. She felt that somehow the image was very important, especially the gap.

Unable to decipher her experience, she let the matter be. She determined to leave the decoding to her subconscious. It was like trying to remember a name: focusing on it did no good, but if she did something else for a while, the name would simply pop into her mind.

As she had hoped, the meaning of the pattern began to come to her an hour later. It represented something she had seen recently, something important to the investigation—but what and where? The answers eluded her again, and she went to bed, still puzzled. She fell into a restless sleep, dreaming heavily. However, she awoke the next morning with the insights she was looking for, and they were startling. She knew she needed to talk to Jeremy and that he and Tony must travel to Clairmont with her—urgently.

But she hesitated. There was still an important part of the puzzle missing, and at any rate, how could she expect her colleagues to take her intuitive suspicions seriously? She had some doubts herself.

She arrived at the office that morning still undecided about what to do. She started to read some of her files on the serial murder cases but couldn't concentrate. She sighed and got up from her desk to get some coffee. She knew she couldn't sit on the matter any longer. She had to risk opening up to Jeremy. She walked into his office and sat down without a word.

Jeremy looked at her curiously.

"Jeremy, remember I was telling you about the old book on spiritual development I had inherited?"

"With the red eagle on it, right?"

"Yes, I've begun following the meditations in it almost every night."

Jeremy gave her a curious glance. "How's it been going?"

"It isn't what I expected. I've had some interesting and … strange experiences."

Jeremy nodded. He'd had more than a few unusual meditative experiences himself. But he wasn't ready to acknowledge that quite yet. "So, tell me about them."

She inhaled and let out her breath slowly. She was uncertain how this was going to be received. "Well… I saw an image during mediation. It began as wavy lines and eventually formed into a geometric pattern of interlocking rectangles. There was a gap in a part of it. A brilliant light flashed from it. Then the image disappeared."

Jeremy looked perplexed. "That's it?"

"No, the rectangles had an orangish tint, and their borders were grayish white. I was baffled about what the pattern was, though it seemed familiar. But later the answer came to me. It has to do with the Chartrand case."

Jeremy's eyes visibly widened.

"I realized the pattern I saw was the brick driveway behind the Clairmont museum, where she was abducted. There was a gap or a crack between two bricks near where her car had been parked…. I'm left with the strongest feeling that there is something important to the investigation lodged in that crack."

"What?"

"I don't know," she said sheepishly. "But I feel we should get out there and see if it's true."

Jeremy was silent for a time. He flashed back to a few of his more notable meditations on the river.

He'd had insights into some of his cases, which had panned out, but nothing this dramatic. What she's saying could make sense, he thought. He knew meditation tapped the memories of the subconscious mind, which might figure into all of this. After all, she had been at the abduction site.

She took his silence as skepticism. "At worst, we'd only waste some travel time, but we'd know."

"Yeah, that's true. What have we got to lose? This case has been going nowhere." He smiled to himself, despite his grim observation. Tony was going to take a lot more convincing, he mused.

"What are you going to say to the sheriff?"

"I'll say we've got some potential information on Marlene's abduction that we need to check out at the scene. If anything turns up, we'll let him know. Simple as that."

Monica smiled, relieved Jeremy seemed to have remarkably little resistance to what some would dismiss as paranormal nonsense. "Sounds diplomatic enough to me."

"I think it will pass muster."

CHAPTER THIRTY

Jeremy, Monica, and Tony arrived at the Clairmont museum's driveway at the rear of the building. It was a sunny morning at about the same hour as they had first inspected the area the day after Marlene's murder. Tony lagged sullenly behind the other two. He had been reluctant to do the trip, complaining that the whole thing would come to nothing.

Monica approached the crack in the bricks near where Marlene's car had been parked the evening of her abduction. She stopped several feet from the crack, orienting her head at different angles. "Look at that crack from different angles," she said to Jeremy, a few feet behind her.

He followed her instructions, suddenly looking surprised. "There's a glint of sunlight coming from it," he said.

"That's what I see," she said in an exultant tone.

Jeremy put on some latex gloves and took out a small kit from his pocket, from which he drew out a pair of tweezers. He peered into the crack and withdrew a small metal object. "It's a gold-covered metal plate," he announced. He turned it over. "There appears to be a speck of blood on it."

Tony looked at Monica in amazement and took several photos of the retrieved object and of where it had been lodged.

"If that's the murderer's blood, we've got our DNA evidence," Jeremy said.

"Hurray! Let's get it right to the lab," Tony blurted out, now completely on side with the proceedings. He thrust out a hand for a high five, and Monica reciprocated.

Jeremy bagged the find and grinned as they headed for the van. "It'll be interesting explaining to Jack how we found this."

As they drove away, Tony's expression transformed from elation to bafflement. "What *are* we supposed to make of all this?" he asked. "How did you know it would be there, Monica?"

"I didn't know for certain," she said. "An image came to me in a meditation, something I later figured out was the crack in the museum's driveway. I somehow knew there was something important there that we had missed. It was a kind of intuition."

Tony looked even more baffled.

Jeremy spoke up. "I think there's a scientific explanation for all of this. We had to be at just the right angle of observation to spot the flash from the crack at this time of day." He looked at Monica. "When you were walking through the scene the day after the Chartrand abduction, the flash might have been very brief due to your motion and changing angle on the crack. It could have been so momentary that your conscious mind may not have registered it…."

"What are you saying, Jeremy?"

"My point is that your subconscious may have picked up the flash that day and remembered it. Subliminal perception, right?"

"So you're saying it was this subconscious memory that emerged as the image during my meditation?"

"Basically, yes. It's a well-known psychological process."

Monica smiled. She decided to let Jeremy have his "psychological" explanation. "It's plausible," she said, "as far as it goes." But she had some questions. Why would she have had such a powerful feeling that something important to the investigation was in that crack—so important that she felt compelled to go to Clairmont to try to find it and risk involving her colleagues? And why did all of this emerge after that particular meditative exercise? Furthermore, what about her feeling that Marlene Chartrand had attended her own funeral or the dream she had about her? Was all of this due to the subconscious too? There had to be something else going on that she did not yet fully understand.

Tony was more pragmatic. "Whatever happened, you found evidence that everyone missed, against all the odds. If it's not Marlene's DNA on that metal piece, the case could be blown wide open." He put on an upbeat rock and roll song on the sound system as the van reached Highway 3.

***

Two days later, the three met with Jack for a much-anticipated briefing. The lab results for the mysterious object found at Marlene's abduction site had just arrived.

"The lab findings are very interesting," Jack said. "The bloodstain on the object is Marlene's." He felt the mood index in the room plummet. "I know it's not the murderer's DNA that we were all hoping for, but at least it ties the object to Marlene. The other consolation prize is that we now know what this object is and likely how it got there. It turns out to be a small, gold link in a wristwatch band for a high-end Swiss watch. Whoever owns it is likely well off. It's a man's watch, and given that people who grew up after cell phones became popular don't wear watches much, we assume that the watch belongs to someone about thirty-five years old or older."

"Finally, we're getting some demographics on this guy," Jeremy said. "And they fit either of our suspects, Madera or Vallencourt. I'm guessing, Jack, you've looked at the techs' photos of their jewelry collections?"

"I did," Jack replied. "Unfortunately, that brand of watch does not show up in either collection."

"Of course, either may have gotten rid of the watch or stashed it somewhere once they realized the link was missing," Jeremy said.

"It would have been too risky to go back to the crime scene to try to retrieve the link," Tony added. "So, yeah, the watch could have been dumped or hidden."

"We could also verify with Mrs. Madera if he had this brand of watch," Jeremy suggested. "She might be able to verify if it had been damaged."

"There are a lot of angles to tracking down this watch," Jack said. "We'll get the team working on it."

"By the way, I think I can see how the watch link got there," Monica said. "There was evidence of a struggle outside of Marlene's car that evening. She may have torn off the murderer's watch defending herself, leaving her blood on the link. The watch and link likely fell off. The murderer picked up the watch but didn't see the missing link, which fell into the crack."

"That's the way I see it, too," Jack said. "By the way, that was some sleuthing, Monica. I don't know how you did it, but it was brilliant. Keep up whatever you're doing."

Monica beamed as she absorbed the rare compliment from Jack.

CHAPTER THIRTY-ONE

Less than a week after the savage murder of the student, there was more bad news. The three found themselves attending another case conference with Jack. The team lead's face was grim. "There's been a disturbing development," he began. "Last evening, a young female cadet at the state military academy did not return to residence after her early-evening jog. Apparently, she was in the habit of jogging alone at that time, along trails in the heavily forested areas around the academy. A security camera on the trail picked her up at about 8:00 p.m., but another camera farther down the trail failed to register her. A search is ongoing in the area, led by Detective D'Angelo. Of course, we don't yet know if there is a link with the serial murders."

Jack felt the tension level in the room rising. He already knew what the others were suspecting. "We also received a report from our tail on Vallencourt late yesterday afternoon. Vallencourt made the unusual move of going to work in his Jeep. The vehicle departed from his estate at his usual time in the morning and was followed to the parkade at his office. The Jeep left the office at about 4:30 p.m. It proceeded downtown at rush hour. The Jeep cut in and out of traffic lanes abruptly, and a bus got in between the Vallencourt vehicle and the tail. He lost the Jeep at a set of traffic lights. The tail didn't know if this simply reflected impatience on the part of the Jeep's driver or if it was a deliberate effort to lose him. The Jeep returned to the estate about

11:00 p.m. Thus, it was missing at the time of the cadet's disappearance. Whether this is simply a coincidence or not remains to be seen. We'll see first how D'Angelo's investigation unfolds. I'll keep you posted on the situation."

He had more dismal news. "The lab results from the student's murder are in, and they're unrevealing. As the techs predicted, no DNA from the murderer was identified. The indigo fibers matched the structural and dye characteristics of those on the other victims. Once again, the victim was attacked in an area where security cameras are sparse, and there were no witnesses either. The same MO was used to brutalize the victim. The signature removal of the ovaries was performed. She is definitely another victim of the serial killer."

"Who's demonstrating the same careful attention to planning as in the other murders," Jeremy commented. "We're still getting practically nothing to go on."

"We'd better get creative about it," Jack countered. "People are panicking. Businesses open in the evenings are escorting their female employees to their vehicles or transit stops. The crowds in the Quarter are thinning at night, except for a protest on Bourbon Street last night about the city and police not doing enough to stop the murders. That caught the mayor's attention, and the chief got a dressing-down."

"Have we got the results yet from the search of Vallencourt's property, Jack?" Tony asked.

"Yes, I was about to mention it. We found indigo fibers matching those of the victims in Vallencourt's mansion, more densely in older parts of the place. This is not unexpected, since the Vallencourts were manufacturing these fibers way back into the 1800s. But indigo dye and textile making was common in the area at that time, and we'd likely find fibers like this all over the Clairmont region."

"Wouldn't there be variation?" Jeremy asked.

"Yes, but probably not enough to differentiate fibers from various producers, since similar manufacturing techniques were used. So we can't yet pin Vallencourt on that one."

"Anything else found, Jack?" Tony asked.

"Nothing directly related to the murders. There was no DNA material from the victims. All the wooden crates that could have held victims' bodies at one point were destroyed. No trophies, such as the victims' clothing or jewelry were found. No recordings of victims or any sadosexual materials whatsoever. But we did find that Vallencourt has been closely tracking our investigation on media sites."

"Which could indicate a murderer wondering how close we are getting to him," Jeremy said.

"Or an innocent man worried about the police launching mistaken or trumped-up charges against him," Monica replied.

"Another thing is that we found he likes movies and books with violent themes of murder and horror," Jack said.

"So, is he one of the millions of fans of this genre, or is this all entertainment or fantasy for a real murderer?" Monica asked.

"What did the surveillance cameras around Vallencourt's property show the night of the student's murder?" Tony asked.

"There were no indications that he left the property that night."

"But?"

"We can't have surveillance everywhere," Jack said. "The property is a huge acreage, and much of it's forest. He could have left by a side road without being detected."

Tony shook his head in frustration. "There are always question marks about this guy."

"Talking about question marks," added Monica, "have we heard anything yet about Jenny Thibeault?"

Jack's downcast look answered her question before he found the words. "No, nothing," he replied. "Since she's disappeared, there's been no activity on her electronics or on those of her friends regarding her. Nor has there been direct contact with her school friends in New Orleans, according to our tails. No contacts with boyfriend Billy, electronic or otherwise, have been noted, either. She's made no credit or bank card transactions. We've monitored Billy's bank account, and there have been no major withdrawals—not that he had a lot in there to begin with.... It's not looking good for her. It's doubtful a young girl like that could run away and pull it off that well for all this time."

Jeremy sighed. "An abduction appears more likely," he said gloomily as the meeting broke up. "The question is by whom and for what reason?"

CHAPTER THIRTY-TWO

The trio did not have to wait long for Jack to update them on the cadet's disappearance. A few hours after their morning conference, Jack and Tony made a call to Jeremy's office. "She hasn't been located yet," Jack announced, "but a trail of blood was found in the woods near the site of her disappearance. We don't know if it's her blood, and samples have been sent to the lab. Also, the academy's security service reports that last night they had trouble with cameras on the public road on the perimeter of the property near the search area. Two cameras went dead around the time she disappeared, and a third produced a distorted video. The blurry outline of a vehicle passing on the road shortly before the disappearance was picked up. It was either a dark SUV or a Jeep, but no other details were identifiable. The security people say they do have periodic glitches with some external cameras in highly humid weather, such as we've been having lately."

"There was a camera issue the night of the Kazinski murder, too," Monica pointed out.

"We put it down to poor viewing conditions," Tony reminded her. "And washed out tapes."

"But tampering can't be ruled out," Jeremy said. "It's interesting how no camera has ever picked up the murderer."

"There are enough loose ends for us to have an initial look at the disappearance," Jack said. "I understand Detective D'Angelo and his team are still searching the woods and have not yet interviewed anyone."

***

In another hour, the three pulled up in the police van at the gate of the Andrew Jackson Military Academy. They checked in with the security officer who opened the gate of the high wrought-iron fence surrounding the extensive grounds of the academy. Cameras were placed on either side of the gate, and an ATV was parked nearby.

"How could they have a security problem in a place like this?" Tony asked as they drove in.

They approached a cluster of buildings about a quarter mile up the main drive. One was the administration and classroom building, an old, three-story brick structure with lofty stone pillars marking the entrance.

Tony parked near the main parade square. As they walked through the square to the entrance, they noticed the statue of General Andrew Jackson, the victor of the 1814 battle of New Orleans against the British. Small groups of cadets in their tightly pressed class uniforms lingered outside the main entrance, while others walked to and from the nearby residences.

The investigators were met by a decorated adjutant and escorted to the office of the commandant, Colonel Grisholm. The colonel rose from behind his massive oak desk to greet them. His desk was flanked by U.S. and Louisiana state flags. The walls behind him displayed portraits of former commandants, going back to the 1800s.

“Thank you for coming so quickly,” the colonel said, giving firm handshakes to each. He turned toward another officer who had risen from her chair as the others entered. “This is Captain Demers, the academy’s counselor.”

The colonel gestured the others to their seats and promptly got down to business. “I’m very concerned about Cadet Marchand’s AWOL. It’s out of character for her. Let me tell you about some of her background. She’s a third-year cadet, a legacy from one of Louisiana’s best military families. She rose quickly in the ranks to become a cadet sergeant this year. Her grades are top-notch, and she is dedicated to her projected career in the military.” He paused to look at the others. “My point is that it is highly unlikely the cadet’s AWOL was of her own making. She would not jeopardize her studies here or her career.” He glanced at the other officer. “Perhaps you would like to apprise the investigators of your findings, Captain.”

Captain Demers peered at her tablet. “Upon the suggestion of the colonel, I spoke today with her roommate and closest friends, also third-year cadets. They are shocked and puzzled by her disappearance, reporting that she gave no warning signs of this happening. They said she was not unhappy at the academy or troubled in any way that they were aware of. To the contrary, she was typically quite cheerful and seemed in a good mood last night, looking forward to her routine jog. She liked jogging as a physical and mental release—not to mention as a means of staying in top physical shape, which she took pride in.”

Monica spoke up. "Sometimes students can be under a lot of pressure to measure up to the expectations of others, even though they might not show it. You mentioned she was a legacy with a tradition of high achievement in her family."

"I asked about that to the cadets and her instructors," the captain said. "She showed no signs of performance anxiety in any way. In fact, the impression is that she seemed relaxed both in the classroom and in her studying. There were no tell-tale signs of general anxiety or depression, either. She has not come to my attention as a counselor at all until now."

"What about her relationship with family?" Jeremy asked.

The captain scrolled down on her tablet screen. "Her relationships with family members are reportedly close. The parents are both career army officers. Her father is currently a colonel and her mother a major. An older brother is a captain in the Marine Corps. She grew up as an army brat with the usual transfers from base to base, although apparently she did not mind army life. She seemed proud of her family's military accomplishments and kept in regular email contact with them. That's all I know of the family so far."

"Any boyfriends?" Tony asked.

"There is a young man in New Orleans she's been seeing during her leaves. He's a third-year university student in computer studies. She talks a great deal about him, and they seem to have a happy relationship. There were no indications of any falling-out between the two lately, and her friends said they would know otherwise. The couple hoped to be engaged after their graduations, although there was some worry on her part about being transferred away from him when she joins the military."

"Another question," Tony said. "Has anyone inspected her room?"

"No," the colonel replied. "Detective D'Angelo told us straightaway that her room was off limits and was to be locked up. The roommate was temporarily relocated and relieved of her keys."

The captain added, "Her roommate did tell me that Cadet Marchand apparently did not remove anything from the room last night, except for her cell phone. Her purse was still in her drawer."

"Any indications of bullying or ostracism toward her by other cadets or vice versa?" Monica asked.

The colonel shook his head. "We keep close tabs on the behaviors and morale of the cadets. Neither bullying nor rejection is tolerated here. We'd get word quickly if either had occurred."

Monica looked inquisitively at the captain.

"I asked her roommate and friends that specifically," the captain said. "They emphatically denied behaviors like that were happening. They said she was a popular leader among the cadets."

"Isn't it possible that a cadet who is a rising star might be resented by some of her peers or seniors?" Monica asked.

"Not that we've noted," the colonel replied. "As I say, we monitor the cadets closely, including their relationships with other cadets. After all, they're being evaluated for how they would fit in the military chain of command." He paused solemnly. "It looks like foul play has occurred, doesn't it?"

"It's too soon to conclude anything, Colonel," Tony said, "but Detective D'Angelo will keep you informed."

"Is there anything else we can help you with?" the colonel asked.

Tony looked at his colleagues…. "I guess not, Colonel. Thanks for your time, and the captain's. This has been helpful."

The colonel nodded and rose from behind his desk, signifying the end of the meeting.

As they walked toward their van, Tony reached into his pocket for another gum. "I hate to say it," he said, "but it's likely the colonel is right about the disappearance."

"It looks that way, so far," Jeremy replied. "But we need to keep in mind who we were talking to."

"What do you mean?" Tony asked.

"The colonel is top of the command chain at the academy. He has a vested interest in presenting what may have happened to the cadet in the most favorable light for himself and the academy. It would not look good for him if she did have serious personal problems or behaviors, which he was unaware of, or worse, which he might have ignored. The same applies to the counselor, whose job it is to have her finger on the pulse of such matters."

"Are you saying they may have lied?"

"No, but we can't rule out that they may have been biased in their accounts."

"I'd imagine having the daughter of a prominent military family disappear on his watch is on the colonel's mind," Monica said.

“And his response may be to blame it on someone outside of his control—an intruder,” Jeremy added.

Tony clicked his remote to open the van doors. “Okay. Detective D’Angelo will question the cadets and staff himself and look at her electronics. We’ll see if that squares with what we heard today.”

CHAPTER THIRTY-THREE

Two days after the cadet's disappearance, Jack sent the trio back to the academy grounds. He had received an early-morning call from Detective D'Angelo. The cadet's body had been located in thick bush about a quarter mile from the jogging trail.

The technicians were already combing through the crime scene when the three arrived by ATV. They were met by Detective D'Angelo.

"What have you got so far, Sal?" Tony asked.

"The body—what's left of it—fits the description of the missing cadet," D'Angelo said. "Facial photographs of her matched up, and the body is the same height and approximate build. The cell phone found on the body was hers, too."

Tony nodded. "What about physical injuries?"

Detective D'Angelo sighed. "You guys will be familiar with them: signs of abdominal mutilation, possible rape, indications of torture and bruise marks on the throat. It looks like we'll be turning the case over to your team."

"Will you walk us through how the body might have gotten here, Sal?"

"We figure she was nabbed on a jogging trail between two of the security cameras. The first showed her jogging past; the second didn't. We searched the area in between. There were signs of a struggle in the bush at a spot near the trail, a half mile past the first camera: trampled bushes and broken branches and a blood trail. There wasn't enough blood to suggest she was murdered there; we think it was right here." He pointed to a small, grassy depression in the moist ground where the body lay on its back, posed lewdly. A dank, musty smell filled the air.

The depression was surrounded by oak trees heavily covered by hanging gray clusters of Spanish moss. They reminded Jeremy of funeral drapes.

"How did he get her here, Sal?" Tony asked.

"I was coming to that. There's an abandoned ATV with a trailer concealed in the bush twenty feet to your right. There are no plates, but we're checking to see if it was stolen."

"Which is likely," Tony remarked. "Any idea how he got into the academy grounds?"

"There's an old side gate next to a little-used public road not far from here on the academy's boundary. The chain was cut, we figure recently since there is no rust on the severed portion of the chain. Also, ATV tracks similar to the vehicle here were found going through the gate."

"Anything else found?"

"Just duct tape, which looked like it was used to bind the victim's hands and feet and to secure her to the trailer during her transport to here. The techs are examining the tape and the ATV and trailer for prints and DNA now. We haven't received word yet if they've found anything on the body."

"Any ATV tracks to the jogging trail?" Jeremy asked.

"There are many old trails through the bush area used for light infantry exercises. They interconnect, and a number come out to the jogging trail. It's like a maze in there. We walked through most of the trails, but nothing evidence-wise has been found so far. The hard-packed clay surface of the trails did not register any ATV tracks."

Seeing his colleagues had no further questions, Sal left to observe the techs still at work on the ATV. The three huddled together under a particularly large, old oak tree. "There are a few puzzling things," Jeremy said. "The academy is certainly not the easiest environment in which to commit a murder. There's the security check at the entrance, security patrols of the grounds, cameras, and the place is enclosed by a six-foot iron fence. The curriculum lists training in hand-to-hand combat for its cadets. So she was probably not a pushover as a victim. The signs of struggle in the bush attest to that."

"Perhaps it was the very challenge of an attack on a high-security environment that attracted him," Monica suggested.

"That would fit in with his psychology," Jeremy replied. "But how would he know that there were jogging trails on the grounds where cadets might be more vulnerable?"

"Unless it was someone from the academy who did it," Tony offered.

Jeremy nodded. "I understand the students are confined under curfew to the academy grounds on weekdays, and we know that several of the serial murders took place after hours on weekdays. That makes it unlikely it was a student who committed the other murders."

"But instructors have no curfews, and some may live off the grounds. What about them?" Tony queried.

Monica was skeptical. "Why would the murderer take the chance of committing murder at his work place?"

Tony looked unconvinced. "Just in case, we should check out alibis and backgrounds of the staff. There's a sign-in/sign-out book at the security gate, which should be crosschecked against the dates and times of the murders," he added.

"We also need to check out Vallencourt's whereabouts the night of the cadet's murder, as well his Jeep," Jeremy reminded his colleagues.

"I'll get the warrants," Tony said.

It began to drizzle, and the three huddled more closely under the tree, brushing away the moss and flies. They watched the techs place plastic covers over the body, the ATV, and trailer.

"It's going to be a long day," Jeremy lamented.

CHAPTER THIRTY-FOUR

Another week passed as Jeremy, Monica, and Tony investigated the death of the cadet. They met with Jack for a mutual update on the case.

Jack noticed that the three looked tired and listless, so he knew news wasn't encouraging. He offered coffee to liven them up. His brew had been getting stronger by the week.

"I've got the coroner's report for the cadet," Jack said, passing around copies. "I won't need to tell you this is the distinctive work of the serial killer, right down to the last detail. This includes the absence of any evidence from himself on the body or in the crime scene—indigo fibers excepted, of course." Jack produced a heavy sigh. "I hope you've got more than I have."

"Not much," Tony said. "Our techs went over Vallencourt's Jeep, and nothing came up related to the cadet's murder, not even the fibers. The Jeep does have a hitch with the same ball size as the ATV at the murder scene. But it's a common size, and there's nothing to tie the Jeep's hitch with the ATV trailer either."

"What did Vallencourt have to say?"

"We spoke with him and his driver about their whereabouts when his Jeep went missing. It was hard to get anything out of them, at first, which was suspicious. But they caved in. The two said Vallencourt visited a high-end escort during the period when the cadet was killed. We talked to the escort service. Under pressure, the manager admitted that Vallencourt was a customer. She said one of her escorts was with Vallencourt that night. The escort, who is apparently a favorite of his, verified this."

Jack gave Tony a skeptical look. "Vallencourt might have arranged for the service to provide him with a false alibi for that night."

"We told them we'd shut them down if we found out they were lying, but they stuck to their story."

Jack sighed. "Vallencourt could afford to pay the service a huge sum under the table if they covered for him. Besides, even if we do shut them down, they'll soon redo their business cards and set up somewhere else. So the threat of closing them down might mean nothing to them."

"There's another question, though," Jeremy added. "Why would Vallencourt be in such a hurry in rush-hour traffic just to see an escort? Or was he just trying to lose the tail?"

Jack shook his head. "The usual trail to nowhere, when it comes to Vallencourt.... Is there better news about the academy staff?"

"I'm afraid not," Jeremy said. "All of them were interviewed. None had the red flags in their background usually associated with violent criminals or serial killers. All had well-established alibis the night of the cadet's murder and the nights several of the other women were murdered. We doubt it was an inside job."

"There's still the question about how the murderer knew about the jogging trail and knew that he'd need an ATV to get around," Tony said.

"I think I have a plausible answer to that," Monica offered.

The others looked at her curiously.

"I checked the academy's website. It describes the recreational benefits of the academy —probably to improve enrolment. The site details the academy's extensive forest lands, lakes, and jogging trails. The co-ed nature of the academy was also touted. It mentions that the academy features advanced learning in a secure setting. All of this could conceivably have caught the eye of the murderer as he sought new victims in a challenging environment."

"If so, it's highly ironic," Jeremy observed. "A pre-military school that prides itself on its security practically issues an invitation to a watchful killer."

Monica took advantage of a lapse in the conversation. "On another topic, Jack, is there any news on that high-end watch?"

Jack shook his head. "Nothing good yet. The FBI has tracked down a number of registered owners of this type of watch, locally. None are suspected in the murders. However, there was apparently one old, highly collectable watch that was sold in New Orleans to an unknown buyer ten years ago, which could be still around. Vallencourt and Madera are not on the list of owners, but it is interesting that both are collectors. So far, no evidence of the watch in question has turned up in their financial records. Another search of their residences has also found nothing. The same for their businesses. However, they may well have gotten rid of the evidence by now.

“Vallencourt denies ever owning such a watch, if that is to be believed. Mrs. Madera says she’s not aware of her husband owning the watch we’re interested in. But she says that he was in the habit of buying expensive jewelry to impress his playmates. He knew she disliked that, so he wouldn’t tell her if he did buy it. That’s it so far. The bottom line is that we can’t pin the watch on either yet, but we also can’t rule out either one as the owner.”

Despite the sobering discussion at hand, Jack looked uncharacteristically buoyant. His colleagues regarded him curiously. “I do have some interesting information for you on the Elena Martinez case,” he announced. “As you know, Detectives Lapierre and Menendez have been following up on the case. Her friends reported that she had recently involved herself in the BDSM scene. She hung around at a seedy nightclub called the Purple Peacock. Some of her older friends had warned her that she might be getting in over her head because she was inexperienced with BDSM. They were particularly concerned when she said she going to meet with an older man for edge play the night of her death. They did not come forward with this information until today. Apparently, they did not want her parents to know of the true circumstances surrounding her death: that she was in the BDSM scene and skipped school that night to meet an edge player who may have killed her.” He looked expectantly at the others.

“So, a possible link with Madera?” Jeremy asked.

"Plausibly," Jack said, "though none of the individuals at the club who would talk ever saw her with him."

"He certainly wouldn't go near the clubs these days," Tony said. "He would have met her on the sly."

"We suspect his pattern has been to pick up the young and naïve ones like Ms. Martinez," Monica added, "and this murder falls right on the heels of his trying to knife Jeremy."

"There's one thing that bothers me, though," Jeremy said. "The murderer has, so far, been very careful not to link himself to the crimes in any way. If it is Madera, why would he now call attention to himself by murdering a BDSM person?"

The four reflected on this in silence. Monica was the first to voice a possible explanation. "Maybe he wasn't his usual self in this murder. It could have been a more impulsive act. After all, look at the stress he's been under with the breakup of his family and his failure to exact full revenge on us. And he almost got killed in the attack on Jeremy and me. He's on the FBI's most wanted list. All of this may have caused an acute psychological deterioration in him. The psychiatrists call it decompensation."

"He's falling apart?" Tony asked.

"Possibly, and as a part of that, perhaps some of his planning and organizing abilities may have been diminished," Monica suggested. "For how long, we don't know. It may just be a temporary aberration."

Jeremy nodded. "He's extremely angry at his wife abandoning him and leaving with his children. He hasn't been able to take it out on her so far, and maybe this resulted in an impulsive attack on the nearest woman, who happened to be his playmate at the time."

Jack nodded. "Let's just hope his carelessness continues, for whatever reason. We are going to nail him if it does."

CHAPTER THIRTY-FIVE

After all the danger and tragedy of the past few weeks, Jeremy sorely needed a break. He was glad when his father visited him on the weekend.

The two spent a relaxing Saturday cruising the river and fishing in the nearby bayous. Their luck had been good, and that evening they had an excellent, traditional bass dish. Afterward, they enjoyed some of Jeremy's best liquors that he saved for special occasions. Jake took out his pipe in preparation for some of the usual conversations about sports and politics. But Jeremy was not in the mood for either. He did not exactly know the reasons why, but he was about to break the great, unspoken rule in the father-son relationship.

Jake noticed his son's silence. "What's on your mind, Jeremy?" he asked.

Jeremy leaned forward in his chair. "Dad, how long have we been getting together a couple of times a month?"

"Oh, I guess it's been almost fifteen years. Since your graduation from college."

"And in all that time, how often have we spoken of Mother?"

"I don't recall that we have."

"Right. That's because we haven't. It's been somehow inadmissible to speak about her."

"And you think it's time we did?"

"Yes, I think it's time I know what happened."

Jake carefully packed his pipe bowl and adeptly ignited it. "That would bring back hard times. Bad times. Are you sure you want to hear all that? That's the reason I haven't talked to you about her, Jeremy. I was afraid it would reopen old wounds for you."

"And for you too, Dad?"

Jake blew out a stream of fragrant white smoke. "Yes, for me, too. But you're an experienced PI now who knows that things go wrong with marriages and what human nature is like. I guess I don't have to protect you anymore, do I?"

"Or maybe yourself anymore, either, Dad. It's been over thirty years." Jeremy sat back, surprised at how well his father seemed to be taking this. He had expected him to simply evade the topic and call it a night. Perhaps his father was more ready to talk about the matter than he had thought.

"What has brought you to this, Jeremy? Your sister's been analyzing you again?"

Jeremy smiled. You can't fool the old man, he thought. "She denies it, but that's what she's been doing all right. The thing about it is that she knows how to get to the truth in other people."

"And she's finally hit the mark with you?"

"Maybe. I'm not sure yet."

Jake set his pipe down in the ashtray and poured himself another Scotch. "I guess I'll need this," he said, resigning himself to the fact that Jeremy was not about to let him back out of this. But there was also a part of him, he knew, that wanted to finally speak the unspeakable. He took the first faltering step. "I don't want you to think less of me, Jeremy."

Jeremy shook his head. "This is not a blame game, Dad."

The older Hale nodded, still looking uncertain. "It takes two to make or break a marriage, Jeremy."

Jeremy leaned forward again. "So what happened, Dad?"

"A lot happened. The problems began after you were born. Your mother became depressed, and it was bad. She could barely get out of bed, let alone take care of you. We didn't know what it was then, but now they call it postpartum depression."

"I've heard of it," Jeremy said. "It's something hormonal, isn't it?"

Jake took another puff on his pipe. "That's what the doctor said years later. But it was more than that. She had very little confidence in being a mother, and that contributed a lot to her depression, because it worsened how she felt about herself—her self-worth. Her own parents were neglectful with her and her sister as they grew up. She simply didn't have a good parenting model."

"Did she get any help?"

Jake Hale sighed. "I tried. My sister tried. But we couldn't get through to her. I was hamstrung by work. You remember, I was on graveyard shift for years and couldn't get off it. When I'd get home, I needed my sleep until early afternoon. I'd take over with you until dinnertime, but it wasn't enough. All of this spilled into the marriage. We fought. I began to drink a lot."

"Did she receive therapy or you two any marriage counseling?"

"Not much. We weren't well-off and couldn't afford private services. My benefit plan was very limited. We had to rely on public services, which were overloaded and underfunded. We could only get in every few months, and that was practically useless."

"Nothing through the regular doctors?"

"She went on antidepressants, but they were new then, and there were very few of them. She tried several, but none were effective, and there were side effects."

"So, what happened?"

"Well, she did eventually improve. I think the involvement of the parish priest, who had some counseling experience, helped. She seemed to feel better about herself, and he referred her to a parenting class. My drinking got better, too. Eventually, we felt we were well enough to have a second child, and along came Kathy." His face fell. "But the same thing happened, only worse. She didn't recover this time, and neither did our relationship. She decided to leave. You know the rest."

"That's just it. I don't know the rest. I didn't hear a thing from her until she called Kathy and me when I was thirteen. It was as if we didn't exist until that time. How could she do that?"

"If I remember correctly, she called you a number of times, and I encouraged you to call back. You would have no part of it."

"Yeah, she'd abandoned me and Kathy."

"So you shut her out like you felt she shut you out?"

"I was very, very angry with her. I felt she didn't care, and everything was her fault."

"I was angry too, for many years, for much the same reasons. But I realized it wasn't really her fault. She didn't know how to be a parent, despite her classes. There's a great deal of difference between learning about it in a book and having it shown to you by your own parents. Add hormones to that and the lousy ways I often tried to handle things with her. No, it wasn't her fault, and it wasn't for lack of caring on her part, either."

"But why a couple of phone calls to me in thirty-three years?"

"I've heard bits and pieces from her sister over the years and did some reading in psychology to fill in the rest. I think she felt terribly guilty about her parenting and for leaving as she did. She was a devout Catholic who believed that she was sinful in abandoning her children. But Mary was never able to bring herself to confess any of this and gain absolution, creating more guilt. If she had visited us during those first eight years after she left, it would have brought her face-to-face with that guilt. She was poorly self-imaged to begin with. It would have destroyed her, I think."

Jake poured himself another drink. "But she received extensive therapy eventually that gave her enough confidence to make those calls. Kathy responded to her and ultimately forgave her. But she knew you were still angry and did not want to be involved with her. This is not blaming you. You were still a kid. As an adult, she could have chosen to go on trying to reach you, but I think despite therapy, she was still too insecure to deal with you. However, her sister said you were never far from her mind. The sister would often call me to keep up on how you were doing and would tell your mother. You were never forgotten. Not by a long shot."

“That’s what Kathy says, too. But as I said to her, it all sounds like rationalizations that she’s made to make herself feel better or maybe you’ve created to make yourself feel better about her never seeing me again.”

“I can see why you would think that, Jeremy. But no. I believe that what I’ve just told you is the truth, as far as I can know the truth. It’s not a big dodge or a deception. That’s all I can really tell you about it. You’re going to have to work this out within yourself, son.”

There was a long, thoughtful silence. Both realized they had taken the matter as far as they could for the time being. Jake tapped his pipe in the ashtray and reloaded it.

Jeremy took another sip of his drink. “There’s something else on my mind, Dad, about you and me. I know you’ve become a well-read man, especially since Mother left. Yet all we talk about are things like sports or politics. Nothing deep. But I know your readings are. Why is it you’ve never discussed them with me?”

Jake looked at him, surprised by what had surfaced. “Well… I wanted to share my readings with you, but you’re a practical man of the world, a professional man. I guess I didn’t think you’d be interested in the kind of abstruse subjects I fill my head with.”

“And I thought you wanted your readings to be a private part of your life, so I didn’t ask you about them,” Jeremy confessed. As he said this, he thought how easy it was to misunderstand even someone you’re close to and think you truly know. “I’d like to hear some of your thoughts on these esoteric subjects, Dad. There's more to life, after all, than practical details."

"Okay. I was reading Einstein's prediction of gravity waves has recently been verified. Want to hear about it?"

Jeremy smiled. He had read a little physics, but his father was really testing him on this one. He rose to the challenge. "Let's have it."

***

Jake Hale left for home at nine that evening. Jeremy sat at his desk in quiet contemplation. Tonight's discussion about his mother had been eye-opening. He had never realized just how bad it had been for her, especially in the early years before she left. Kathy had tried to tell him, but he had always shut out her message. His standard line about his mother always using her problems as excuses no longer seemed as convincing.

As he thought of her now, he found it more difficult to hold on to his anger. Instead, there was a glimmer of an unfamiliar feeling toward her. He let it develop. He was startled to discover it was empathy. Then came a cascade of other feelings about her: sadness, hurt, and guilt over his having taken such a hard, intolerant stance over the years.

He remained in this unsettled state overnight, sleeping only intermittently. At 3:00 a.m., he finally gave up trying to sleep. He made himself some strong coffee, hoping it would relieve his emotional hangover, but to no avail. It was then he knew what he must do. He needed to find his answers on the river.

He turned over the powerful diesel and checked his instruments as the engine warmed. In another few minutes, he cast off and swung the boat toward the open waters. It was still dark, so he turned on the forward lights. He felt the force of the Mississippi on his bow as he turned the boat into the strong currents. Already, the sky was beginning to lighten in the east, and the stars were fading.

In half an hour, Jeremy reached his farthest point north and turned the boat around. He cut the engine, surrendering to the currents and the winds. He sat back in his captain's chair, feeling the river take hold of the boat. The first golden-yellow glow of sunrise appeared in the eastern sky.

Jeremy imagined his confused feelings falling into the river and being swept away by the currents. With each deep, slow breath in, he visualized himself absorbing energy from the river. He felt a sense of inner calm and clarity developing, which seemed to deepen as the sun rose higher on the horizon and began to warm the bridge. Then came the familiar feeling of merging with his surroundings.

***

Jeremy found himself at the buoys marking the entrance to Bay Bayou Marina. It never ceased to amaze him how he could drift so many miles downriver and be practically oblivious to the passage of time. It was like coming out a deep daydream, but his experience had been much more. The calm, clear feelings he had encountered earlier on the river were, to his relief, still with him. The gut-wrenching emotions that had seized him overnight now seemed no more than a bad dream.

He started the engine and pulled into his mooring spot at the marina. After securing his boat, he sat down on a bench on the dock. He pulled out his cell phone, weighing it in his hand for a few moments. He dialed the number for his mother.

CHAPTER THIRTY-SIX

Jeremy was returning home from another late evening at the office. As he stepped out of his car, he carefully scanned the shadowed parking lot, as was his habit since the attack by Madera. Nothing seemed amiss, and he headed quickly for his boat. The tension he so often carried in his neck let go as soon as boarded the boat.

He read a few more chapters of *The Hound of the Baskervilles* before falling asleep with his book beside him. He'd barely had time for a dream when he was awakened by his phone. It was Tony calling. What was so important this time of night? He picked up the call, feeling the tension creeping back into his neck.

"Sorry to call this late, Jeremy. The undercover guys monitoring the decoy made an emergency call for backup at Canal and Grange Street. I don't know the details, but meet Monica and me at that locale."

***

Earlier, Monica's evening had begun pleasantly enough. She meditated at the bay window overlooking Bourbon Street, then she had a light dinner as she watched one of her old murder-mystery movies. She slept restfully afterward—until the nightmare came. She dreamed of a scene from the movie: the stormy black night and the murderer's malevolent eyes staring out of the dark closet as he waited to strike his unsuspecting female victim. But the dream was not just a replay of the movie. Strangely, the victim in the dream was not the character in the film; it was someone she did not recognize. The victim had felt she was safe in her home, but the murderer had crept into the house through a decrepit basement door. That was different than the movie, too. Monica awoke with a start and answered Tony's late-night call.

She dressed hurriedly and drove to meet Tony and Jeremy. On her way, she thought about the unknown victim in her dream. She knew some theories hold that dream figures are simply masked projections of the dreamer. So could she have been the victim in her nightmare, after all? Before she could consider the matter further, she arrived at Canal and Grange Street.

Jeremy arrived at the scene a few minutes later. There was a huge collection of police vehicles, their lights flashing. A police line was formed around the intersection. Sparks from a cutting torch sprayed out in a nearby alley.

He spotted Tony and Monica with Jack Claye. Jeremy pulled his teammates to the side. Tony's pallid face revealed the seriousness of the situation.

"What's happening, Tony?" Jeremy asked apprehensively.

"The undercover boys were tracking Officer Crosby, the decoy, from their vehicle, not more than two hundred feet away. She was in radio contact with the officers, who kept her under night vision, too. They also had an electronic tracker on her. At about 11:20, she was walking past the mouth of that alley." Tony pointed toward the white-hot sparks. "Suddenly, the surveillance equipment went dead, distracting the undercover officers. In a few seconds, the equipment kicked back on, but she had dropped off the night vision. The undercover officers heard muffled screams through the radio connection and then silence. They made it to the alley in seconds, but she was gone. The tracking signal stopped just behind the old, abandoned abattoir near a heavy steel door off the alley. The door was either locked or jammed from the inside, and they weren't able to gain entry. The rest of the building's entrance points are bricked up. So there's a welder trying to cut through the door now. We've also got a perimeter around four blocks, including the docks."

Jack Claye approached them in a hurry. "They're through the door! Let's go!"

The team rushed into the dilapidated, near-empty interior and dispersed in the cavernous dark building. Crisscrossing flashlight beams darted into the black recesses along the brick and cement walls and upward into the thick timber rafters. Most of the old machinery had been removed long ago, with only their large steel anchors protruding from the floor. There were some broken cutting tables. A few rusted chains and hooks hung from the ceiling. A dusty, cobwebbed sign displaying the name Boutilier's Meat Company leaned forlornly against a wall. Jeremy recognized the company; his father used to buy its ham and bacon until it had gone out of business ten years ago. Now, the derelict building was a potential murder scene.

The trio spread out. Monica coughed as she inhaled the musty, stale air. She shone her light in the direction of a rustling. She shuddered as the beam caught a large brown rat disappearing around a barrel. Tony, in turn, poked a metal rod he had found into a large pile of rags on the floor, raising a cloud of dust but encountering nothing solid. Jeremy ventured off into what seemed to have been an office area. Papers, along with some damaged computers and bent filing cabinets, lay scattered over the floor.

Some of the searchers had already gone into other smaller rooms branching off from the central area. Suddenly, the silence was broken by a frantic shout: "Here! She's here!"

The team followed the shout, rushing into a scene from their worst nightmares. Several beams of light converged on a bloody mass suspended about eight feet from the floor. It was the body of the undercover policewoman, naked below the waist. Her eyes stared down at them blankly, her tears still fresh on her face. A large gash in her lower abdomen had bled out into a large pool on the floor, and the body was extremely pallid. She was cruelly hung from a hook through her back, like a piece of meat, suspended by a chain from the ceiling.

Exclamations of shock, horror, and anger made their way through the crowd of officers. Monica looked over at one of the undercover officers who had been tracking her before her disappearance. He looked shaken and was held up by two of his colleagues. "She was his friend," Tony whispered to Monica.

Monica stared up at the body. She flashed back to her nightmare and the bulging eyes of the murderer waiting for his victim. She wondered if the real murderer had been tracking Officer Crosby at the very moment of her dream. She knew her grandmother would have said the dream was no coincidence and that there was a psychic connection between her dream and the actual murder unfolding. She shook her head. This was no time for paranormal musings.

Jeremy motioned to Tony and Monica to join him. “How did this guy get in here?” he asked. “Unless the door to the alley had been unlocked already somehow. But there’s no evidence of street people using the building. So, if the door was unlocked, it wasn’t for long. Even more puzzling, how did he get out after the murder? The building seems totally sealed, and there is a police perimeter around it.”

Monica flashed back to her dream of the murderer creeping in through the basement door. She drew in her breath sharply. “Maybe he went under the building.”

Jeremy nodded. “Let’s see if the place has a basement.”

“Basements are hard to find in New Orleans because of the high water table,” Tony said.

“Yes, but I’ve heard some downtown commercial buildings have them,” Jeremy replied. “They’ve got drainage systems.”

Tony shrugged. “It’s worth a look.”

The three returned to the main room and inspected the floor more closely. Behind a pile of barrels and boxes was what appeared to be a trap door. The door lifted surprisingly easily. Jeremy’s flashlight revealed a shaft dropping ten feet or so to a floor below. There were rails on each side, which looked like the remains of an old freight elevator. A chain hung down the shaft to the floor.

"Well, if our murderer is athletic, he could have shimmied down the chain," Jeremy suggested.

The three looked at one another questioningly.

"So, who's in good enough shape to do it?" Tony asked. "And what about your arm?"

"You've gotten to be a sedate family man, Tony," Jeremy said. "And my arm is pretty good." He took hold of the chain, testing it with some of his weight. "It feels solid." He slid down the chain and played his light around the floor below. "There's not actually a basement here," he called up to them. "There's a large brick tunnel sloping downward in the direction of the river." Jeremy's light disappeared from view. "I'm heading down it."

"Okay. Watch it," Tony cautioned. "He may still be down there."

"This may answer our question about how the murderer got in and out of the building," Monica remarked.

Ten minutes later, Jeremy appeared behind Tony and Monica, who were still peering into the shaft. He cleared his throat, startling the other two. "The tunnel leads right under the police line to the dock. I think that he used the river to make his escape. He must have had a small boat tied up in the understructure of the dock, where it was difficult to spot. I've informed Jack, and he's called in the river patrol and a couple of helicopters to search for it. A patrol boat will pick us up at the dock in a few minutes."

The three headed around the perimeter of the building to the dock. They soon boarded a patrol craft and headed upriver, the searchlight sweeping over the black water and the shadowed bank on their left. They noticed another police boat focusing on the opposite shore. A brilliant beam from a helicopter swept the river in front of them.

They travelled for nearly twenty minutes, encountering only a few freighters and barges making their way upriver.

Tony shook his head in frustration. “It’s so dark. A small boat could be hidden anywhere along the banks.”

“There’s no doubt about it,” Jeremy said. “This guy’s been one step ahead of us or more tonight. Another demonstration of his cleverness.”

“Unfortunately, he’s using his intelligence for the wrong purposes,” Monica said. “It’s hard to find words to describe what happened to that poor woman tonight—taken right from under the noses of the police. One of the undercover officers looks traumatized, too.”

“Yeah,” Tony said. “Officer Dupuis took it very hard. He lost a fellow officer and friend on his watch, despite keeping close tabs on her.”

“Unfortunately, the murderer was tracking her even more closely,” Jeremy remarked. “With the elaborate way he set this up, he had to know she was a decoy. He was expecting a tight chase from the police. It was to show us all up—that he was smarter than us and that not even the police could protect one of their own against him.”

“Exactly,” said Monica, “and you can imagine what the reaction is going to be in today’s news. This is more evidence he’s trying to instill fear in the public and the police. His sadistic nature is coming out on several levels.”

A call came in on the boat's radio. It was the helicopter pilot reporting that he had spotted a small boat, which was partially concealed in the tangled, dark bushes on the riverbank. The pilot indicated he would maintain position until the patrol craft arrived.

The driver gunned the motor, raising the bow over the water. The boat travelled upstream only a few minutes before encountering the helicopter's spotlight focused on the bank of a small bay.

The police boat pulled up near the shore, focusing its own light on an open aluminum boat about sixteen feet long, with netting and branches partially covering it. It had a black, fifty-horsepower outboard and a small electric trolling motor.

Jeremy asked the driver to pull up near the stern. He reached out, almost touching the larger motor. "It's warm," he confirmed. "The trolling motor may account for the boat making it out of the dock without being heard."

Tony shone his light on the dirt road ascending the muddy bank above the small boat. "There are tire tracks up there…. Wait! It looks like the back end of a boat trailer jutting out of some bushes, too."

"Perhaps our murderer has made his first mistakes," Jeremy surmised.

"It could be," Tony said. "Let's see if he's made any more. I'm calling the techs to go over everything here." He took down the boat's registration number and the make of the outboard motor. "I'll run these. But the chances are everything's stolen." Tony radioed the helicopter to search the road further for a vehicle. He sighed.

"The road doesn't show up on the map, but I'm betting it connects with Highway 4 and the murderer's left the area."

All the three could do at this point was sit tight and await the techs. Jeremy turned to Monica. "You were right on this one too. I hope you're not going to tell me an image of the tunnel came to you in a dream or vision."

No, but something pretty close to that did, she thought. She smiled and said nothing.

CHAPTER THIRTY-SEVEN

The case conference had just broken up. Jeremy, Monica, and Tony emerged together from the conference room and walked down toward Tony's office.

"That had to be the most depressing meeting we've had yet," Tony lamented, looking down at the featureless gray carpet on the hallway floor.

Jeremy agreed. "The gloom in that place hung over us like a fog on the Mississippi."

"The murder of Officer Crosby is a huge loss for everyone," Monica added. "Utterly demoralizing."

"And the murderer knows it," Jeremy said. "I'm certain that was one of his intentions in the first place."

"The press sees it that way, too," Tony said. "Did you read the coverage in the *Sentinel* this morning? We come out as a bunch of bumblers. There's even an article in the financial section that downtown businesses say there's been a big-time drop in sales since the murders began. Female customers are too afraid to shop in the evening."

"This is also what the murderer wants. To control others through fear," Monica observed. "He's going to be laughing all the way to his next crime."

The three turned into Tony's office. "We were outsmarted at every step of the murder," Tony complained as he sat down at his desk. "He knew exactly when he was going to grab her and how he was going to cut us off from the old slaughterhouse."

"And likely how he was going to display the body in the most horrific way possible," Monica said. "Then his finishing touch: executing his escape under the police line and onto the river."

"That being said, the decoy team set up the bait well," Jeremy added. "They had to make sure the route and times of the operation were predictable, successfully luring the murderer. But they were too confident in their tracking technology. It was indeed sophisticated, but it proved fallible and failed at a critical moment. It will be interesting to see what the techs eventually make of that, but right now, the shutdown of the system seems very suspicious. It played right into the hands of the murderer. If he had anything to do with that, he is indeed technologically skilled, and we are dealing with a more formidable opponent than we thought."

"Jack tells me that, naturally, our female police officers have been very nervous since the murder," Tony reported. "They're afraid the murderer is going to try another attack on female staff. The women are being rescheduled to daylight hours, operating with male officers at all times. This is pretty tough on the whole department."

Jeremy noticed Monica seemed preoccupied.

"I've been feeling the same way," she confided. "On edge most of the time, especially when I'm alone in my apartment. But I'm jumpy just walking downtown. Yesterday, someone behind me said, 'Excuse me,' and I actually started to reach for my gun. It turned out to be a tourist asking for directions."

"Well, it's understandable, with Madera still on the loose and now the murder of Officer Crosby," Jeremy empathized. "Who wouldn't feel vulnerable?"

Tony nodded.

Jeremy noticed Monica's face flush. "There's something else, isn't there?"

She hesitated and then spoke her mind. "I think there's someone following me."

Jeremy and Tony looked at one another uneasily. "What makes you say that?" Jeremy asked.

"I can't definitely say. It's more of a feeling. It's like what Jenny Thibeault told her boyfriend, Billy, before she disappeared."

"Have you actually seen someone tailing you or watching you?"

"I noticed a man in a black hoodie and sweats behind me on Main Street on two occasions. But I can't say for sure that it was the same person each time."

"What did he do?" Jeremy asked

"He hung around when I stopped walking, but each time I went into a store, he was gone when I came out."

"Anything else?"

"A black SUV stayed behind me on the way to the office this morning for a number of blocks. It kept turning with me when I deliberately tried to lose him."

"Did you get his license?" Tony asked.

"No. As I said, he was behind me, and I couldn't get a look at the plate. I can't imagine why Louisiana has only rear license plates."

"Louisiana cops have said so, too. Anyway, the SUV's making the same turns could be a coincidence," Tony said.

"There's always the possibility," Jeremy suggested, "that Jenny's reports and the dark SUV or Jeep picked up by the academy's cameras might be playing on your mind. You may be projecting your fears out there."

Monica looked unconvinced. "There's another parallel with Jenny. Billy disbelieved her and even labeled her as paranoid when she told him of her suspicions. Then she disappeared."

"I don't disbelieve you," Jeremy replied, "or think you're paranoid, for that matter. I'm simply saying that because you feel something to be true, that doesn't necessarily make it true. But we won't take any chances, either. I'd be glad to accompany you back to your apartment, after work, from now on."

She smiled. "I would appreciate that.... And I think I'll stay away from crowds for a while, too."

"Not a bad idea, right now," Jeremy said. "And if you have any more of these experiences, be sure to let me know, okay?" He reached out to take her hand.

Her smile broadened as she took his.

CHAPTER THIRTY-EIGHT

Jeremy, Monica, and Tony visited Professor Greenwood in his office in the Social Sciences Building a few days after the loss of Officer Crosby. Her murder and the helpless feelings that pervaded the team afterward added a sense of urgency to the trio's visit. Monica wondered if something in them needed to be told what to do by an "expert"; perhaps it was a child-like part of them seeking parental guidance in a time of threat.

Monica immediately noticed how functional the office was. The professor had lined his office walls with all manner of psychology books and dissertations he had supervised, with a section dedicated to serial murders and criminology. The office displayed no photos, knickknacks, or even paintings. This was a place for a thinker, not a sentimentalist or an aesthetic, she thought.

The professor sat behind his desk as if he was addressing his grad students. "Our visit with one another is long overdue," he said. "It's unfortunate that it occurs in the shadow of Officer Crosby's death."

Tony nodded. "Everything that could have gone wrong went wrong," he said disconsolately. "The murderer turned the tables on us."

"And I'm sure that was his plan," the professor said grimly. "To beat the police at their own game. Like many of the infamous serial murderers in history, this is part of their thrill-seeking and lust for power. Jack the Ripper in 1880s London is reputed to have written letters taunting the police and bragging about his future crimes. Indeed, the motives of serial killers have not changed in centuries—perhaps only the technology used by them."

"Well, the 'Ripper' ultimately won his game," Jeremy remarked. "He never got caught."

"Let's hope there will be no repeat of that in this case," the professor replied. "Interestingly, the taunting by some of these vicious killers actually worked against them, providing leads to the police. Perhaps a strategy might be to try to psychologically ensnare this murderer—bait him to communicate with us or make public statements. His own ego may give him away."

Tony sighed. "Well, we'd better do something different. The bugger seems to be winning so far. We had better get a break pretty soon.... By the way, Professor, you've got a point about technology. Our techs say that Officer Crosby's killer used an electronic jammer to scramble our surveillance equipment and distract the undercover guys just before she was nabbed."

"This is indeed sophisticated," the professor observed. "Scramblers have been developed by the military for electronic warfare."

"That's exactly what the techs said," Tony replied.

Professor Greenwood nodded. "I read your transcript of the interview with Charles Vallencourt. Didn't he say that his chief of security was an ex-military intelligence man who was knowledgeable about electronic surveillance?"

"Yeah, he did," Tony confirmed, impressed. "We need to follow up on that."

"I like the concept of psychological entrapment," Jeremy said. "It's a different angle."

Monica also seemed taken by the idea. "Do you have some research on the topic, Professor?"

The professor went to his bookshelf, pulling out a tome, which he handed to Monica. "This is my psychohistory book on serial murderers I was telling you about. It describes some of the psychological strategies used by police in the past."

"Any other tips for us, Professor?" Tony asked.

"About Vallencourt, yes. I've noted in the sheriff's report that his early background and development included experiences of powerlessness, humiliation, and trauma. The psychoanalysts believe that serial murderers re-enact these experiences during their killings. The victims are symbolic of whoever it was that originally tormented the murderer. The murderer expresses his rage about that on the victim. Likewise, the murderer tries to dominate and control the victim, as he had been dominated or controlled as a child—only in a much more extreme way. Mutilating, torturing, and finally killing the victim becomes the ultimate revenge and means of domination."

"But yet we know," Monica said, "that any of these factors alone or in combination will not necessarily produce a serial killer later on."

"I absolutely agree, Monica. Allow me to use the analogy of a mixture of flammable gases and oxygen. It will not explode until there's a spark to create ignition. Likewise, serial murderers need some triggering event to finally go over the edge, the point of no return. That often happens at a critical juncture in their social development. We need to know Vallencourt's trigger."

The others listened in silence, absorbed in the professor's words.

"Talking about Vallencourt," the professor continued, "I would imagine you'd like to borrow the Clairmont history book I found." He went over to a cabinet and unlocked its thick oak door, fetching a small, faded green, cloth-covered book with a loose spine. He handed it to Jeremy. "It's fragile, so take good care of it," he advised in a sober voice.

Monica smiled. "A devoted book collector," she observed.

Jeremy, however, was curious. "So I hear you picked this up at a book sale?"

"Yes. I understand an anonymous donor gave the book to a church sale. It was part of a personal library of books from this person's estate after he or she had passed."

"That's a pretty lucky find, Professor. The Clairmont Museum's late curator said there was only one copy to her knowledge."

"I was curious about that, too. I sent for a printing history of the book from the publisher, who is still around. There was an initial run of twenty books printed in the 1950s, intended for local Clairmont consumption. So there is a likelihood there are more out there still. The curator was probably mistaken."

"I expect you've read the book, Professor?" Jeremy asked.

"I have, and it contains very significant information about the history of the Vallencourts and the bodies found in the Clairmont area. I won't bias you with the details right now. Have a look at the book for yourselves."

Monica gave the professor an admiring look. A true academic, she thought.

***

After the meeting with the professor, the three drove to Leo's for a late lunch. They found some privacy at a corner table in the back of the restaurant and soon had their salads delivered to them.

"The professor came up with some good ideas," Tony commented, waving a carrot stick in the air.

"I can hardly wait to get into his book," Monica said. "It could prove useful."

"There might be potential there," Jeremy agreed. "Let us know what you come up with, ASAP. We should also look for a scrambling device at Vallencourt's and question the security chief about what he knows."

"Let's do it," Tony agreed, "but I expect he'll be tight-lipped, if he even meets with us. These military guys are sticklers for loyalty, and I'd be surprised if he gives anything away on his boss. He might also be under a gag order not to reveal the details of any technology he may have learned about in the military."

"The professor was certainly suspicious about Vallencourt," Monica remarked. "I suppose it's difficult not to be, given his recent reading material on the Vallencourt family. It'll be interesting to look over the documented reports on the bodies in the Clairmont area."

"The professor has refocused us on Vallencourt, and I think that's justifiable. We've been distracted, to say the least, by all the drama with Madera," Jeremy said.

"If we find precipitating factors in Vallencourt's background that the professor suggested, that would really put him up on our suspicion list," Monica added.

"True," Tony said. "But how in the world are we going to come by that information? He's a guy who keeps to himself a lot. Who would know personal things that happened to him, especially just before these murders began?"

"Hmm," Monica began. "He does have a favorite escort he sees. Men are sometimes known to confide personal matters to escorts. We could talk again with her."

"It might be worth a shot," Tony said.

"Yeah," Jeremy agreed absentmindedly.

"You seem preoccupied with something, Jeremy," Monica observed.

Jeremy didn't reply immediately, and then he slowly voiced his thoughts. "What are the chances of this history book surfacing like this out of the blue?"

"It's just one of these happy coincidences," Tony responded. "They happen. Maybe, like the professor says, there are actually a number of copies still around out there. Somebody died, and up pops a copy nobody knew about."

"I just don't know, Tony. PIs don't believe in coincidences, happy or not. If they do, they soon wind up dead."

Tony laughed. "You're getting suspicious in your approaching middle age, Jeremy. What do you think, Monica?"

She thought for a moment. "There's a part of me that wants to believe this may not be a coincidence."

"What!" Tony said.

"Yes. As illogical as it may sound, maybe it's synchronicity."

It was Jeremy's turn to laugh, but Tony looked utterly bewildered.

"Synchronicity refers to supposed connections between events that science and logic can't explain," Monica said. "As you said to the professor, we needed a break in this case. And now this book comes along, which may give us that break."

"So I'm supposed to believe that wishing for a break somehow brought the book to us?" Tony asked.

"You're definitely a pragmatist, Tony. But what if there is a deeper meaning, sometimes, behind events that seem to be random or coincidental on the surface?"

"Maybe, Monica, your spiritual side is finally coming out—in a metaphysical way," Jeremy offered. He smiled. "Just don't tell Jack about it."

Tony looked at him, amused. "I said the same thing to you about your relationship with the river."

"What relationship?" Monica asked.

"It's a long story," Jeremy said as he shot a reproving glance at Tony. "Anyone up for croissants?"

***

The next day, the three drove to the escort service office to meet with Moxie, who apparently was Vallencourt's favorite. Moxie was in her mid-thirties, with long, dyed blond hair and bright red nails. She wore a short skirt and tight blouse, which accentuated her stronger physical attributes. She sat with her arms and legs crossed, a churlish look on her face.

Moxie had some unfriendly words as the investigators sat down. "I already talked to you guys. What do you want now? I don't get paid to sit around."

"We need more on Charles Vallencourt," Tony said.

Moxie looked even more uncomfortable. "About what? I told you enough already."

"Why? Because he's a rich guy?"

"I got to make a living too."

Tony leaned toward her. "If we don't get what we want, you won't be working much longer, Moxie. We'll shut the place down and charge everyone with prostitution, including yourself."

"Okay, okay. What do you want?"

Jeremy took over. "We understand you're Vallencourt's favorite girl. Does he ever say anything about himself?"

"Like what?"

"Like his problems. Anything that's happened to upset him."

Moxie sighed impatiently. “He keeps a lot to himself.”

“But sometimes not?”

“Yeah. He did tell me one thing, about eight months ago. There’s a woman he knows. Somebody who worked for him. He had a thing for her. Began to bring her gifts, complimented her looks, and asked her out. She went a few times. Then she dumped him and quit. She said she wasn’t okay dating the boss. But he didn’t believe her. He took it real personal. You know, a brush-off. Got really choked over it. Said he’d got too much of that from women. He even stopped seeing me for a while. When he did come back, he made me promise I wasn’t going to dump him, too. I got the feeling she was the only one he’d asked out in a long time.”

“Did he say anything else regarding her?”

“No, and I didn’t ask. But I think he’s still choked.”

“Any more?”

“No, that’s it. That’s all I know.”

“Okay, Moxie,” Tony said. “Nothing happens right now. But get in touch with us if something comes up about him. If you don’t, we’ll find out and there’ll be trouble for you.”

On the way back to the van, Jeremy asked the question on everyone’s mind. “Do you think we’ve got a triggering factor for Vallencourt, if he is the murderer?”

“We don’t know for sure, but it might be,” Monica replied. “He seems to have taken the refusal of his past employee as a serious rejection, possibly replaying similar childhood experiences. We know he acted his anger out back then.”

"But we don't know if he did anything to her," Jeremy said. "There are no complaints concerning him on file from any female. It would be nice to get into his company's personnel files to see if a female employee quit about eight months ago. We could pay her a visit."

"That would be great," Tony replied. "Except I have a feeling we're not going to have enough to get a warrant for something as confidential as a personnel file on someone who isn't even our suspect. Jack probably won't go for that."

***

It was Monica's meditation time again. She was especially looking forward to leaving her anxieties and troubles in the world behind her for the rest of the evening.

She easily moved into a deep meditative state. She became that single, irreducible point of consciousness, a beacon of light in the darkness, signifying she existed. She enjoyed the peaceful feeling gradually enveloping her. It was a state of contentment, with no needs, wants, or desires to distract her from the business of being.

She became aware of a stirring in the darkness. The stirring became something she felt. It was like a very subtle, gentle breeze passing over her. She took a deep breath, absorbing the breeze, feeling uplifted and invigorated by it. She stayed with the experience until it dissipated on its own.

She returned to ordinary consciousness, feeling calm but buoyant. Curiosity was there, also. What did the breeze signify? Why did it have such a powerful effect on her? As usual, the answers weren't forthcoming. She wondered if some meditative experiences were beyond the ability of thought to comprehend them.

But she was curious about something else. She had now come to the last spiritual exercise in the old book and wondered what it held for her. The title of the last chapter was the most mystical and mysterious so far: “Merging with The Oneness of All Things; The Power of The Turquois Stone.” She had no intention of using these final prescriptions tonight but decided to study them closely.

CHAPTER THIRTY-NINE

The next morning found Jeremy and Monica going over the notes and photos for the case. They had been hoping that somehow, in the mass of details, a lead might appear. There were depressingly few of them right now.

Jeremy was about to open the Clairmont history book when his cell buzzed with a text from Tony. Jack had asked for a meeting with the trio right away. Tony didn't know what was on the agenda. Jeremy's stomach tightened. Had yet another body been discovered?

The two left hurriedly. The downtown traffic was civilized this morning, and it didn't take them long to cover the few blocks to NOPD headquarters. They found Jack and Tony in the former's office, peering at a printout. The team lead looked up. "I have major news on the Martinez case," he announced. "Detectives Lapierre and Menendez have been swamped with tips from the public, including a couple of crazies who falsely confessed to the murder. None seemed credible until last night. An anonymous male called. Said he saw Madera the night of the Martinez murder. Madera stopped at a traffic light at Levine and Rose at about 9:00 p.m. You'll recall the estimated time of Martinez's death was between 9:30 p.m. and 12 a.m. The caller said Madera was driving a large black SUV but didn't notice its make or license plate. He stated he saw a young woman in the passenger seat who looked like Elena Martinez. He said he was sick and tired of Madera terrorizing the BDSM scene and the cops needed to get this 'scum' off the streets."

"So, if our informant is correct," Jeremy said, "it could be the first connection of Madera to the murders."

"It looks that way," Jack said with an uncharacteristic smile. "The intersection is not far from the Purple Peacock and on a direct route to the murder location. All in all, the call appears to fit with a disgruntled BDSM person who's fed up with Madera."

"Well, if it was Madera, he's changed vehicles," Monica observed.

"Probably stolen," Tony commented.

"Detective Lapierre is already checking that out," Jack added. "If the vehicle was stolen, it might be ditched somewhere, and we may be able to place Ms. Martinez in the vehicle."

Jeremy looked pensive. "We know that a dark Jeep or SUV was picked up on the academy's cameras near where the cadet's body was found. We've been focusing on Vallencourt, but now we can't rule out it might have been Madera's vehicle."

***

That evening found Jeremy trying to relax on his boat, reading another classic murder mystery. But his mind kept returning to the tumultuous events of the day. Lapierre had discovered that a full-sized black SUV had been stolen in the city about a week before the murder. It had not been recovered, and the vehicle was now the focus of an intensive search. Was it the vehicle reportedly used by Madera? Was the case about to break? He got up to pour himself a drink from his liquor cabinet and sauntered over to a porthole facing the dock. It was so dark that the neon lights on the dock barely managed to illuminate it.

A call came through on his cell. It was Monica, and he picked up, uneasy about the lateness of her call.

"I think you better get over here," she announced, her voice pitched unusually high. "I just checked my security system record for the day. I do it before bedtime. It went down for half an hour today when I was at work. It's never done that before. I ran the diagnostics, and nothing came up."

"You've checked through your place? There's no chance that an intruder might be concealed somewhere?"

"I've checked. I'm okay so far, and the door's locked, of course."

"I'll be right over." He disconnected and went to his desk drawer for his gun. He strapped it on under his jacket.

He hurried down his gangplank but then told himself to slow down and not rush headlong into the deeply shadowed parking lot. What if all this was a setup? If the murderer broke into Monica's computer, he'd know the time of night she checked her security program and that she might then call him. The murderer could be waiting to ambush him outside. He walked around the periphery of the parking lot and then stopped to look over the area. Seeing nothing suspicious, he walked quickly to his vehicle. He checked the backseat before he got in and locked his door immediately afterward.

In another fifteen minutes, he pulled into the visitors' parking at Monica's building. His first move was a quick walk around the building, looking for anything or anyone suspicious. In another few minutes, he was at Monica's apartment. She seemed relieved to see him as she opened the door but looked a little sheepish as well.

"Maybe I'm overreacting," she said. "I shouldn't have disturbed you."

He dismissed her reservations. "I'm glad you called. Given what we're up against, we should take no chances," he said. "So far, so good, though," he added. "I looked around the outside of the building and up the stairwell to your floor. Nothing came up. Why don't you show me the gap in your security recordings?"

She brought him over to her PC and logged into the security system. "See? Between ten thirty and eleven this morning, there's no record, no video recording, nothing. The rest of the day, the system was normal. No power outages occurred, either."

"That's very odd," Jeremy agreed. "I could get Tony to ask one of the police techs to check out your system. It could take a couple of days, though. If you want, you could get your own security company to look at it."

"I'll wait on the techs," she said. "I don't know if the security company could identify sophisticated tampering if it happened. Besides, I've panicked enough for one day."

Jeremy smiled. "Maybe it's simply prudent caution," he said. "At least get your security code changed ASAP. Did you notice anything else amiss or unusual in the apartment?"

"There's nothing moved or missing…. Hmm. Now that I think about it, I thought I detected a whiff of a sweet fragrance, like cologne, when I came in. But I had a screen window open; it could have been from the street."

"Did you sweep the place for bugs or micro cameras?"

"Not yet."

Jeremy spent the next fifteen minutes going over the apartment for surveillance devices but came back empty-handed. "That's one less thing to worry about," he remarked. "Does the building have security cameras?"

"Only in the two entrances."

"Okay. Tomorrow we'll get Tony to come by and ask the superintendent about viewing the videos. In the meantime, I've got a camera I can conceal in the planter at the end of your hallway. It'll broadcast right to your computer. You'll be able to record all the activity in the hallway 24/7. I imagine that will be quite exciting. By the way, I'll be glad to stay over, if you'd like."

"I've put you out enough already," she protested.

"There's no imposition. I'll crash on your couch, and I promise to make you breakfast tomorrow with one of my favorite galley recipes."

She smiled. "Well, I can't pass that up. I'll get you some blankets."

CHAPTER FORTY

The next evening, Monica returned to her apartment building after another late Wednesday at the office. Jeremy dutifully escorted her once again. As they arrived at the building's front entrance, a call came in on his cell phone. He picked up and listened for a few moments. "I'll be right over," he said.

Monica gave him a curious look.

"It's the office security company calling. There's been an intruder alarm at the office, and the police have been called. I'd better get down there."

Monica nodded. "I'll be okay from here," she said, watching Jeremy leave hurriedly for his car. She opened the front door and stepped into the foyer, pausing to unlock her mailbox. She examined a few pieces of mail. There was an official-looking letter from the Louisiana State Board of Private Investigator Examiners. It must be the results of her PI exam, she thought excitedly. She tore open the envelope and smiled as she read the letter. She had passed her exam and was eligible for her license. Monica felt a surge of elation; she had dreamed for a long time of becoming a certified investigator. Things were working out for her in New Orleans. Jeremy had been a good mentor and her an eager student. Unexpectedly, she was also getting in touch with her spiritual roots. But as she reached to relock her mailbox, her elation suddenly turned to terror. Everything went black as she felt a suffocating hood being pulled over her head and then the prick of a needle in her arm.

She staggered back and began to lose consciousness; then she felt herself being dragged into a nearby room. She still had some fight in her and struggled with her captor, but the drug was too powerful, and then there was nothingness.

***

Monica awoke being jolted up and down and from side to side. She slowly realized that she was strapped into the seat of a moving vehicle. The vehicle stopped, and she again felt the sting of a needle. As she blacked out, she heard a low voice, though she couldn't make out the words.

Monica awoke again in a small, dim room. Her body was stiff and sore, particularly around her upper arms and shoulders where she had been roughly grabbed. But some of her discomfort came from lying prone against the cold, damp floor. She felt the floor with her fingers. It was a coarse concrete surface. She had an ache in her forehead as well and brought her hand there to sooth it, but her forearm felt heavy. She looked down to see a steel cuff around her wrist. It was attached with a chain to a metal ring mounted in the concrete wall behind her. She felt the first surge of panic. She was a shackled prisoner. But held by whom? Was it that madman, Madera? Vallencourt? She knew her unconscious was already searching through its memories, seeking to identify the mysterious, low voice. Whoever he was, he had to be the serial killer! She had been caught in his trap!

Monica felt another surge of panic. She was in great danger—more danger than she had ever been in before. She knew that the prospect of rescue from a horrible fate was slim at best. The chances were also remote that there had been a witness or that the security cameras were functional in the apartment building. This murderer had a history of skillfully evading detection. Despite her fears, she was powerfully curious about the identity of the killer. She would find out soon enough. His face might be the last thing she would ever see.

Her intuitions had been right, after all, she thought. The murderer had been tracking her, coldly planning and calculating to bring about this day. She had been a fool not to take more precautions than she did—to fail to assess where all her vulnerabilities would be. The first-floor postal alcove turned out to be one of them. She realized she had most likely been taken into the janitor's office. From there, she was probably dragged through the basement into a nearby alley.

Her heart jumped as she heard the door lock click open. Someone was coming in! A brilliant light flooded into the room as the door opened. She closed her eyes, pretending she was still unconscious, but kept a sliver of her eyelid open. A man was silhouetted in the harsh light. He bent down and placed a water bottle near her and a thin mat for her to lie upon. His cologne was familiar! As he stood up to make his way back to the door, she saw the side profile of his face. A chilling, electric feeling ran through her as she recognized him! The dark mystery was finally laid bare.

CHAPTER FORTY-ONE

Jeremy disconnected his call to Monica. He had reached her voicemail for the third time. He paced around his office. It was almost 10:00 a.m., and it was not like her to be late—let alone not to call to notify him. His pacing quickened as he thought of Madera still being at large. Finally, he decided to go to her apartment. He tried to reassure himself that she probably had just slept in; after all, she'd been working long hours lately. At most, he would encounter Monica's mildly disapproving look at the door and her reminder that he was too protective of her.

In a few minutes, he pulled into the visitors' parking at her building. He noticed her car was still in its parking spot. He walked over to it and tried the door. It was locked. All about it seemed normal, he thought.

He walked into the main entrance. His eyes were immediately drawn to the mailboxes on his right. Her box was open, and some of her mail was scattered on the floor. He scooped it up and buzzed her apartment, but there was no answer. At that moment, another tenant opened the inner door to the building's main hallway and with a smile let him through. His heart beating fast, Jeremy took the elevator to the third floor and knocked on her door. There was no answer. He looked around to ensure that he was alone and then picked the lock and quickly entered. Her security system was armed, and he was greeted by a threatening computer voice warning of an imminent alarm. He took one of his cards out of his wallet, and noting her security code, punched it in to disarm the system.

"Monica?" he called out as he anxiously explored the apartment. "It's Jeremy. Are you all right?" The dead silence was ominous.

Finding her bedroom empty, he braced himself, in a sweat, against a wall. He was probably overreacting. There could be a benign explanation for what was going on. He went to her computer and accessed the security camera recordings. They showed that she had not entered her apartment after he left her at the building last night. She had never made it beyond the mail alcove. Frantic, he called her cell number again, reaching her voicemail once more.

He hurriedly left the apartment, running down the stairwell on the off chance that he might find her incapacitated there—or worse. But it was empty. His hands shaking, he took out his phone to call Tony.

***

The cell door opened, and a small, thin man came in. Monica couldn't see him very well in the bright light radiating through the open door. As she adapted to it, she recognized the man standing in front of her in her tiny dungeon. "Doctor!" she said. "Thank God you're here. The professor is the murderer and is holding me hostage. Get me out of here!"

Dr. Tremblay produced a thin smile. "I'm afraid I can't do that, my dear. You see, he'll be gone for a while, and I'm to keep an eye on you, as—how shall I say it—you're unappreciative of our hospitality."

Monica's face turned ashen. "You! You're in on it, too!"

"You could put it that way."

Monica was too shocked to think of a possible retort. Her mind went blank for a few moments. Then came a confusing rush of feelings: anger, fear, profound disappointment, and betrayal. Her words finally came. She tried to shame him. "How can you possibly have done all this as a pastor and a doctor?"

The doctor's anemic smile transformed into a toothy grin. "As for the former," he said, "I am not a man of God. That's just a convenient role that I play and rather well, don't you think? No, I do not have any need for God, but you see, others do, and I cater to that for my own and my brother's advantage."

"Your brother!"

"Yes. It's a long story, and maybe I'll get around to it sometime, if you're well behaved."

"So you and your brother have been doing the killings together!"

"Well, yes and no. My brother did the killing and the brutalizing; I was the surgeon. Isn't that unique in the annals of criminology?"

Monica was too shocked to reply.

"Clever covers, are they not? Who would ever suspect me and my professional brother to be involved in serial killings and abductions?"

Monica found her voice. "Diabolical, you mean." She gasped as she suddenly remembered something. She pointed an accusing finger at her jailer. “Marlene Chartrand. You and your brother killed her, didn’t you? And then you had the despicable gall and irreverence to preside over her funeral! You dominated her right up to when her casket was entombed.”

“Yes! That was supremely delightful. It was every serial murderer’s dream: control over the victim till the very last!” He let out a wild cackle that Monica likened to the laugh of the devil himself.

Monica shook her head in disgust. “I suppose you’d follow her into the afterlife, if you could? Don’t. You are destined for Hell!”

Dr. Tremblay was amused. “You are a feisty one,” he remarked. “You’ll last a long time during our procedures.”

“Procedures? You act as if you are a physician in this gruesome business, not the enabler of murder you actually are. You have shamelessly broken your Hippocratic Oath.”

“Not really,” Dr. Tremblay said. “I was playing at that too. Besides, Hippocrates is passé. Don’t we have medically induced death today? We call it euthanasia. But aren’t the doctors just executioners in that scenario?”

“No, because death is a deliberate choice of the patient. A welcome release for the sufferer. You are clever at rationalizing your dishonor and cruelty, but you do not have the truth on your side.”

“And you do, I suppose? What do you think about prisoners, convicted murderers, who are put to death in the correctional system? Do they welcome death? Is it their choice? Why not call the doctor who administers the fatal injection a state-sponsored murderer? Has he kept his Hippocratic Oath?"

Monica stared at him in disbelief. "Though I don't approve of capital punishment, it's never the less a result of a considered, lawful process, which has led to a murder conviction. It's hardly torturing and strangling some innocent person in the street."

"Capital punishment," Dr. Tremblay repeated acidly. "Nice words to sanitize an execution. My brother and I have no need to sugar-coat what we do. We know who and what we are."

Monica ignored his reply. "I'm puzzled," she said. "The recordings of your autopsies showed you were at the morgue at the times of all the serial murders."

The coroner gave her another cold smile. "I'm a doctor in more than one way; I doctored the time and date of the recordings. It was almost fool proof."

"How did you manage something like that?" Monica asked, trying to find out as much as possible about her captor.

"High-tech, my dear. My brother and I are quite good at it. Remember how the police technicians thought the surveillance devices had been jammed the night that delicious decoy was taken? They were right. We used an electronic scrambler built from scratch—talented siblings that we are."

"But I'm sure the techs would have checked out your autopsy recordings for tampering."

The doctor snorted. "You have misplaced faith in your fellow professionals. They, too, were subject to the halo effect. Unconsciously, none wanted to look too deeply into someone who is both a pastor and a doctor, a man well known to the community and a member of the sheriff's investigative team. We're all one big, happy family, aren't we?"

"What are you going to do with me?"

"So curious! But I see no harm in satisfying your need to know. After all, none of this will ever get beyond these four walls."

"Then answer my question."

The doctor gave her another grin. "Patience. Patience. All will be answered in good time. For now, let's just say you'll be our guest for a while."

"Guest? A guest is not chained to the wall. You don't give me the slightest comfort. Oh, excuse me. I have this hard mat to lay upon."

"If you're requesting some empathy and kindness, I've never had them, and neither had my parents."

"So, when you gave the eulogy for Marlene Chartrand and saw her grieving family, there wasn't one moment, a single instant, when you felt some semblance of pity?"

"Don't try to find something within me that isn't there."

"That's strange, because for a moment during the service, you looked as if you were moved."

"Probably by the supreme irony of the situation—nothing more, I am sure. By the way, don't think that I am unaware of what you are doing: trying to get into my head to exploit me. You can't manipulate another manipulator, my dear. I see through your desperate game; in fact, it amuses me, and I am turned on by it. My brother and I will ultimately win the game. Don't you know that?"

Monica ignored the comments. “Why do you call me ‘my dear’ and not by my name? Is it a condescending term? Or do you not want to know me? Is it easier to be cruel that way?”

The doctor put up his hand to silence her. “Enough for today,” he commanded and abruptly walked out of the dingy cell.

Monica heard the key turn in the cell door and then a bolt slide into place. She was once again alone with her thoughts in the semi-darkness. The exchange over Marlene Chartrand lingered in her mind. She flashed back to the dream of the lightning strike on the church where the doctor/pastor had given her funeral oration. Then she remembered the dream image of Marlene’s corpse reaching out to her. She hadn’t understood the meaning of the dream then. Could it have been a warning about the doctor? If only she had seen that was a possibility then, while she still had time. But this was only wishful thinking, she knew. It would not help her now.

She refocused on her current predicament. She was surprised she wasn’t panicked by her grim situation. She had every right to be, she knew, but she was in much more physical discomfort at the moment than mental or emotional. However, that could change, she realized. Sensory deprivation might start to set in. She remembered the experiments she had studied in college. The mind begins to break down with little or no sensory input from the environment. Psychotic symptoms—hallucinations and delusions—could well occur. She must remain calm and keep herself together, at all costs, to stand the slightest chance of surviving.

She would work out how to do this. She recalled reading that some of the inmates in concentration camps in World War II prevented themselves from going mad by learning to live in the inner world of the mind. They managed to detach from the horrors around them. She would recall accounts of how they did it. She rolled her pendant between her fingers. She had tactics of her own, too.

She thought about her attempts to influence the doctor in her favor. Perhaps that was what had calmed her, too. She sensed there was a chance she could get through to him. She knew that at some point in Marlene's eulogy and when she first met him at the sheriff's, there was a glimmer of warmth in him. He was not all cold, indifferent, or triumphant. If she could elicit one small, positive feeling or action from him, she could build on that and perhaps begin to shape his behaviors to her advantage.

CHAPTER FORTY-TWO

The evening after Monica's disappearance, Jack convened an emergency meeting with the whole investigation team. He surveyed the group around him. Despair and tension hung heavily in the room. Jeremy sat in disconsolate silence, looking preoccupied; Tony fiddled nervously with his pen; others shuffled distractedly through their papers.

"We're very sorry about Monica," Jack said to the two. For once, his face showed his true feelings, but despair was not one of them. "We *will* find her," he said reassuringly. "Let's get going at it. Tony, I believe you have a report for us."

Tony touched the screen on his tablet. "As far as we know, Monica disappeared at about dusk last evening after being escorted to the entrance of her apartment building by Jeremy. She had reported feelings that she was being followed for some days before, but there was no hard evidence of this. Jeremy first noticed she was missing at nine o'clock this morning, when she was overdue at work. We believe she didn't make it to her apartment door but was grabbed near the mailboxes in her building as she was retrieving mail. Her box was open and her mail scattered on the floor. Nothing else unusual was found in the hallway. However, a nearby janitor's door was unlocked. Upon entering the room, we saw that a chair and small table were knocked over, as though a struggle had occurred. The room connects to a boiler room in the basement, which leads to a door to a back alley.

This door was also unlocked. The janitor tells us that these doors are regularly locked. All this indicates she was likely taken to the alley and transported from there."

"How about prints?" Jack asked.

"We have numerous different prints from the areas, including the doors. We ran them on the databases. There were no hits."

"Any witnesses?"

"The team fanned out through the building and neighborhood, door-to-door. Eighty-three locals were questioned. Only one, a street person who hangs around in the area, noticed activity around dusk last night at the alley side of the building. It was too dark to see much, he said, but he saw what looked like a large vehicle idling near the alley door. He approached it, looking for a handout, but it took off fast."

"Any security cameras in the area?"

"There is one in the alley, but it wasn't working. A security camera in the building hallway near the mail alcove was also not operating. Our techs say both were deliberately disabled."

"All too familiar," Jack remarked. "Anything to add from the state police or FBI?"

The state police detective spoke up first. "We have, of course, put out a missing person's bulletin on local, state, and national media, in conjunction with the FBI."

Professor Greenwood cleared his throat. "This has all the earmarks of the serial killer, not the least of which is his tendency to leave the crime scene bereft of clues. To my mind, his grabbing her is a logical follow-up to the murder of the police decoy.

Some of his intentions in that murder were to outwit the police and demoralize them. The seizure of one of the prime investigators on his case furthers those aims."

Jeremy raised his voice. "Monica is missing, and the killer has probably got her, and we're still talking, for Christ's sake, about the killer's motivations. Just what are we going to do to find her?"

The FBI liaison spoke up. "We should continue to focus on our current suspects. The facts are that Madera and Vallencourt are the only two external people who knew she was on the investigation team and who would want to do her harm. One of them took her. I believe the murderer has made his first mistake: he has allowed us to close in on him by exclusion. In that regard, I'm authorized to double the number of agents on the case, and I've done so today. We'll continue our search for Madera in the areas he has frequented in the past, namely the downtown and BDSM scene. We're banking on the likelihood he will be unable to resist contacts with playmates and prostitutes. The search for the black SUV he was reportedly driving also continues. As well, we advise doing another search on the Vallencourt property. We'll bring in portable ground-penetrating radar units to probe any suspicious disturbances in the ground, aided by drone surveillance."

One of the NOPD detectives added, "We'll put the word out on the street about her disappearance. If we're lucky, one of our informers may have picked up some information on her."

"Okay," Jack said. "I'll be setting up a twenty-four-hour situation room staffed by myself and two senior officers. All information or developments will be funneled through the situation room." He handed out contact information cards. "Furthermore, there will be a daily conference at 5:00 p.m. sharp with the entire investigation team, until further notice."

As the group disbanded, Tony approached Jeremy, who was still sitting at the conference table. "How are you doing, Jeremy?" he asked, placing his hand on his friend's shoulder. "You were pretty quiet at the meeting today, until you tore a strip off everybody."

Jeremy shook his head in anger. "There was very little new today," he complained. "The same old approaches. The same worn concepts. We keep hammering on the usual suspects, thinking we're going to get different results. Meanwhile, Monica's life hangs in the balance, if she hasn't already been murdered." He banged the table with his fist.

"I think you're angry at yourself, too, Jeremy, and feeling guilty over her disappearance."

Jeremy lowered his eyes. "I let her down, Tony. I didn't cover all her vulnerabilities, and he got her. And to think I worried she wouldn't have my back. I ended up not having hers."

"You got distracted by that security alarm at your office."

"Yeah, it was likely the murderer snookering me. I was taken in like an amateur."

"We can look back now with twenty-twenty vision, Jeremy. But before she disappeared, there was no hard evidence she was being followed. It really looked like she was unnerved by the decoy's murder and by what Jenny said. She seemed to be overreacting to things. We've got to get a grip. Beating ourselves up isn't helping Monica, either."

Jeremy exhaled slowly. "You're right, Tony. This is getting us nowhere."

Tony nodded. "And some good things did come out of this meeting today. The FBI liaison said it: 'The murderer has made his first mistake' by taking Monica. She was right. It's got to be Madera or Vallencourt. We're on the right track, Jeremy." He noticed Jeremy's grimace. "What's on your mind?"

"Nothing."

Tony was not convinced but let it go. "I think you might be underrating Monica, too. She's smart and knows how to defend herself if she gets a chance. She was surprised at her mailbox, but if the murderer cuts her any slack—if he doesn't watch his back around her—he'll regret it."

"I hope to God you're right, Tony."

"There's one more thing. I think doubling down on our informers is a good idea, too."

"That's worth a further shot," Jeremy agreed. "I'll be calling in the debts for all of mine in the next hour and a half.... I'll tell you something, Tony. This is more than either Madera or Vallencourt. I have a feeling about all of this that keeps on coming to me. I don't see how yet, but the answer to the murders is there, staring all of us in the face; we just don't see it yet, because we don't expect it to be there. The problem is our mindset, Tony."

Tony stared at Jeremy in silence. He knew Jeremy did not have a rational explanation for his feelings. While Jeremy's hunches were often right, he could also sometimes be wrong—spectacularly wrong. For the time being, Jeremy had to work out these feelings for himself, Tony thought. At the very least, it might give his friend hope in this dark time.

CHAPTER FORTY-THREE

Jeremy slept restlessly the night of the case conference. He awoke several times agonizing about Monica's disappearance. Her body had not yet been found. Was she still alive, or were they all in for a gruesome shock? A grim consolation crossed his mind: If she were dead, they would soon find her body. The murderer would see to that.

He anguished further. What were the missing pieces he needed to find her? Why couldn't he come up with them? He remembered what he had said to Tony after the conference: "Our mindset is the problem." He knew that, somehow, he had to change his own. But how?

Jeremy mulled over the investigation throughout the early morning. His thoughts ultimately concentrated on one central theme. He knew Tony would be skeptical about it but called to arrange a meeting with him regardless.

The two met at Tony's office at nine. Tony noticed Jeremy looked pale and haggard, but there was a kind of fire in his friend's eyes.

"Do you remember I was talking to you about changing our mindset?" Jeremy began, almost breathlessly. "I keep on thinking about Officer Crosby's murder. It went without a hitch for the murderer—too smoothly. We attributed this to his intelligence and impeccable planning."

"What are you getting at, Jeremy?"

"I mean, I'm wondering if the murderer had advance notice of our plans to decoy him that night."

"But that's impossible. Nobody outside of the team could have known."

"Right. Nobody outside of the team."

Tony gaped at Jeremy. "Are you suggesting that the murderer is someone on the team?"

"I'm seriously thinking about that. He's managed to skillfully evade detection in all of these murders so far. What if all of this is an inside job?"

"You can't be serious, Jeremy. It's got to be lack of sleep that's talking. Maybe your grief and shock. It's paranoid."

"But let's look at this some more, Tony. The FBI profiler recommended we focus on Madera and Vallencourt in Monica's disappearance. Her reasoning was that they were the only ones who knew she was on the investigative team and would want to kill her. But that excludes the investigative team members themselves, who also have that knowledge."

"So you think one of the team made off with her?" Tony asked, completely dismayed.

"Isn't it a possibility that the killer infiltrated the team since the very beginning?"

Tony looked flabbergasted. "But everybody's vetted. Nobody has the background or personality profile to be a serial murderer."

"That we know of. But what if all the information wasn't available to the FBI or other police agencies in their background checks? What if the murderer managed to conceal his red flags?"

"You've got a suspect in mind?"

Jeremy's face darkened. "I've never taken to the professor from the start."

"Professor Greenwood?" Tony asked, his voice betraying his astonishment.

"I know it sounds crazy, Tony."

"It *is* crazy. For starters, the guy has an airtight alibi for the night of the Martinez murder. He wasn't even in town."

"Look, Tony. We'll come to that. For now, let's set the alibi aside for a while. Let me point out a few things."

Tony shrugged. "Okay. Let's have it."

"First of all, a general impression. There's something phony and unemotional about him."

"He's a professor, an academic. The guy's a thinker, not necessarily the feeling type."

"It's more than that, Tony. I've watched his eyes during the briefings. They were cold and unempathetic—even when the worst details of the murders came out."

"Say that's true," Tony said. "You and I both know it takes more than lacking empathy to make a serial killer. Is that all you've got on him?"

"What were his lunches with Monica all about?"

"Is jealousy behind your suspicions about the professor?"

Jeremy ignored Tony's question. "We know the killer studies his victims before he murders. What if he was gathering information about her habits, her likes and dislikes? Maybe he was trying to determine when and how she would be most vulnerable."

"Or maybe he was simply flattered by her interest in him."

"Okay," Jeremy replied. "What about this? He came across the missing Clairmont history book, apparently by chance, at a book sale. This book may be the only copy in existence, as far as we know, and likely contains circumstantial evidence against the Vallencourt family. What are the odds against that happening?"

"Jeremy, we've been through all this. The professor explained there could be nineteen other copies floating around. That makes the odds better."

"Would you bet on the horses with these odds?"

"So you think that the professor stole it?"

"More than likely. And he was trying to frame Vallencourt by miraculously finding a 'copy' of it for us to examine."

Tony shook his head. "Jeremy, if you brought that as evidence to the district attorney, he would throw you out of his office. We both know that."

Jeremy was unfazed. "There's one more thing. When we met with Professor Greenwood in his office, he unlocked a cabinet to retrieve the history book in it. As far as I could see, there were just a bunch of old books in it. Why would he have them under lock and key?"

"Well, he's a book collector, and maybe these books are valuable. He knew the history book was rare, and maybe a piece of background evidence, too."

"I hear what you're saying, Tony, but what if the lock wasn't only to protect what's in there, but to conceal something that's in there?"

“Like what?”

“I don’t know. It’s a hunch at this point.”

Tony sighed. “Anyway, let’s come back to the basic fact that the professor has an iron-clad alibi; he was in Washington at FBI headquarters the night of the Martinez murder. He couldn’t have been in two places at the same time. He couldn’t have murdered her. That blows away your whole argument.”

Jeremy smiled. “You’re right that he couldn’t have been in two places at once, Tony. Maybe he didn’t have to be. What if he had an accomplice to do the murder?”

“What!” Tony said. “We’ve never picked up any signs of an accomplice. How do you prove that?”

“I can’t. But if it is the professor, that’s what must have happened.”

“Jeremy, I know you’re trying to get a new point of view on the case, but all of this is a bunch of guesses right now—some of them pretty wild. You can’t talk about this to anyone else. Jack would drum you out of the investigation if you did.” But his friend’s face told Tony he wasn’t going to give up on the matter. How far would he go with this?

CHAPTER FORTY-FOUR

Monica dreamed she was a child again. It was one of her family's August vacations. She frolicked on the warm, sunny Massachusetts beach with her brother and sister—another carefree day in a never-ending summer.

She awoke slowly, forgetting where she was for a few moments; she had managed to escape her dire situation for a while. Then her senses were assaulted by the harsh, dark reality of her cell. Her body protested as she sat up on the cold, hard mat. She felt a sharp pain in the back of her neck and the aching stiffness in her back.

She heard the door unlock. She was blinded once again by the intense light as the door opened. The doctor did not greet her but silently placed beside her a bowl of unsweetened gruel with a little milk and a bottle of water.

She left her meal untouched. "I see I've got a continental breakfast this morning," she said.

The doctor smiled. "A cutting sense of humor," he said. "I like that. I have something else for you."

He produced a roll of foam as an underlay for her mat.

She resisted another sarcastic comment and simply thanked him. Breakfast aside, she thought, it was his first act of kindness toward her. Was she correct about his having some small measure of good in him?

"You do have a heart, after all?"

"If that's a metaphor for kindness, my answer is no. I was only thinking we need you supple and fit for our procedures, no more."

She didn't believe him. He was just reluctant to reveal to her a softer side, which she would ruthlessly exploit. He might be in conflict over what he was doing, and she would bring that out to her advantage, too. Meanwhile, she needed to elicit more of this kindness. She rubbed her wrist where the steel cuff had chaffed her, hoping to play to whatever part of the doctor remained within him. "This is going to get infected."

He left for a moment and returned with a Band-Aid and antiseptic, which he applied to her wrist.

She thanked him once again. She felt a small burst of hope. Against the odds, she seemed to be succeeding in drawing some caring from him. But she reminded herself not to be too confident and overplay her hand. He was smart and might recognize what she was trying to do.

She began to eat her gruel, looking at him between spoonfuls. "Not bad," she said. "Yesterday, you said you would satisfy my curiosity. Does that still hold?"

"Certainly, why not?"

Monica nodded approvingly. "A man of your word, I see." She brandished her spoon as she spoke. "I was thinking about Charles Vallencourt last night. Were you two trying to frame him with the murders, all along?"

"That's very perceptive of you, Monica. I only told you about how we used the scrambler to cast suspicion on Vallencourt, but you've correctly generalized from there. Very good."

Monica perked up another notch. Hearing her name had never meant so much. It was the first time he had used it. He was recognizing her as a person.

"We've been trying to frame him since day one."

"Like Marlene's body in the cemetery?"

The doctor's eyes lit up with undisguised glee. "That's right!" he said. "That was one of our best ploys. Placing the body near Vallencourt's back quarter and salting it with the cocoa tree materials, which existed only on his property, were masterful strokes, don't you think? But the *coup de gras* was placing some of her blood in the cocoa grove to suggest the body had been there at some point."

"So, where was she killed?"

"In the cemetery."

"Why there and not on Vallencourt's property itself?"

"Because the body might never have been found if it was done somewhere on the Vallencourt plantation. The graveyard was close enough to Vallencourt's to cast some suspicion on him and would add to the general horror of the murder, would it not?"

"All of that was quite ingenious," Monica said. "You're like Conan Doyle's Moriarty."

The doctor grinned. "I admire him as a villain."

"I can understand the attraction of one master criminal to another," Monica said. She knew that the doctor was just getting warmed up in recounting his and the professor's exploits.

"We carried out a number of interesting gambits," he said. "Take the Clairmont history book, for instance. We stole it from the museum hoping Vallencourt might be suspected of the theft, and it succeeded brilliantly. Unfortunately, the curator talked about Jeremy visiting her at the museum and that she had told him that she had read the entire book and knew the history of the bodies on the outskirts of the Vallencourt property. We killed her, hoping to raise suspicions that Vallencourt did it because she knew too much. And then we had her body for the cocoa grove and cemetery ploys."

"It doesn't get any more devious than that."

"Precisely. And we even had Jeremy wondering if his visit to the museum had something to do with the curator's murder—that her murder wasn't just a coincidence."

"How did you know about that?"

The doctor smiled. "He told Tony, and from there it got back to Jack and the investigation team."

"And of course, since both of you were so brilliantly placed, you found that out. I'll bet you got a lot of useful information as team members."

"It was the perfect scheme, wasn't it? If you want to get away with a crime, infiltrate the police. We knew your every move; we knew exactly what was known about us by the police at all times," he said with a note of triumph.

"So that's why Officer Crosby's murder went off that smoothly. You knew everything about the operation to begin with."

"*Voilà*! And the decoy met her end. We beat the police at their own game, completely demoralizing them. We laughed the whole way as we made our escape upriver that night."

"Once again, I can't help but admire your ingenuity and your total control over the situation.... I suspect you and your brother also used his position on the investigating team to try to frame Madera with the Elena Martinez murder," Monica said.

"You *are* a deep one!" the doctor said. "Yes, we knew of his preference for young playmates and eventually tracked the Martinez girl. My brother posed as an experienced edge player and arranged a rendezvous with her. Of course, we knew Madera would immediately be suspected of her murder once it was learned she was in the BDSM scene. The finishing touch was the anonymous telephone tip my brother made to the police implicating Madera in the murder." He smiled and looked at his watch. "But I'm afraid I must tear myself away from this enchanting conversation; I've got to prepare for when my brother gets back."

After the doctor had left, she became solemn and anxious. Perhaps, she thought, she was greatly overestimating her chances of influencing the doctor. In fact, she was probably kidding herself that she could turn him around. After all, he was a conspirator in multiple murders, rapes, and mutilations. She stood a good chance of simply winding up like the others. No one knew where she was. She couldn't expect rescue and had a zero chance of escaping. Most certainly, no one had a clue these evil brothers were at the root of the murders or that they were even brothers. As the doctor said, they would never be suspected.

She felt a surge of panic. Then the panic turned into anger. It was an unbelievable situation, she told herself. What were the chances of ending up a captive of two serial murderers? Why her? Life, maybe God himself, had pulled a fast one on her.... But her rational side began to argue back. Neither luck nor fate had anything to do with it. She had made a conscious choice to catch criminals as a career. She had always understood that there was an element of risk in that. The criminals could also come after her, and in this case, they did. And less than a few weeks ago, she and Jeremy could also have been killed by that madman, Madera. She had to quit worrying and feeling sorry for herself and find a way out of this.

Her thoughts turned to her confinement. It was rare that serial murderers confined their victims. Why would these two go to all the trouble of stalking and abducting her, only to confine her for days like this? What were they trying to get out of it? And what was so pressing that the professor apparently wasn't even around? By all she knew about serial murderers, she should have been dead by now.

Were they just toying with her, keeping her alive, literally in the dark about when she was to be finally brutalized and killed? This would fit with their needs to dominate and take pleasure in another's pain. But if so, why was the doctor doing small favors for her? Was he playing a counter game with her? Was he stringing her along to believe that she was eliciting kindness from him, building her hopes for survival? Perhaps, any day now, he would pull the plug on her. He would have the last laugh, and as he said, ultimately win the game.

She mulled over these questions for what seemed a long time, though she had no way of tracking time or even knowing if it was night or day. Was all that an attempt to disorient and torture her?

She felt her heart speeding up and her breathing shallowing. She knew she was on the verge of panicking again. She needed to regain emotional control and began by slowing and deepening her breathing.

As she calmed, she remembered the last spiritual exercise she had read in the old book but had never carried out. She decided to try it; she hoped it would measure up to its lofty promise. She needed nothing short of a miracle right now.

She touched her pendant, which she had read would help connect her with the one consciousness. She focused her attention inwardly to ever deeper levels of awareness....

After an unknown lapse of time, she opened her eyes and gradually became aware of her dark cell. She couldn't recall if she had carried out the full meditative exercise or not. She may have fallen asleep. Then she remembered the nightmare. She had been lost in a forest at night. It was so black that she could not see any paths she might follow. A storm came, the lightning periodically illuminating the sky and the trees, though not enough for her to find her way out. The thunderous skies frightened her.

She was pelted by a cold drizzle. She sensed that there were predatory animals lurking unseen around her. She heard something in between the thunderclaps: the cry of a bird high in the sky. But then she had woken up—or thought she had awakened—in the deep shadows of her cell.

CHAPTER FORTY-FIVE

Monica began another morning in her bleak cell. At least she thought it was morning, since the doctor was there with her breakfast. This time, he'd added a little sweetener to her gruel.

Monica thanked him again. She found herself eating with a surprisingly good appetite given her perilous situation. Perhaps it was the sweetener, she thought. "I have a question," she announced.

"That's not unusual for you," he said. "What's on your mind?"

"Is your brother back yet?"

"No, but he'll be here soon."

"Will you tell me where he's been?"

"I suppose it'll do no harm to answer you. He'd taken a holiday to abduct you, but he had to cut it short."

She looked at him curiously.

"Jack, your team leader, had asked that the whole team meet for daily briefings at NOPD headquarters. You see, they're frantically searching for you, including hordes of FBI agents and state police. Your boss, Jeremy, and his sidekick, Tony, are the most frantic of them all. You're also quite a celebrity in the media.... But they're burning a lot of gas and flailing about uselessly as, according to my brother, they have no clue yet who actually took you or where you are. They're focusing on the usual bogus suspects, Madera and Vallencourt, as we hoped. In fact, this was our main intention in seizing you in the first place. At any rate, the police are tearing up the woods and bayous around Vallencourt's and dredging the social cesspools in the city in search of Madera." The doctor laughed. "It couldn't have worked out any better."

He paused to gauge her reaction. Getting none, he went on with his account. "There's more good news. My brother thinks the team meetings will soon be reduced, since they are accomplishing nothing. He believes the team will be asked to be available if needed, so he'll be here soon enough. I would imagine that's unsettling for you," he remarked with a smile.

Monica said nothing. She was not going to show fear to him under any circumstances. Instead, she made a provocative statement. "Everything seems to depend on your brother. He seems to be running the show."

The doctor's smile faded. "He was always the dominant one, if that's what you mean—even when we were kids. He used to be the neighborhood bully and was to me too, if I didn't cooperate with him."

"What would he want you to do?"

"To be an accomplice in his bullying. I'd set up other kids so he could corner them. Of course, I'd also be the loyal witness whenever angry parents would confront ours about the bullying, and that was often."

"That must have been quite a burden on you."

"For a while. At first, I wasn't much for violence and used to feel guilty about it. But the guilt went away in time, and I began to enjoy it, too."

"As much as he did?"

"No. He took particular pleasure in it and began to view sadistic sexual material."

"But you didn't?"

"No, I never did make the connection between sex and violence."

"Because of guilt?"

The doctor didn't answer.

"It sounds like you got pushed into it, helping him with his deviant sexual acts. That must have made you angry on some level."

The doctor remained silent, but Monica saw his jaw muscles tighten. She knew she was pressing the right buttons. "You and he appear quite different," she said. "I think you've spent too much of your life tied to your brother's whims and wishes—even today."

There was no reply from the doctor once again. Monica noticed the tension seemed to spread to his neck and shoulders. Could she make use of the anger she was tapping into? She must not overdo it, though. He could easily rebuff her attempts to plumb his emotional depths and simply walk out. She could not afford that. She sensed her time was running out.

She changed the topic. "So, you were the surgeon in the murders. The NOPD coroner said the surgeries were very masterful…. I'm very curious. What was done with the ovaries afterward? Were they kept?"

"Yes. My brother froze them as trophies."

"Trophies of what?"

"They represented his victories: total dominance over the female victims and the destruction of their female physical identity."

"And they were used for his sexual gratification, I assume?" The doctor's silence confirmed her guess. She decided to press on with the topic. "So, here you are, enabling his sadistic sexual fantasies, though they probably revolt you." She saw that his entire body had stiffened. "Did your parents know of the bullying toward you?"

"Of course they did. They were bullies themselves, especially Jean."

"Your mother?"

"If that's what you want to call her."

"She was particularly violent?"

"Yes. She called it discipline, but really it was simply daily beatings. We never understood why most of the time, but we do now. It was all part of the family shaping us to become violent ourselves. It was the family tradition."

"What do you mean?"

"The family's tradition—indeed, its legacy—is murder. This is the family's dark secret. They are really intergenerational murderers, going back, at least, to their arrival as settlers in Louisiana in the eighteenth century. And we assume that their murderous history went back a long time before that in Acadia and France."

Dr. Tremblay was amused at Monica's look of total surprise and shock. "Yes, it's true—unsuspected even by you, a seasoned criminal profiler. It isn't in the criminology journals, is it? You see, each generation of the family carefully groomed chosen offspring, mostly the boys, to learn the art of serial murder. The knowledge was passed on like other families pass on their religious beliefs or their family lore, or their skills. Organized crime families, like the Mafia or Cosa Nostra, pass on their criminal skills, including murdering, to each generation and have for hundreds of years. Our family, too, passed on the motivation to murder and the skills to do so, including how to evade detection. These were core to the very identity of the family."

"So your family was responsible for the long history of murders near the Vallencourt property?"

"Of course. The Vallencourts were the intended scapegoats for our family's crimes for over two hundred years." The doctor laughed. "We even started the rumor that they were Louisiana werewolves, the rougarous, to raise the suspicions of the more superstitious locals. My ancestors changed the story of the so-called ghost ship that arrived outside of New Orleans in the late 1700s. Most of the passengers and crew had died of a virulent, infectious disease, but my family told the locals that all had been killed by a rougarou, which escaped and now lived among them as a Vallencourt near Clairmont. Of course, the Vallencourts' eccentric, reclusive traits gave more credibility to the story for some and helped our efforts to frame them in general."

"I'd imagine planting the indigo fibers on the victims' bodies was part of your attempts to frame Vallencourt?"

"Exactly. This was a family tradition that my brother and I kept up. We knew the police would find remnants of indigo fibers on Vallencourt's estate, which were originally produced there in the old dye and textile sheds in the 1800s."

"Exactly how did your family groom its children to become murderers?"

"They programmed our young and vulnerable minds; they brainwashed us, using techniques perfected by previous generations."

Monica leaned forward, mesmerized by these bizarre statements. "Like what?"

"They used methods that spoke to children. Stories that told how the family murdered and justified that as moral. These were like children's tales, which often advise young listeners on matters of conduct and morality. Our family's stories were the dark flip side of this. The stories were even told to us before bedtime so their messages would replay in our dreams and lodge in our unconscious minds. It resembled hypnosis."

"The word 'diabolical' comes to mind again," Monica said.

The doctor laughed. "The stories were diabolical, indeed— the devil's doctrine, no less."

"But yet, unlike your brother, the psycho-programming didn't work with you entirely, did it?"

"I've always had a stubborn, individualistic streak," he said. "Whether that's hereditary or the influence of other people in my life, I don't know. But that part gradually became buried."

"But not completely, because you don't do the killing."

Thc doctor seemed disturbed by her assertion but did not reveal his feelings.

"There's a contradiction here. The night of the Martinez murder, your brother was away in Washington. That left you to commit the murder, which you say you don't do. How do you account for that?"

The doctor smiled. “You are a thinker, aren’t you? Contrary to what you may believe, I played my usual role that night. An accomplice we hired actually did the murder and the other brutalizing. He was a contract killer from New York—the first and only third party we’ve involved.”

“And that gave your brother the perfect alibi.”

“Yes, presenting a workshop at the FBI! Alibis don’t get any better, do they? We thought we’d better do that for at least one murder, as a bit of insurance, you understand. Otherwise, someone on the team might eventually get the idea that the murders were an inside job.”

Monica was satisfied that the doctor wasn’t the actual serial killer. This gave her a better chance of influencing him to her advantage. She went on to ask about how the brothers’ family could have gotten away with such crimes over so many generations.

“Because their murdering skills were honed by centuries of practice,” the doctor said in a matter-of-fact tone. “Law enforcement was also minimal to non-existent for many years around Clairmont, and the police that were present were often bribed by our family to look the other way.” He laughed again. “It is ironic that the locals suspected the Vallencourts of doing the bribery. This suited our purposes. As long as the Vallencourts were the focus of suspicion, we were safe from exposure.”

“So how is it that you and your brother ended up with different surnames?”

“We were adopted out when he was twelve and I was nine. This followed a schoolteacher reporting us to Child Welfare for child abuse. Though their policy was to work with families to keep them together, the abuse was judged to be so serious in our case that an exception was made, and we were taken into care. They were unable to find an adoptive home that would take both of us, so we were separated and took the surnames of our adoptive parents. Some years later, our adoption records were lost in a flood, and my brother and I lost contact. A few years ago, we located one another through a former member of my parent's household staff. By that time, our biological parents had died."

"So you came under your brother's spell, again?"

"In a sense. It did not take long for my brother to start talking to me about his violent ambitions and carrying on the family's traditions. He persuaded me to cross the line from what had been aiding his bullying as kids to helping him murder as adults."

"Did something cause him to cross that line?"

"It was a young woman. He began having a sexual affair with a graduate student at the university, but she broke off with him when he tried to introduce her to sadistic sex. He couldn't take the rejection, and this seemed to be his trigger."

"Do either of you have heirs to continue on with the family tradition?"

"No. My brother was planning to have children for that very purpose, but I stood my ground on that. I said I'd help him with one murder spree but on condition we would be the last generation of murderers.... You will be our last victim." He noticed the pleading look in her eyes. "There's nothing I can do about that," he added.

"You can if you choose to. I know there's some decency in you."

"Too much is made of free choice. I made a pact with my brother, and as you say, I am a man of my word. This will finally bring an end to the killings."

"By murdering me? Don't you see the madness in that?"

"But it would be for the greater good, wouldn't it? One more murder saves many lives."

Monica gaped at him.

The doctor had some chilling final words. "I wouldn't try to engage my brother on this matter. He's not as tolerant as I am. He's a man of action."

After the doctor left, Monica lapsed into a twilight state. Her captor's last words reverberated in her mind. She knew the professor's return was imminent. She had never experienced such a total feeling of helplessness and vulnerability. She pressed her pendant tightly between her fingers, trying to regain emotional control. But fatigue from the shocking dialogue with the doctor overcame her, and she fell into sleep.

She experienced another dream, or, more accurately, a continuation of her previous dream. Once again, she was back in the stormy forest, lost, afraid, and unprotected. The cold, wind-driven rain pelted her mercilessly. There were growling sounds from what she thought were wolves in the dark bushes nearby. Panicked, she ran away blindly into the night. The shadowy animals followed her, slinking low to the ground. Then she heard the bird, once again, coming ever closer to her. She saw the yellow eyes of an eagle as lightning flashed across the sky. The great bird circled above. It had discovered her.

CHAPTER FORTY-SIX

The doctor returned after what she thought was many hours. He brought her a hospital gown and a pail of water to wash herself. For the first time, he brought a second meal: a sandwich and some salad.

"Your brother's here, isn't he?" she asked.

He nodded.

"So, is this the last meal before the execution? Part of the preparation of the sacrificial victim?"

He gave her a wry smile and left.

She ate the sandwich ravenously, but she refused to wash and gown herself. She would not give them the satisfaction.

Her hunger satiated, her thoughts returned to something even more basic: survival. Dr. Tremblay's warning not to engage his brother reverberated in her mind. If the professor showed up in her cell, how should she handle him? He was the murderous sibling, after all, and could well snuff out her life, right then and there, if she tried to dialogue. She dared not contemplate what he might do to her first. Her heart started throbbing, and she took in a few deep, slow breaths. If he came close enough, she might be able to aim a knockout karate kick to his throat. Maybe he had the key for her cuffs. But how realistic was a move like that? She was weak from inactivity and minimal nutrition and might not be able to land the blow successfully. And what if he fell backward, out of reach? No. A kick was a last resort.

She'd have to ad lib it—look to him for cues to what she should do or not do. She would initiate nothing. If he began to talk, she would mirror him. She knew also never to show fear to a sadist or to seek empathy. He would scorn both.

If he began to talk to her without antipathy, there were a few tactics she could employ. She knew that he enjoyed admiration. She might be able to use that, as she did with his brother. She knew of his love for the psychohistory of serial killers. Engaging him on that should buy some time. He was also a logical guy, that is, outside of his sadistic killing. It was his strength, but hers as well; she might be able to turn his into a vulnerability by boxing him in logically. She could even begin to sow the seeds of sibling discord by implying that his brother was critical of him and might even betray him. This was particularly dangerous, she knew. Another last resort.

Some hours later, she heard the sounds of the heavy door being opened again, startling her out of a daze. Her heart pounded as she saw the tall figure in the blinding light of the doorway. It was the professor, the epitome of evil itself. She rose from the floor to a standing position, hoping he would come within range of her feet. But he did not. He stood there in ominous silence. His features became more evident as her eyes adapted to the light. He stared at her without blinking; his face looked hard. She had never seen the cruelty in his features until now. How did she ever miss it?

Her heart accelerated wildly. She held her breath to try to control it. Was he going to kill her at this very moment? No fear! she reminded herself, and in turn, she stood silently, staring back at him, expressionless.

A thin, cold smile crossed his face. "The fly in the spider's web is defiant," he remarked in a mocking voice. "Apparently unafraid of the sting to come."

"The spider may think itself omnipotent, but it can also become the prey," Monica retorted, looking him directly in the eye.

"But not by you, little lady. In case you haven't noticed, my pursuer is now my prisoner." His smile broadened.

She straightened up as far as her chains would allow. "They're looking for me, you know. Right now. They won't give up until they find you and then your brother."

"You forget I'm on the investigating team. I know they haven't the slightest idea where you are or who has you." Monica decided to chance it. "But there's someone on the team who's on to you and making sure you're out of the loop on this." She hoped she'd get away with the bluff.

Professor Greenwood laughed harshly. "A very clever ruse," he remarked. "Tell me, what is he or she supposed to have on me?"

"A lot. Beginning with the question of how you really came into possession of the Clairmont history book."

He wagged an accusing finger at her. "My brother told you that."

She, too, poked a finger in his direction. "I knew it before your brother spilled the beans."

His smile faded. “And what else do you claim to have? We’ll go easier on you if you reveal what you know.”

“You’re aware of how evidence trails develop. By now, everyone on the team knows it was you. Think about it. What have you done or left out there that has already provided the final clues to identify you as the murderer? They’ll find you, and if you harm me, they won’t be reading you your Miranda rights. They’ll kill you. Let me go now, and you can still make your escape, change your identity, and disappear somewhere.”

For a moment, he looked as if he would lunge at her, and she readied herself to inflict a disabling, if not fatal kick. But the fury left his face suddenly, and he seemed to relax.

“All in good time,” he said in a veiled threat.

She made the pretense of relaxing. “But how much time do you really have?” she warned.

He said nothing and turned to go out the door. As he turned, she saw his wristwatch. It was the expensive brand of Swiss watch they had been searching for…. The puzzle was finally coming together. But would she survive to tell the tale?

Dr. Tremblay brought her supper shortly after his brother had gone and then left without saying a word. This was the second time he had been silent with her. Was he instructed not to engage with her, or did it signify something else? She spent a restless night after that. She was awake much of the time, limbering herself up with whatever stretches she could do and practicing karate kicks.

She heard her cell door suddenly unlock and open. She stood up in in a half-karate stance, praying it wasn't too evident. She hoped it was Dr. Tremblay—the lesser evil of the two—but it was not. The feared silhouette of the professor presented itself in the doorway. He stood there silently once more.

She stared at him pensively. What was he thinking about? Was this her last conscious moment upon the earth? She ran through the karate moves in her mind once again. If he went down and was still breathing, she'd finish him off by wrapping a chain tightly around his throat. The gruesome image gave her some satisfaction.

She felt rage galvanizing her body—partly for retribution, mostly to survive. She flashed back to what Jeremy had said about how his body had taken over his mind in his desperate fight with Madera. This must be how it begins, she thought.

He stepped toward her. Her moment of vengeance seemed imminent. The murderer lurking within her was poised for action.

Then her abductor paused just outside of kicking range. He grinned at her. He had not missed her DEFCON 1 readiness level. "Don't worry," he said. "It's not your time yet. And by the way, don't expect me to get within five feet of you until I'm ready."

"But your time is running out," she reminded him. "They're going to be here any moment. Free me and leave while you still can. It's the logical thing to do, is it not? You'll survive."

He laughed. "As good a bluff as I've ever encountered. You'd make an excellent poker player."

The stakes are a lot higher than that, she thought. She set her jaw and gave him a look of defiance.

"You can stand down now," he said. "I'm only here to bring you breakfast." He backed out of the door and returned with a food tray.

"I suppose it's drugged," she remarked.

"No, no," he countered. "When it's your turn, we want you fully awake; otherwise, what's the point?" He pushed the tray over to her with his foot.

She ignored the food. "So what *is* the point?"

The professor smiled. "You're the cutting-edge profiler. You tell me."

"I could provide you with a whole list, but what turns your crank?"

Professor Greenwood chuckled. "You are a clever one, stringing me along as much as you can. You hope to find that ingredient in me you can turn to your advantage. I admire that. We're not so different, you and me. You're an exploiter, like me. I sensed that right away in you. It was that and your cleverness and spunk that drew me to you in the first place."

"Well, I'm glad to see our luncheon dates were not only to gauge my vulnerabilities," she said sarcastically.

"That was there, but I was attracted by the challenge you would present to me to abduct you. Actually, I was a bit disappointed in you and Jeremy. He fell for the security-call ploy like a sap, and you were ridiculously easy to capture. It was, as the saying goes, like a walk in the park. Though you're making up for it now with your brilliant resistance. But keep in mind there is danger in this, for I always rise to a challenge."

"That's it, isn't it? You always have to win, don't you? That's why you're here now: to prod me into ever greater resistance, forcing me to become ever more resourceful in opposing you. It turns you on."

He threw his head back and laughed uproariously.

"You don't deny it. So, it's true then. In fact, your ultimate goal is to outdo all the serial murderers of the past. This is the biggest reason you're so fascinated by the psychohistory of these vicious killers. You want to know about the competition."

He looked at her admiringly. "You get an A plus for identifying the key factor in my profile." He smiled. "But where does that get you?"

She smiled back, ignoring his question. "But don't you see? With your record of serial murders, confounding the police for so long and even infiltrating their investigation team, you've already accomplished your goal of being the best in history. It's time to get out before the police take away your title by killing you. Free me and go write a memoir staking out your claim."

"Ingenious arguments. Highly creative! But you overlook one thing."

She looked at him quizzically.

"What if my crowning achievement and my claim to the title depend on my murdering one of the police team's principal investigators—you? And then I can retire." He grinned triumphantly.

She found herself lost for words, frozen by the cold fear rising within her, despite her desperate effort to control it.

The professor waited a few moments for her reply. Getting none, he turned to walk to the door. “Checkmate,” he called back.

Monica had never felt such despair and anguish. She knew now that, despite her wiles, she had failed to convince the professor to release her. She knew, too, that he was too cagey to allow her to take him down physically, even if she had the strength.

She asked herself why she had not seen through him in the past. She knew that psychopaths could be deceptively charming, but there was more to it. She needed to admit that she had let herself be mesmerized by his intellect and knowledge, instead of allowing her intuitive side to guide her.

She took further stock of her situation. Her meditation and use of the stone seemed unhelpful so far. At best, they may have been linked to two dreams the meanings of which were not at all apparent to her. Was there no way she could alter her fate? She had no answers to that, except praying for a miracle. She felt it ironic that this was her last choice. She remembered telling Jeremy how she was not a good Catholic and even had doubts about the Trinity. But she must pray now to whomever or whatever might listen.

She closed her eyes and began her prayer, pressing her pendant tightly in her fingers. After a few minutes, she experienced what she thought was a vivid daydream or perhaps a vision; she couldn’t tell which. She was back in the dark, stormy forest.

The eagle now descended from the sky and landed on the soaked ground next to her. She felt a gentle breeze from its wings as it landed—the same breeze she had experienced in a meditation before her abduction. The eagle closed its huge wings around her to protect her from the storm. The wings were warm, powerful, and loving. She was reminded of the presence she felt when she dreamed of her grandmother after Marlene's funeral.

She awoke in her cell, or perhaps she was in that twilight state again. There, in the near darkness, she saw a great red eagle standing on the floor. She stared at it, astonished. Was it, too, a vision, a paranormal image of the dream eagle or maybe of the eagle on the cover of the old book? Or was it a hallucination produced by sensory deprivation and extreme stress? She didn't know, but did that matter? As illogical as it seemed, she felt that whatever it was, it brought hope. The eagle would show her the path forward. She pressed the pendant even more tightly between her fingers.

***

It was late evening on the river. The sun was setting in an explosion of color. Jeremy pushed his boat's throttle as far forward as it would go, demanding every ounce of power from the old diesel.

As he plowed upstream, he mulled over his dark suspicions about the professor, once again. Many questions swirled in his mind, but no certain answers about the professor's guilt. The logical side of him agreed with Tony. He could prove none of his many suspicions. However, his intuitive side would not relent. It said his answers would come but warned they wouldn't be necessarily logical. The change in mindset that he needed was likely not a rational one.

He reached his turning point and swung the boat around to drift downstream. It was time to contact the river.

CHAPTER FORTY-SEVEN

Jeremy arrived at the Psychology Department's main office shortly after 9:00 a.m. He was gripped by a singular, irresistible aim. A vivid image of the professor had come into his mind on the river last evening. At that moment, he'd had an overpowering feeling that the professor and the serial murderer were one and the same. He'd also strongly felt that evidence of the professor's guilt lay hidden in his office cabinet. He'd ascertained from the professor's voicemail message that he had left for a couple of days' vacation. It was now a perfect time to find out what was in that cabinet.

He walked down to the professor's office, noting the position of a security camera in the hallway. There was a note on Dr. Greenwood's door to his grad students, which confirmed his absence. But where was he? Jeremy returned to the main office and greeted the young secretary who came to the counter. He noticed her coffee mug had a picture of a pink heart on it. If she was the caring type, he might get something useful from her, he thought—providing he played his cards right.

The secretary smiled and leaned slightly forward on the counter. "How can I help you, sir?"

Jeremy matched her smile and also leaned forward on the counter. "Well, I would appreciate a little help," he said. "I'm Dr. John Clement, an old college friend of Dr. Greenwood. I dropped by to see him, but I see from the note on his door that he's off on vacation." Jeremy produced a profoundly disappointed look. “It’s been years, and I really don’t have that much time in town.”

The secretary gave him a sympathetic look.

“I was wondering. You wouldn’t happen to know where I can find him?”

“I’m not supposed to give out private information like that—even if I did know it,” she said. “But perhaps you can speak to a colleague of his, Professor Jamison. He’s in, and I’ll see if I can find him for you.”

Jeremy smiled again as she walked away. So far, so good.

A few minutes later, an older, refined-looking man came to meet him. “So, I take it you’re a friend of Daryl’s?” the man asked.

“Yes,” Jeremy said, offering his hand. “John Clement’s the name. We were psychology majors together in college.” He chuckled. “We both did term papers as grad students on the psychohistorical roots of infamous serial murderers. That’s where he got his ideas for his dissertation.”

The professor smiled. “Yes, and he’s been obsessing about the topic ever since. I understand you’re trying to get in touch with him. I heard he has a fishing camp somewhere in the bayous south of Clairmont. He may be there, but I can’t tell you exactly where it is.”

“That’s a start,” Jeremy said. “There might be some fishing lodges along Highway 3. They could know. Appreciate the help, folks.”

“Good luck,” the professor said.

I’ll need it, Jeremy thought. Nevertheless, he smiled to himself as he walked down the hallway, pleased with his performance.

His next stop was the janitor's office. He took the elevator to the basement and checked for security cameras in the area, but fortunately, there were none. He knocked on the janitor's door, relieved there was no answer. Determining he was alone, he quickly jimmied the janitor's lock. He soon found what he was looking for: the janitor's cleaning cart and uniform.

In a few more minutes, he was pushing the cart down to the professor's office in janitorial garb, his back to the security camera in the hallway. He was soon in the office; he went directly to the cabinet and pried open the lock. Jeremy peered inside at the contents. His heart leaped as he noticed a dusty photo of the professor holding up a fish in front of a cabin. Why was this locked away in a cabinet? Was this the missing piece he needed to find Monica? He wiped it off and was gratified that it was a sharp image of the cabin. He took two photos of it with his cell. Then he saw something else. There was a black and red cloth-covered book that was highly ornate and personalized-looking. His excitement grew as he read the first page. He photographed the page and five pages after that, carefully replacing the book in the cabinet. He hurried out into the hallway, pausing to lock the office door. In another five minutes, he managed to get out of the janitor's uniform unobserved and walked out the front entrance of the Social Sciences building.

Jeremy called Tony to let him know he thought he had the lead they were looking for to locate Monica and was on his way to meet him.

"How did you pick it up?" Tony asked.

Jeremy's response was terse. "I'll explain it to you later."

Tony had heard this line before, usually whenever Jeremy had come up with something from his experiences on the river.

The two soon met at NOPD headquarters. Jeremy came right to the point. "Okay, I've got a photo of where I think she is right now." He handed Tony his cell phone. "It's located somewhere in the bayous south of Clairmont."

Tony raised his eyebrows. "At a camp behind the professor in a fishing photo?"

Jeremy nodded. "Don't ask me how I got it."

Tony shook his head reprovingly. "You'll lose your license if you're caught."

"But I wasn't," Jeremy retorted. "And to hell with that anyways, Tony. We need to get to her. There's not much time."

"But how do you know she's really there?" He gave Jeremy a sharp look. "I suppose you're going to ask me to believe in some kind of a vision you received? I don't understand this any more than I understand your connection with the river. I'm a cop, for God's sake, not a psychic."

"Look. There's nothing remotely paranormal about this. It's simply another level of mind at work here; that's all.... But I ask you, Tony, don't you find it strange that he kept this photo, frame and all, inside a locked cabinet with a solid hardwood door?"

"Maybe he was just temporarily storing it."

"It had thick dust on it. He was either a helluva procrastinator or he was trying to conceal it,

Tony…. And there was something else I photographed in that cabinet."

Tony scrolled down to the next photo. "What's this? The title page of a book: *Odes to the Great Ones*? What in the world is an ode?"

"It's a poem praising some event or person. The ancient Greeks originated it. Scroll to photo three."

Tony read again for a few moments. "Why, it's praising a serial murderer!"

"Yeah, look at the next."

Tony's eyes widened as he quickly scanned the fourth photo. "It's the same thing … through each of the three stanzas!"

"Doesn't it look to you that the professor has a little more than an academic interest in the topic? And look at the title page again. You'll see there's no author's name. I wonder who wrote it?"

Tony looked both confused and worried. "Jeremy, if we go after him and we're wrong, our careers are over. I can kiss goodbye to my detective's shield and you to your license."

"But could we live with ourselves if we were right and did nothing?"

Tony saw his friend's look of desperation and finally threw up his hands. "Okay. Okay." He sighed. "I imagine you've checked the land registry for a title in that area listed for the professor?"

"I did on the way down here, and nothing came up. But there are two people who would know about it."

"The Boisvert brothers, right?"

"Yeah. The fastest way to get there is by helicopter."

"Jack's not going to release one on the basis of a hunch against a member of the team. Don't even try."

"We could rent one privately."

"But by the time we arrange it, we could be halfway to the Boisvert brothers' lodge. And there's one detail. I doubt they're around. It's not their maintenance day."

Jeremy phoned the lodge and handed the cell to Tony. He responded to a voice message that came on. "This is Tony Vasquez, NOPD. We need to get a hold of you as soon as possible on an urgent matter. We'll be arriving in about one hour at your lodge." He gave the cell back to Jeremy. "You know that reception is bad in the bayous, if they're out with a tour right now."

Tony and Jeremy sped off in the police van, but the mid-afternoon rush soon slowed them to a frustrating crawl. Tony weaved from lane to lane to make time, but after a half an hour, they hadn't even reached access routes to Highway 3.

"Damn it," Jeremy shouted. "Everything is conspiring against us today."

"Okay, plan B," Tony answered. He placed a flashing light on the driver's side roof and turned on the siren. "You know if we hit somebody, we're going to have to explain why we're in emergency mode and speeding. Good luck to us on that."

Traffic became more congested the closer they were to Highway 3. Vehicles tried to get out of their path, but there was often no room. It was now more than a full hour since they started. They were late for the Boisvert brothers, assuming they'd received the message.

Jeremy pressed the Boisvert brothers' number once again with a sweaty fingertip. "Jeremy Hale, PI, calling. Detective Vasquez and I have been delayed in traffic and will be at least another hour."

The exits for Highway 3 finally appeared, and as they merged onto the highway, the traffic was faster. Jeremy was relieved to feel their vehicle accelerating.

The highway trip was uneventful. Tony then had to negotiate the tangle of gravel roads leading to the Boisverts. The GPS was useless, but fortunately, he remembered the route from his first visit.

They arrived in a cloud of dust at the lodge. The front door was locked, and they encountered a note that the brothers were on a fishing tour and wouldn't arrive back until 6:00 p.m., at least.

"Damn," Jeremy said. "We're losing a lot of time." He felt deep down that each minute that passed could make the difference between seeing Monica alive again and her death under horrible circumstances.

CHAPTER FORTY-EIGHT

Jeremy and Tony headed out to the largely empty docks. Only one boat, which looked under repair, bobbed at the end of its rope to the dock. Tony sat down in a disconsolate mood on the edge of the dock, while Jeremy paced up and down. Both kept an eye on the entrance to the bayous in the west. It was getting late. The sun was lowering, and Jeremy worried that if they didn't locate the fishing camp before dark, they'd have to wait till daybreak.

After an interminable hour passed on the dock, Jeremy's anxiety transformed to despair. Then it happened: the sounds of powerboats in the distance. Both stood straining their eyes for any sign that it was the Boisverts' boats returning. They saw the flashes of aluminum hulls heading fast for the lodge. The two craft pulled up to the dock, and Jeremy and Tony secured their lines.

As fishermen proudly weighed and took photos of their catches, the brothers approached the investigators and huddled with them beyond earshot of the others. "Got your message," Mike announced. "It was just luck we got it; it was so far back in the bayous. We left right away. Can't say our customers were very happy about that, though. If it wasn't for the great catches today, we'd have to do refunds."

"We don't have much time, Mike." Jeremy showed them the photo of the professor's cabin. "Do either of you recognize this?"

“Yeah,” Mike said. “It’s an old fishing camp on Bayou Noir. Been there for as long as I can recall.” He turned to his brother. “Bud, get the map out from under my seat, will you?” He spoke again to Jeremy. “Nobody knows who owns the place.”

Mike kneeled down and spread out the map on the hot, gnarled dock. “Here,” he said, pointing a wrinkled finger at a remote island deep in the bayou. “I’ve never seen anybody there, but the place has been kept up over the years, so somebody was using it.”

“Have you ever seen the guy in the photo?” Jeremy asked.

“No. He’s never come by here. But there’s a public launch a few miles from here, and that’s how a lot of fishermen from the city get into the swamps.”

“We need you guys to take us to the island—now,” Jeremy said. “It’s a life-or-death matter.”

The brothers looked at one another, taken aback by Jeremy’s urgent, demanding response. “Okay,” Mike said. “We have to gas up. It’ll take only a few minutes. Do you want us to take our 303s with us?”

Jeremy looked at Tony, who nodded. “We may need them,” Tony said.

Within five minutes, the four had boarded the larger and more powerful of the two boats. Jeremy sat in the bow with Bud in the captain’s seat. They cast off, and Bud swung the eighteen-footer around. He gunned the powerful motor, leaving behind a turbulent white wake as the bow lifted up in the water. The craft soon entered the main channel leading to the bayous beyond.

"How long do you think it will take to reach Bayou Noir?" Jeremy asked.

"At this speed, half an hour at most," Bud replied.

It was going to be a fast trip, but Jeremy's furrowed brow betrayed his anxiety. He looked back at Tony in the stern of the boat. Tony's face was pale with apprehension. They had every reason to be worried, Jeremy thought. They might be too late; the professor might have already done his gruesome work. And it was likely he wouldn't surrender. He was probably armed, and there would be a gunfight. The next hour would tell it all.

Bud skillfully maneuvered the boat through numerous bayous and connecting channels without consulting his map. They passed several fishing boats, giving them as wide a berth as possible because of their strong wake. Jeremy saw the startled faces of the occupants as the boat roared past.

"We're coming up to Bayou Noir now," Bud shouted over the engine noise. "The island's in about a mile or so. How do you want to approach it when we sight it?"

"We need to cut speed now," Jeremy advised, "and hug the shore. Then we use the trolling motor to approach silently. You be the judge about when to do this."

Bud nodded gravely.

The island came into view, and Jeremy focused his binoculars on it. Tony came up and leaned over to him as Jeremy described the scene. "There are two cabins on the property. The main one is on the water's edge, and a secondary one is thirty or forty feet from the other in the middle of the island. The main cabin has two floors and a front deck level with the docks. There's an open porch with stairs facing the other cabin. The other is a small, single-floor affair. I can't see any windows from this angle. I'll bet she's in that building."

He inspected the main cabin more closely. "It's difficult to see if it's occupied. The windows are shuttered and the back door closed. There are no boots or other paraphernalia on the porch to suggest anyone is there. There's a powerboat with enclosed cabin tied up at the dock. No sign of occupants. If this is his only boat, he's got to be on the island."

Jeremy swept the binoculars around the island's circumference. "There's cover at the end of the island closest to us, and there may be a direct line of sight to both cabins." He gave the binoculars to Bud, who immediately scanned the nearest shore.

"Bud, head for that cover and get as close to the shore as possible. Tony and I will jump off there. You two stay with the boat." He and Tony checked their handguns and strapped on their protective vests.

As directed, Bud quietly steered the boat into a tangle of brush and grass at the eastern tip of the island and cut the trolling motor. Tony and Jeremy jumped over the bow. They then crept up to some trees and kneeled behind them, peering at the cabins to ascertain if they had been detected. Except for the background of swamp noises, the island was quiet. There were still no signs of anyone there.

Jeremy began to have his first doubts. Were the professor and Monica really here? What if his suspicions were merely a work of fiction created by his desperate desire to find Monica? What if all this was for nothing? A quick look at Tony's face told him that his friend was also having second thoughts. God, he was beginning to feel like a fool.

They were just about to make a run for the side of the main cabin when they heard a loud creaking sound to their left. The heavy metal door of the smaller cabin suddenly swung open. A small man in camouflage clothes stepped out and looked around. Then he turned to motion behind him, revealing that he carried a sidearm. He began walking toward the main cabin. Two women trailed behind him, their hands bound by a rope. The free end of the rope was being pulled forward by their captor, as if the two were dogs on a leash.

Jeremy's heart fluttered. One of the captives was Monica! They had found her. She looked bedraggled and exhausted, but she was alive! The second woman, who appeared much younger, sobbed deeply as she stumbled along.

Jeremy whispered to Tony. "Let's wait till they get to the bottom of the stairs. He'll be focused on getting them up the stairs, and that's when we make our move."

Holding their breath, Tony and Jeremy waited behind the trees as the group made its way slowly toward the main cabin. The camouflaged man reached the stairs and climbed to the top, awkwardly trying to pull the women up to the porch. This was the cue for Tony and Jeremy to act. They ran forward to within twenty feet of the group, guns drawn and aimed. "Hands over your head!" Tony shouted at the man.

The man turned to look, completely surprised. For the first time, Jeremy could see his face clearly. He was shocked as he recognized Dr. Tremblay, the coroner.

The doctor pulled his gun out from his side holster. Distracted, he dropped the rope, enabling the two women to run off and dive to the ground. As the doctor raised his weapon, Tony and Jeremy fired almost simultaneously, hitting him in the upper chest and throat. His eyes rolled up in their sockets, and he coughed blood out of his mouth before falling face first, sprawled over the steps.

At that moment, another much taller, camouflaged man appeared from the front of the cabin facing the bayou with a look of hatred and fury. As Jeremy had suspected, it was the professor. The professor aimed his assault rifle and pulled twice on the trigger, bringing down Tony behind Jeremy. Jeremy shot at him twice, hitting him once in the arm. But his opponent could still wield his weapon and leveled it directly at him. Jeremy was about to take another shot but stumbled over uneven ground and fell to his knees. He stared for a second at the barrel of the rifle pointed at his head, expecting his life to end in the next moment.

Then he heard a shot from behind him. The professor was struck by a bullet squarely in the chest, throwing up his arms over his head in a death spasm. He fell off the edge of the deck into the swamp water. As his body quickly sank, Jeremy saw a pair of knobbly eyes moving toward where the body had gone down. He thought it was a fitting end for a serial killer: consumed by a vicious predator of another kind. He looked back to see where the fatal shot had come from. He saw Bud standing about forty feet away, his 303-rifle raised.

Bud lowered his gun and shrugged. “I never was much for following orders,” he said as he walked over to untie the two women.

The next thought on Jeremy’s mind was Tony. He hurried over to see how badly he had been hurt. The wound on his upper arm was bleeding profusely, and Tony was unconscious. Jeremy ripped off his own sleeve and made a tourniquet on Tony’s arm. To Jeremy’s relief, the wound stopped bleeding almost immediately. He quickly checked Tony’s body for any other wounds but mercifully found him unscathed.

Out of the corner of his eye he saw one of the women running toward him. In a moment, Monica hugged him tightly and began to sob. He put his arms around her to console her and drew her close. “Thank God you’re safe,” he said. “I don’t know what I would have done without you.”

“I–I didn’t know–if I’d ever see you again,” she managed between sobs.

Suddenly, Jeremy felt another pair of arms embrace him from behind. Still hugging Monica, he turned to see it was the young woman, her face bruised and swollen. “Who are you?” he asked.

“Jenny. Jenny Thibeault.”

“Well, I’ll be damned,” Jeremy said, grinning broadly. “We’ve been looking for you for quite a while. It’s a miracle you’re alive—that both of you are alive.”

Jeremy noticed that Monica was distracted by something behind him. He turned and looked along her line of sight. Perched on the thick bough of a swamp cypress was a large bird. It was dark, but its feathers were lustrous and caught the reddish orange rays of the setting sun.

The bird attracted Bud's attention as well. "It's an eagle, and a big one, too. I've never seen one in the bayous in my seventy years here. They nest much farther to the south. Maybe they're moving north for some reason."

"They must be," Jeremy said. "I was out in my boat last night, to the north, when I noticed a large eagle repeatedly circling above me. Its wingspan must have been seven or eight feet. I've never seen that before either."

Monica smiled and touched her pendant.

CHAPTER FORTY-NINE

Jeremy walked down the austere hallway of Our Lady of Assumption Hospital. He introduced himself to the burly officer guarding a trio of hospital rooms and produced his ID. The officer asked if he was wearing a gun, and, receiving an affirmative answer, held out his hand. Jeremy turned his weapon over but was frisked, nevertheless.

Jeremy knocked on the first door and took a muffled reply from inside as permission to enter. He found Tony sitting upright in his bed, his bandaged arm in traction since the surgery two days before.

Jeremy placed a hand on Tony's good arm. "I see you rate a guard these days," he joked.

Tony laughed. "Madera will think twice about visiting."

"Unless he wants his tail end flamed again," Jeremy added. "I see Monica's room is next door. It was a good idea to check her in for a while, after what she's been through. Talking about tough breaks, how's the wing, Tony?"

"The professor got me right between the shoulder and upper arm. They managed to repair it okay, but I'm told the scar tissue might cause trouble. They don't know how much yet. It's lucky it's my left arm."

Jeremy gave a sympathetic nod. "I hear that physiotherapy can be really helpful, Tony. They'll get you back in shape. So don't get your hopes up for a gold watch yet."

Tony smiled. "It could have been a lot worse. They tell me you stopped the bleeding. You saved my butt, buddy. My family and I owe you one on this."

Jeremy knew this was as close to a thank-you as he would get from Tony. "That's what buddies are for," he said. "I'll always remember when you saved me from a pounding by that bully at St. Vincent's."

"Oh, yeah, Bruno Vittorio. I swear that guy had yellow eyes. You know, like a wolf."

The two laughed. "I think when you heal up, we should pay a visit to the Boisvert brothers," Jeremy said. "They're the unsung heroes in all of this."

"I heard about Bud from Jack."

"Yeah, he took an amazing shot at the professor. Told me he was a crack rifleman from his alligator hunting days."

"Lucky for us he disobeyed orders."

"For sure. I don't know how much Jack told you, but the professor had a bead on me with that assault rifle. I thought for a second it was all over. Then I saw him go down. Center shot to the chest. He fell backward off the deck and sank in the water. We haven't recovered the body, and I don't think we will. I saw an alligator moving toward where the professor disappeared."

"That's some way to go," Tony remarked. "I heard the doctor bought it, too. I figured as much. But I never would have guessed it was those two or that they were brothers. Who would have thought it?"

“Nobody. It was a perfect setup. Their covers were flawless: well-respected professionals on the investigation teams, one of them vetted by the FBI. It was no wonder they got away with what they were doing for so long.”

“And they managed to snooker us with their frame-up of Vallencourt, right to the end,” Tony remarked.

“Not to mention framing Madera. Did Jack mention it was the professor who phoned in the false tip on him?”

“Yeah, they thought they had everything sewn up, huh?”

“Did you hear their family had been murdering for multiple generations?”

Tony’s eyes grew wide. “Jack started to tell me about something like that when I dozed off. I’ve never heard of serial murdering being passed on from generation to generation. It’s got to be pretty rare.”

“I think it is. How many families have a legacy of murder? Even the Mafia murder only for specific purposes like retaliation, power, or protection—not for murder itself.... It’s hindsight, I know, but what were the alternatives, really? Copycat murders for two hundred years? A serial murderer who was two hundred years old? I think none of us wanted to seriously believe that intergenerational serial murdering was any more possible than the alternatives. I think we were all in denial.”

“You were right about our mindset, Jeremy. And all of this comes from Monica, huh? Have you seen her yet?”

"No. I was giving her some time to pull herself together. And when she was first hospitalized, she spent hours with a therapist and Jack recounting the whole experience. The team listened to it and read the transcript. It was something to behold."

"Did she get the story from both brothers?"

"Mostly from the doctor, but the professor rounded out a few details."

"God! What she must have gone through! It's a miracle she survived. I hope they didn't get too far with her before we got there."

"It was mainly verbal, but she was kept in the dark with little food, not knowing whether she would live or die horribly from one moment to the next." Jeremy's voice broke.

"Those bastards!" Tony shouted.

"They got what was coming to them," Jeremy said.

"But how did you know, Jeremy, that it was the professor? I know you had bits and pieces that you put together, but these weren't enough. How did you finally zero in on him? You even broke into his office and practically strong-armed me into driving you to the Boisvert brothers."

Jeremy looked at Tony in silence for a few moments. "Jack asked me the same question. I shrugged and said it was a good hunch. But it was much more than that. A vivid image of the professor came to mind, and I had a strong feeling he was the one, and that there was something in his office cabinet that would back up my suspicion. All the pieces that I was mulling over for days came together."

"And this happened out on the river?"

"Yes. I was drifting south again, the evening before we discovered Monica." Jeremy looked at Tony and smiled. "Tony, I should get a photo of how mystified you look right now."

"Well, I'll tell you, Jeremy. Whatever happened out there, it broke the case. It's a miracle."

Jeremy smiled again. "So, no more razzing me about the river?"

"Who am I to argue with the river? By the way, who was that other woman tied to Monica?"

Jeremy grinned broadly. "You'll never guess who."

Tony waited expectantly.

"It was Jenny. Jenny Thibeault."

It took a few moments for Tony to process what Jeremy was saying. "Jenny!" he said at last, stunned. "They kept her for all that time? We thought for sure that she was a goner. What are the chances?"

"Incredibly low. But I think the professor kept her for his extended sadosexual pleasure. She's in intensive therapy now and on my visiting list today, if she's up to it. Which reminds me, I'd better get on with it and let you rest up."

"Not so fast. I suspect one of those bags you're holding is for me."

"Oh, I almost forgot." He gave Tony a large, heavy bag. "That should hold you for a while."

Tony read out the label on the bag, "One Thousand & One Sugarless Bubble Gums." He pulled out a gum, eagerly unwrapped it, and popped it in his mouth. His eyes beamed. "Strawberry and banana. My favorite flavors!"

Jeremy waved at the officer as he walked out of Tony's room and down the hall. He pointed to Monica's room. "Visit number two," he announced. The door was half open. He knocked gently. "Anyone home?" he asked.

"Come in, Jeremy," Monica said in a somewhat monotone voice.

As Jeremy walked in, he saw she was sitting in an easy chair next to her bed. He went over to her and gave her a strong hug. He didn't get the reaction he expected. She seemed flat, almost indifferent. "Hey," he said. "I made quite a sacrifice visiting you and Tony today. I got frisked and relieved of my gun in the hallway. I feel like a defrocked priest."

She presented him with a poker face.

He looked around for a book and her cell phone but saw neither. "You don't look too busy right now," he observed as he sat down on the bed beside her.

"No," she replied, almost absentmindedly. "I seem to do a lot of sitting around staring."

"Sounds a bit boring," Jeremy said.

"I hadn't really noticed. I'm really not myself."

"After what you've been through, it's no wonder. Has the psychologist been in to see you much?"

"He's in once daily for a session."

"How's it been going with him?"

"Okay. I do a lot of talking about the confinement. He's says expressing my feelings about it is healing."

"Is it helping?"

"I think it's a little weight off my chest, but it's still early in therapy. The idea is to repeat the experiences so frequently that I begin to desensitize to them. He calls it exposure."

"I guess he's trying to figure out what's going on, too?"

"Yeah, he says naturally there's trauma there, and he's trying to see how deep it is. I've been getting flashbacks of the abduction and the confinement. Nightmares about them, as well, that wake me up. Lack of sleep doesn't help either. In general, I feel pretty numb."

"These symptoms go with the territory, I hear. Like all troubles, they'll eventually pass. You'll regain your feelings, your happiness," he reassured her.

"What about you, Jeremy? You had a near-death experience with the barrel of Greenwood's rifle."

Jeremy found himself tensing. "Yeah, I find myself going back to that moment, especially before I go to sleep. It was one of those moments when you're hovering between life and death. You're face-to-face with your own mortality. It's frightening. I also didn't know if Tony was alive or dead behind me."

"How are you dealing with all of that, Jeremy?"

He stared at her for a moment, but he did not hold back this time. "I bring the memories to the river with me," he said. "They become part of my experience drifting down the Mississippi: part of the currents, the driftwood, the winds, and the sky. And for a while, I'm not afraid anymore."

Monica looked deep into his eyes. "So this is what you meant by your relationship with the river?"

"Mostly, but I can gather truths, insights from the experience, too."

"And is this how you found me?"

"Yes," Jeremy said. He noticed a flicker of life coming into Monica's eyes.

"How did it work, Jeremy? What truths did you experience?"

"As I was telling Tony, I was drifting on the river the evening before we found you. I had been thinking about the case and about the many suspicions I had about the professor that I couldn't prove. I was getting nowhere and simply let go of my thoughts, imagining them falling into the river. Suddenly, a vivid image of the professor's face flashed in my mind, and I was pretty sure that he was the murderer, and when I found him, I would find you. I also felt strongly there was something in the professor's cabinet that would add weight to my suspicions."

"Did you go to his office?"

"I did. I broke into his office and the cabinet. I found a book of poems extolling serial murderers. I also found a photo of the professor at a fishing camp. A faculty member at the university had told me the professor had a camp somewhere in bayou country, south of Clairmont, and might be there. I suspected that's where you were. Tony and I rushed to the Boisvert brothers' lodge. They identified the location from the photo and took us by boat to the professor's cabins."

Monica stared at him in awed silence and then spoke softly. "So there had been a lot of deductions going on, many bits and pieces, but it was only when your mind became totally absorbed in the experience of the river that things suddenly crystalized. You virtually knew it was the professor and felt that something very suspicious was in his cabinet."

"Basically, yes, but if you're making this into some kind of a paranormal experience, that's not so. I think my subconscious was at work, like an underground computer processing information. Both of us learned in psychology that the subconscious integrates many disparate pieces of information into a cohesive whole. It forms pictures, images, and feelings. That's what I received about the professor and his cabinet."

"That's all there was to it, then? Psychology 101?"

"I think it's deeper than intro psych. But yes, it was a psychological process."

"There's one factor you've left out of your equation, Jeremy."

He gave her a quizzical look.

"You mentioned when you saw the reddish eagle on the island, that one had circled you while you were drifting on the river. What did you think of that?"

"I thought it was a strange incident. It never happened before."

"Tell me more about it, Jeremy."

"All right.... As my mind began to drift with the currents and the wind, I heard the cry of a bird above the boat. I looked up and saw a huge eagle circling above me. Its feathers were just as lustrous as the eagle we saw on the island. The feathers reflected the orange-red of the setting sun. The eagle circled at least a half a dozen times and then flew off to the northwest into the sun. My mind continued to drift deeper and deeper."

"And then the images came?"

"They did. That was the sequence."

Monica paused in deep reflection for a while. Finally, she voiced her thoughts. "Jeremy, you know that I've been developing myself on the spiritual level for some months now."

Jeremy nodded.

"Ironically, my development reached a culmination point when I was confined at the brothers. I had three dreams, which I believe completed my spiritual training. For days, I lapsed into and out of sleep, waking, and dreaming, which sometimes seemed to merge with one another. After the third dream, on the last night of my imprisonment, I saw a red eagle standing before me in the half-light of my cell. Some might say it was a hallucination—part of sensory deprivation and stress—but I think it was a vision that came to me in my moment of need."

Jeremy stared at her in silence.

"I spoke to the eagle vision, asking it to deliver a message to you revealing the professor as the murderer."

Jeremy remained silent, looking at her curiously.

Monica could imagine the rational wheels and gears turning in Jeremy's mind. "Do you think that the reddish eagle circling your boat was a mere coincidence?"

Jeremy hesitated and then said, "With all due respect, Monica, yes I do."

She met his eyes directly. "I thought you said PIs don't believe in coincidence?"

He still said nothing, but he looked uncertain. His uncertainty turned into a teary, upset look. Suddenly, all the fear, the sadness, and the rage he had felt over the past few weeks burst out in a great catharsis. He buried his head in her shoulder and began to cry. "I thought I'd lost you," he said.

She had never seen him cry. He was always the pillar of strength, the tough-guy PI. She remembered he had once said to her, "Never let your emotions get control of you in this business, or you'll get yourself killed." She placed a comforting arm around him and held on tightly.

His crying became more intense.

In that moment, she realized the depth of his feelings for her, even through the haze of trauma. She had sensed it was there over the past couple of months and had known her feelings matched his. But right now, her feelings were buried somewhere in places she could not fully reach. All she could do was hold on to him.

After he cried himself out, she would have to tell him some hard words. She was going to leave the job and return to Boston to heal. She needed therapy to happen there. She remembered her grandmother's words about balance. She would balance her therapy with spiritual healing. She had to tell Jeremy that she didn't know when she would return, or if she would return at all.

CHAPTER FIFTY

Jeremy stood looking out at downtown New Orleans from his office window. The fog and rain of the past several weeks had finally lifted, and there was a beautiful rainbow arcing perfectly across the sky above the river. If he were a superstitious person, he might take that as a sign of hope, but he wasn't. The dazzling display failed to cheer him up.

It was now a month since Monica had left, with no word of her decision to return or not. Kathy and Tony were always upbeat about the situation. "Give her time," they advised. But with every passing day, Jeremy grew less hopeful that he would ever see her again.

He looked back at the ever-mounting pile of papers on his desk. He'd been trying for days to clear it up, but his mind would wander off, mostly toward Monica. It was oppressively quiet and lonely in the office these days. He sometimes took a nostalgic walk down the hall past Monica's office. Her door was half-open, perhaps symbolic of his place in her life right now.

He would look at a framed photo of Monica and her family on the shelf behind her desk. It had been taken ten years before, but he thought she was even more beautiful now in a mature way. He remembered the workshop in Boston when he had seen her for the first time since college. He laughed at himself for lacking the nerve to introduce himself. But circumstances introduced them anyway and brought them together as fellow investigators.

He began to know her as the deep and complex person that she really was.

He chuckled as he remembered her job interview with him—how worried he had been that somehow she might not have his back when he needed her. He knew now that was unfounded. It was only a projection of his mistrust of women in general. Now that he might finally be ready for a relationship, the person he wanted might be lost to him. How's that for irony? he thought.

***

It was Saturday morning on the river. Jeremy climbed the stairs to the bridge and looked out on the Mississippi. It was overcast but warm and calm—a good day to take the old boat out for a run. This was particularly important today because he was going to play host to his sister and her family. He already heard the chatter of excited children on his port side and turned to see his two nephews, Thomas and Sonny, bustling up his gangplank. He descended to meet them in the main cabin.

The boys exploded into the cabin. "Uncle Jeremy," they cried, running to hug him.

Jeremy beamed. "How are my little sailors today?"

"We haven't got any sailor stuff," Sonny, the oldest, lamented.

"Oh, yes you have," Jeremy corrected. He gave them each a white sailor's cap. "Now you are official crew of the *Mississippi Dream*."

His sister laughed and came over to hug him. He extricated himself enough to give her husband, John, a handshake. "Good to have you guys aboard," Jeremy said. "The ship's day begins with a hearty breakfast from the galley. I was thinking of some eggs with hot sauce and flapjacks with Canadian maple syrup. That should satisfy all crew members and forestall any plans of mutiny."

After breakfast, everyone headed up to the bridge, except John, whose job it was to cast off. Jeremy allowed Sonny to start the old diesel, which rumbled and growled deep in the boat, as if complaining about its disuse for such a long time. Jeremy checked the instruments, and finding all in order, opened a window to tell John to cast off. They were soon reversing in the marina, finally swinging around to face the Mississippi.

In a few more minutes, the boat was out in the main channel, heading upstream. Jeremy allowed the boys to take turns at the captain's wheel. He told them about the different buoys marking the channel and how to steer around them. They came up on the stern of a freighter plowing up river. Jeremy showed his nephews the proper passing procedure, allowing each to blow the boat's horn. The boys stared up in awe at the giant ship as they slowly went by it. Jeremy had to compensate for the strong wake of the freighter pushing them to the side as they passed. It felt good to get out on the river again.

Toward 11:00 a.m., Jeremy reduced speed as his nephews and John went out on the deck to do some fishing. This was the first chance he and his sister had had to talk with one another in months.

"Any news from you know who?" she asked.

"No. Dead air."

"But you seem in a really good humor today, Jeremy."

"Being out on the river helps, but I also decided last night to pack my troubles away for today. No sense in having a depressed captain, right?"

Kathy smiled. "She's gone through a lot, Jeremy—a bona fide living nightmare. It's going to take her time to heal from that. I mean, just coming back to face reminders of what she went through is a challenge. The brothers were traumatic enough, but she was also shot at in her office, for God's sake."

Jeremy had been telling himself the same things, too. But were they actually true, he thought, or just feel-good statements, wishful thinking?

Kathy changed the topic. "I hear you've got another dinner date with Mom next week."

Jeremy nodded.

"She's really happy now that you two are talking. I'm proud of you, Jeremy."

"You weren't proud of me before?"

"Yes," she said. "But I'm even prouder now. Remember I was telling you about the little boy in you who needed to grow up? Well, I think he's grown up. I know you're probably not ready to hear this, but even if Monica doesn't come back, you'll deal with it, Jeremy. I am certain of that because you'll be facing the issue as a strong, mature man. And someday, someone will come into your life. Maybe when you least expect it."

He looked at his sister in awe. As he had told to his father, she had an uncanny ability to discover deeper truths about others, and this felt like one of those times.

He took a deep breath and exhaled slowly. He experienced a feeling that he couldn't quite name, but it was uplifting.

The two heard cries of joy coming from the deck below. Jeremy stuck his head out the open porthole to see what was going on. The boys and John were struggling to control a big catfish bouncing on the deck. Sonny had pulled it out of the river with a little help from his father.

"Get him, boys!" Jeremy yelled. "He's on the ship's menu for tonight."

CHAPTER FIFTY-ONE

The rainy weather returned, and the buoyant feelings Jeremy experienced during his sister's visit had long dissipated. Jeremy sat at his desk on his boat. He was trying to read another Sherlock Holmes book but kept on rereading the last page of chapter two. He finally gave up and put the book down. He listened to the night rain patter and splash on the deck and cabin roof. The boat had been tied up in the marina, drenched and forlorn, for some weeks now. That was the way he had been feeling about his life since Monica had left, he thought—stuck and purposeless. It had been almost two months now since she had gone back to Boston, but it felt to him like eons. The worst was not knowing if she was coming back. He had sent several emails to her, all unanswered.

He heard a knock at his cabin door. Almost reflexively, he opened his desk drawer, exposing his gun. "Who is it?" he asked warily.

"It's Tony, Jeremy. Open up, buddy," came the reply.

He unlocked the door for Tony, who took off his soaked jacket and hung it up. Jeremy noticed he had used his left arm. The arm was getting better, he thought.

"Miserable night," Tony lamented.

"That it is. I'm surprised you're out and about tonight, Tony."

"I was wondering how you were doing," Tony replied. "I haven't heard from you lately."

Jeremy heard the serious tone in his voice. Gone were the usual jesting and banter between the long-time friends. The firefight at the brothers' fishing camp had changed them both.

Jeremy's mind returned to that day often, almost obsessively, despite his attempts to resist the nightmarish memories. Since that fateful day, he felt life was worth too much to simply be laughed off. Tony seemed to feel the same. They had almost lost one another in a few moments of blazing gunfire.

Tony saw the half-empty bottle of Scotch on Jeremy's desk. "How have you been feeling lately?"

Jeremy sighed and sank into his chair.

"That bad, huh? Still no word from Monica?"

"No. She hasn't answered my emails."

Tony poured himself a drink. "She's probably in the middle of therapy, Jeremy. Her therapist may even have instructed her not to contact anyone who may remind her of the trauma or to make major decisions until her therapy progresses."

"How did you pick all that up, Tony?"

"The department had us attend a workshop about trauma last year. Then, too, my wife's friend saw a therapist for trauma. I've heard all about it from top to bottom. I don't think you've got too much to worry about, buddy. From what I've seen, she's got just as much passion for you as you have for her. She'll find her way back to you. I believe she'll be the first romantically inclined woman to cross that gangplank of yours."

"Love always finds a way, huh? I wish I were as confident as you, Tony. It's not the love that worries me. It's the trauma. I saw how numbed out she was in the hospital. It was like someone had turned down the dimmer switch."

"But it's a temporary self-protection, Jeremy. If all the feelings are numbed out, then she won't feel the fear of the trauma, either. It's kind of like going into shock after a serious accident. The therapist will help her clear that up."

Jeremy looked tense. "It's how she might protect herself in other ways that's worrisome, too. I've heard traumatized people can lose trust in others and become detached. After what the perpetrators did or were going to do, what if she loses trust in men?"

Tony nodded. "And maybe disconnects from you? That's a heavy one, Jeremy. I'm thinking you were once in the same boat, only in reverse. But you managed to let go of a lot of your mistrust of women — in your mother and certainly Monica. Why can't she do the same with men if problems crop up there?" Tony looked at his friend for a few moments. Jeremy seemed to lose some of his tension, but he still looked gloomy. "I've got some news that might cheer you up."

"That'll take a bit of doing."

Tony smiled. "First on the list: the FBI got Madera today. He was holed up in some seedy downtown rooming house. There was a gunfight, and he was wounded on the same shoulder that Monica winged him in, if you can believe it. He has a whole raft of charges against him, including two counts of attempted murder—one for you, one for Monica." Tony saw Jeremy's face relax a little more. "So you don't have to be looking over your shoulder for him. Not for another twenty or thirty years, anyway."

"His wife will be relieved to hear that, not to mention the BDSM crowd."

"I've got some good news from Clairmont, too. Charles Vallencourt received visitors at his mansion yesterday: the town mayor and a delegation of councilors. They came to apologize to him on behalf of the town for the mob attack on his place and for all the accusations against him and his family over the years."

"A lot to apologize for," Jeremy remarked.

Tony handed Jeremy a copy of the *Clairmont Examiner*. "Here's a shot of them having iced tea on Vallencourt's porch."

Jeremy managed a smile. "That's quite a switch from a lynch mob to a tea party."

Tony laughed. "Take a look at the photo below, too."

"The Boisvert brothers?" Jeremy read out loud the caption below it: "Local brothers aid in captives' rescue." He grinned. "We still have to pay those two a visit sometime and personally thank them."

"For sure. They really saved the day for us.... I wonder what Sheriff Petit was thinking when he saw all this on the front page?"

"He couldn't possibly miss the irony of it all," Jeremy quipped. "The town making nice with Vallencourt. The victims and the police saved by civilians.... By the way, did he ever charge the clowns who aimed their shotguns at him on the way to Vallencourt's? You know, the car he sent careening into the swamp?"

"Yes. Two of three in the car were charged with aggravated assault on a police officer and something else. I've forgotten what. They'll be going away for a while, too."

"You're brimming with good news tonight, Tony. Anything else?"

"There's some news on Jenny Thibeault. We contacted Child Welfare about her. A social worker helped her get an emancipation order from the court."

"You've got me there, Tony."

"Meaning she'll be legally independent of her parents. She'll be staying for free at a friend's parents' place in Clairmont."

"Louie will have another beef about the state interfering with his God–given parenting rights."

Tony chuckled. "Jenny's also seeing a therapist in the city and, from what we hear, is recovering pretty well. She's even dumped her boyfriend Billy.... There are other good things happening in town. The Clairmont history book stolen by the brothers has been officially returned to the museum."

"The curator would have been glad to see that."

"By the way, another funeral service was held for her at the graveside. The new pastor is quite a reformer we hear. He's getting some New Testament wall murals done for the church."

"Glad to see it's more than fire and brimstone happening on those hallowed walls."

Tony saw that his friend was in a much better humor. "Enough work for one night," he announced, downing another shot of Scotch. "How about a rematch at pool?"

The two picked up their favorite cue sticks and set up for another game of snooker.

CHAPTER FIFTY-TWO

Jeremy arrived at the office on a Friday morning and pushed his key into the door lock. About to turn it, he was startled to see the door open. He opened it a few more inches, enough to look inside. He was disconcerted to find the lights on.

He was sure he had closed up when he left the night before. It could have been the janitor, but he had never been that careless previously. He mentally reviewed the list of disgruntled husbands he had recently caught having affairs. No more red flags than usual came up, but he wouldn't take any chances. He took out his gun and removed the safety. He quietly edged himself around the door into the office and hugged the side wall. There was nothing unusual in the general office area. Jeremy bent down to view his desk at floor level in case someone was concealed behind it, but no one was waiting in ambush.

He heard a metallic noise to his left down the hall. With the hairs on his neck bristling, he moved stealthily along the hall wall. There was someone in the next office! Was it a B & E? Was someone trying to access the files? He reached the edge of the office door. It was wide open. He held his breath. It was now or never. He jumped into a crouch in the doorway, holding out his gun.

A cry of surprise came from the apparent intruder inside. Jeremy quickly lowered his gun. He wondered, for a moment, if he was seeing things—

but no. It was Monica sitting at her desk behind her computer screen!

"You scared the hell out of me!" she reprimanded.

Jeremy felt his face flush. "I–I thought you were an intruder." He castigated himself. Here she was, just back from trauma therapy, and idiot here jumps out at her with a gun. He put the safety back on and holstered his weapon. Monica rose to meet him as he walked around to the end of her desk.

"I missed you a lot," he said. "I couldn't stop thinking about you."

"This wasn't the best of reunions," she replied.

"No. But we can make up for that." He took her face in his hands and kissed her deeply on the lips.

For a moment the kiss took her by surprise; then she returned it enthusiastically. "I missed you terribly too," she said breathlessly.

"So you're back?" he asked.

"Yes, I'm back. For good."

"You didn't call me or email me for two months. I didn't think I'd see you again."

"I'm really sorry, Jeremy. I thought about you every day, too, but my therapist was very strict about my not contacting anyone related to the trauma in any way."

"That's what Tony said," Jeremy replied. "He was right. But don't tell him I said so."

She laughed. "Still jokesters, huh?"

"Oh, we don't kid around as much as we used to. We've grown more serious since you left. I'll tell you about it sometime."

"This I would like to hear. Tony's arm is okay?"

"Yeah, his arm is pretty much back to normal. He's on full-time duty now."

She studied him carefully. "And how have you been feeling, Jeremy?"

He paused for a moment, tempted to fall back on his old avoidance tactics. But no, he wouldn't shut her out. "I've been down a lot. Mostly about you."

She placed a consoling arm around his shoulders. "I *am* really sorry. My hands were pretty well tied."

He looked at her quizzically, wondering if the expression she had used had a double meaning. Was part of it a flashback, perhaps? But she seemed calm and fully present in the moment. "Monica, we do what we have to do. I understand."

She smiled, glad he was connecting with her. "So the river didn't fully help?"

"With the weather being so bad, I wasn't out on the river much."

"How have you been handling your feelings, then?"

"Mostly by talking to Tony and Kathy, but I've been into my liquor cabinet, too."

"You know you need to face your feelings directly, Jeremy."

He nodded. "The first thing I'm going to do tonight is give my Scotch collection to my father. He can handle it. The second is to take the next opportunity to consult with the river. Then we'll see from there."

She smiled. "It seems like a good start."

"But what about you?" he asked. "How have you been doing?"

"I have my off moments, but I'm much more together now." She kept smiling. "In fact, I'm better than I've been in a very long time."

"Good therapist?"

"He is. And I've used other ways of healing, spiritual ways. I'll try to explain some time."

"I'd like that," Jeremy replied. "I see you're still wearing your pendant. Have you given some thought to your grandmother's prophecy that achieving balance with your spiritual side would someday help you survive? Did it come true?"

She touched her pendant. "I guess that's open to interpretation, Jeremy. But my thoughts? I survived that wretched little cell against all the odds, and I'm standing alive in front of you on this beautiful day. That's truth enough for me."

Jeremy nodded and gently squeezed her hand. He turned to look out the window at the clear blue sky. "It's supposed to be gorgeous over the next while," he said. "What are you doing this weekend?"

"Nothing much."

"In that case, how would you like to take a boat ride on the river?"

She looked at him, full of anticipation. "I'd love to," she said.

"Fantastic! We have a lot to catch up on."

THE END

www.ingramcontent.com/pod-product-compliance
Lightning Source LLC
La Vergne TN
LVHW030908080826
845145LV00010B/2804